Praise for Michele Richard

Michele Richard had me on an emotional roller coaster from the first page til the last page. I fell in love with the characters and truly wanted to know what would come of their lives. I felt that she dealt with teenage pregnancy in a very real and down to earth way.

Heather Landry Goodreads

Having grown up in a tourist town which also had a base at one time (Myrtle Beach, SC), this story evoked a lot of memories for me. I viewed the friendships differently than Stella- I saw them as brief spotlights in my life and feel that some people are put in your path for a reason. Michelle really described those feelings of new relationships well and I felt like I was in the scene- the ice scream shoppe, the beach, the base. So this book was more personal for me and thanks for the trips down memory lane.

Amber Vaughn Goodreads

My emotions throughout Mocked by Destiny where all over the place once again. Michele Richard has a way of making it to where you put yourself in the characters shoes. Right away it has you caught up into that world, that life, and all that goes with it. You cry, laugh, get angry, feel their pain, and talk back to the book like some do to their T.V.'s. I love how these two find each other. The way they take their lives into their own hands. With help from one from both sides, possible these two may have a chance of controlling their destiny. Growing up, dealing with so many different issues, more than you will ever know if you just let the title and cover decide how this book goes.

Kim Justice http://breathoflifebookreviews.blogspot.com

● ● ●

Mocked By Destiny

• • •

Michele Richard

Mocked By Destiny

• • •

3

Mocked By Destiny

Second Edition Published by
Renaissance Romance Publishing

Renaissance Romance Publishing
PO Box 22 Clarendon, TX 79226

ISBN-13: 978-0615673318
ISBN-10: 0615673317

Cover art: © Barsik | Dreamstime.com
© Wertes | Dreamstime.com
Cover design by: Laura A. Braley

● ● ●

4

About the Author

Michele Richard is the proud mother of two daughters and has been married since 1997 to a wonderful husband, who for twenty-five years has been her best friend and supporter. Being an overly creative and caring person, she has been a volunteer co-leader for the Girl Scout Troop for five years. She takes great pride in teaching and guiding our future generations.

Her desire to continue her education drove her to attend night classes at Waltham High School. She refuses to just let life be. There is too much to learn to stand by and watch it go by. Though she is not fluent yet in either, she has learned to speak French and Spanish. Her dream is to be fluent in both one day.

"I suppose that makes me a lover of languages. Never stop learning is my motto."

Travel is one of her great passions. Having seen the beaches of the Bahamas, Aruba, and Mexico and the deserts of Utah and Arizona, her personal favorite was bicycling down Mount Vail and standing on top of the Intercontinental Divide, followed closely by the Grand Canyon.

"America is truly a beautiful place to see. I recommend seeing as much of it as you can."

● ● ●

Special Thanks

First and foremost, thank you to Maurice, Danielle, Virginia, and Pat. You supported me as I wrote for hours, days on end. You are my own personal cheerleading team. You are truly the best family I could ask for.

Thanks to Kevin for pushing me to write my first words when I doubted myself. Darlyn, what can I say, you always told me over the years that I could do anything and as always you were right, I could.

Special acknowledgements to Gloria Keenan for all her hard work in the early stages of this story. She was my shoulder to cry on whenever I needed her. I consider her a true friend in every sense of the word. Thank you just doesn't seem like enough, but it's all I can say.

Thank you to Tish, Lauren, Amanda, Donna, Jenn, Lea and the rest of the staff at TWCS Publishing House for all their hard work on this book. Without you working with me on this book it might not have become a reality.

And Lastly: Thank you to the hardworking staff at Renaissance Romance Publishing. Elizabeth, Laura, and Lisa for bringing this 2nd edition to life. I adore you all and am grateful for the long hours and hard work.

● ● ●

Mocked By Destiny

• • •

Introduction

AFTER THREE GENERATIONS HAD MADE THE SAME mistake, you'd think I would have known better. It seems destiny had other plans that did not coincide with my own.

You know when everyone says, "That won't happen to me?" Well, I am here to tell you that it does.

How many teenagers have said that? Countless, I am sure. This time next year, I would have been completing the first leg of the journey to change my destiny, but that dream is long gone. I believe the expression "that ship has sailed" works as well as any other.

"There's always next year" and "It's only one year off, then I will go" are more common excuses that really mean "It will never happen." Right now, I know it will never happen. Fate, destiny, or some other unnatural event has set its eyes on my life and is out to change everything I have worked for over the last seventeen years.

If you have never walked a mile in my shoes, then you have no idea what caused my life to turn out this way. Everyone is quick

● ● ●

to judge, but no one ever took the time to see the string of events that lead me to where I am today.

You see, there is a major downfall to living in a tourist town. You guessed it: the constant turnover of new people. You cannot really connect with anyone because no one is ever there for more than two weeks of every year, if they come back at all. The intruders never think about what happens after they leave.

This is my life. My mom Daisy named me after her favorite movie, *A Streetcar Named Desire.* Her favorite scene was when the jerk of a husband stood in the rain screaming, "Stella!"

I look nothing like my green-eyed, blond-haired beauty of a mother. Therefore, I must look like my father. My mother, like me, grew up in Virginia Beach. My dad was gone before my mother even found out she was pregnant. I wish I could tell you about him, but unfortunately, there is very little information to share. He'd never been around, and my mom was no help either, since she knew very little herself. The most known about him was his name and that he was a Marine.

My little sister Brianna has the same problem. Her dad was in the Navy and vacationing here at Fort Story. It's where all the military personnel vacation with their families. At night, they flood the boardwalk, hitting the local bars, watching the free entertainment, and eating ice cream.

Brianna and I look nothing alike, either; she has chestnut-brown hair and icy-blue eyes. They must be from her dad, too.

I have always been a bit of a loner. Well, I really can't say I always was that way. It started after I turned ten and was allowed to hang around the beach unsupervised. I would spend every day there,

● ● ●

10

playing and enjoying the sun and fun. It was the day I met my first and only best friend, Annie. For two weeks, we were inseparable, and then it happened — she left to go back to Boston.

I made six friends that summer, and every one of them left me, never writing or calling. That fall, I vowed to never again connect with anyone vacationing at the beach. That was, until last March.

You might think I am bitter about my situation, but truth be told, I'm not. I have come to accept my life. The unexpected turns and twists in my world have given me something I never knew I wanted.

There is no reset button on life's lessons. I should know. I learned that the hard way. Once you do something, you cannot take it back.

● ● ●

• • •

Chapter One

Stella's March and the meeting

SPRING BREAK STARTED OUT SIMILAR TO LAST YEAR'S, with me working at Jerry's soft-serve ice cream stand on the boardwalk that stretched along the Virginia Beach shoreline. The job itself wasn't terrible. Bringing grinning smiles to the faces of so many children was always a good job in my book, and it allowed me to continue to save a little money for community college. That's the best I could hope for, given I would be the first to attend college in my family. Sure, I had some of the best grades in my class, but my mom wasn't a saver. It's hard to save when every penny goes to putting food on the table. She never thought college would change who we were. Her view was simple: we are who we are. I already had applied for every scholarship available. However, it would be

● ● ●

months before I'd know if I would receive any outside help.

My mom Daisy was a "free spirit," as she liked to put it. If you asked me, she'd missed the 60's hippie movement. Daisy would have made an awesome love child. In retrospect, she was a love child, just not the kind that danced around with flowers in her hair, singing. Her philosophy on life was carefree, but life had treated her harshly enough that she had sobered up, hardened a little, and even became skeptical.

My grandmother Marie was an unwed mother. In her day, it was looked down upon. When Nana refused to give my mother up for adoption, her parents kicked her to the curb and never looked back. Nana didn't talk about her parents, and I've never met my grandfather; he had just been passing through on his way to a new post. Those were two of the reasons I wanted my life to take a different path. The last reason was the disappearance of my own father; my mom never heard from him after he shipped out. It's no wonder I wanted to change my future. Who wouldn't?

My day started off as quiet and uneventful as every other day of my life, until I went to work at Jerry's stand. It was only ten minutes into my shift when the most gorgeous, raven-haired guy came up looking for an ice cream. He was, without a doubt, the most attractive man I had ever seen. Working and living on the beach, I had seen more than my share of men. Not one of them had managed to turn my head, but this one did. After I made his chocolate cone with sprinkles, unlike most people, he stayed and talked for a while. Since it was quiet, I let him.

"The weather is really nice for March."

I smiled and nodded, not sure if I could actually manage to

● ● ●

speak.

"Is it always this warm?" The gentleness of his voice was so soothing; I couldn't help but gaze into his platinum-colored eyes.

Shaking my head, I answered in a quivering voice, "Not always. Sometimes it is; depends on the year."

Just as he opened his mouth again, my next customers arrived. He stepped back and watched with a smile upon his cotton candy-colored lips while a family with two bouncing little boys pointed to their choices. Normally I'm not one to rush someone off, but I wanted to see what he was going to say before he was so rudely interrupted. Juggling four swirled cones, I hurried to give them to the family. Glancing up, I saw the waving of his hand as he slipped away and disappeared between the mulling tourists and the beach. Sighing heavily, I completed the sale and slumped against the wall. Where did he run off to? Was I that scary to look at?

He surprised me the next day when he came back. This time I didn't wait for him to order. He grinned when I handed him another chocolate cone with sprinkles.

"So, what's your name?" He chuckled and took the cone.

When he looked at me expectantly, I realized I was so lost in the sight of his perfect pout wrapped around the frozen chocolate dessert that I forgot to answer his question.

"Stella, Stella Richards. And you are?" I gushed, feeling rather stupid. I don't know why I asked; I wasn't supposed to care. Right?

"Nice to meet you, Stella. I'm Stefan Sterling. Have you

* * *

worked here long?" he asked between his licks. I couldn't help but stare at the way his tongue made laps around the frozen treat. Ice cream had never looked so delicious. I think he caught me ogling his luscious lips because he laughed.

"Um, yeah, about a year now. So, where are you visiting from?" What was it with me! Why did I feel the need to talk to him? Or stare at him, for that matter.

Okay, I'll admit it. His face was even more beautiful than all the A-list actors in Hollywood. His perfect pointed chin, sharp jawbone, slim-lined nose, and heavy laden, steel-grey eyes all screamed for admiration. Who was I to deny them their rightful adoration?

"My dad just got posted to D.C.; we were in Germany." He sounded somewhat homesick, but I guess if my mom moved me across the world, I would be homesick, too.

"So, you speak German?" I guess he liked the fact that I was showing some interest in his life, because he leaned against the worn counter and started chatting even more.

"Yeah, and Italian. We used to vacation in Italy during the summer; it's really beautiful. Have you ever been there?" His glimmering eyes seemed to twinkle as he thought about his childhood summers.

"Wow, that's great. No, I've never been anywhere but here. Um, excuse me; I have to take care of them." I pointed to the customers that had walked up. He didn't leave as I thought he would; instead, he waited for them to leave and started chatting again.

"You should go. There is a group I heard of going from the

●　●　●

16

base at the end of August. You would love it there, I bet." He smiled.

"Yeah, only if I don't want to go to college or anything silly like that." I was somewhat defensive about his comment. Did he think everyone could afford to just jet off to Italy for the summer?

"I'm sorry. I didn't mean to sound like I was being a snob or anything. I just thought you would look really beautiful on the beaches there. In Liguria, sitting on the beach, you can see sharp cliffs on one side, the crystal clear sea in front of you, and lush, green mountains on the other. It's quite a stunning sight." Did he just say beautiful? No, of course not, he was just being polite.

"It's fine; one day I do hope to leave all this behind." I gestured to my humble surroundings. "But I have to go to school for that to happen." I shrugged, trying to discard the hurt feelings he had inadvertently caused.

That's when he did the unthinkable, the one thing that would change everything. He grabbed my hand and held it. "You'll do it. I can just tell." I swear his warm smile and hot hand melted years of ice off my unsuspecting heart. For the first time in my life, I didn't want to pull away from the touch of a man.

"Thank you." I sighed, my cheeks, I'm sure, glowing red. He was just too sweet for words.

"Stella, I have to head back to the base, but can I come see you when you get off?" Hearing him purr my name sent shivers running down my spine.

Like an idiot, all I could do was nod and breathed, "Six." Yeah, real smooth there, girl!

● ● ●

He nodded in return and released my hand. I continued to stare speechless until he got into his faded, green 1966 Mustang hatchback. For a moment there, I felt like I had grown wings and could fly. Reality definitely sucks when it comes back and bites you in the butt. One minute my insides were jumping for joy, and the next minute my heart was plummeting into my stomach.

Why had I agreed to that? For what? A week or two of companionship? Then he would be gone, like everyone else. Honestly, I didn't even know why I was so worried about it. Stefan would probably forget me as soon as he hit the base, anyway. That was the way things worked around here. It was the one thing you could count on. For decades, the locals dealt with the constant, inevitable invasion of the Users. Users are the life-draining guests that take advantage of the area, then discard it when they head home. Annie, my first best friend, had taught me that little lesson.

After Stefan's short intrusion, the next four hours dragged by at an agonizing, slow crawl. Whenever I was alone, I would fantasized that he had come back and swept me into his arms and we'd stroll away into the sunset. But when I had customers, the harsh reality that he most likely wouldn't come back hit me like a wrecking ball. How is it possible that two brief encounters could leave me reeling, so out of control?

"Are you ready?"

I spun around and gasped. He had indeed come back.

"Almost, I just have to cash out my drawer." I grinned like one of my many toothless five-year old customers.

Thankfully, the cash drawer was perfect, so I only had to count it once. My insides could not decide if they wanted to be one

● ● ●

giant knot or a bowl of Jell-O. By the time I had changed out of my ice cream-covered T-shirt and had let my hair down, I could barely breathe. Each gasp felt as if I was breathing underwater. Shyly, I slipped out the back door to come face-to-face with Stefan, who seemed just as nervous as I was. It was easy to see by the way he shifted his slender hips from side to side, his hands buried deep into the pockets of his long, denim shorts, and how his eyes darted around, looking at the beach.

"Are you ready?" he mumbled, nudging his head toward the beach.

"Yeah, what did you have in mind?" I asked as I watched the breeze make his hair look like black, flowing silk.

He pursed his lips in thought. "How about we walk the beach and maybe grab a bite to eat?"

I nodded and turned in the direction he had started to move toward.

Secretly, I hoped he didn't have something expensive in mind; I only had a few dollars in my bag. It would be embarrassing having to explain that fact to him. Now that I was up close, I could truly admire his physical stature. Was there anything about Stefan that was not perfect? I doubted it.

Following his lead, I sat in the sand just a mere two feet away. "So, have you always lived here?" he asked glancing at me over his shoulder.

"Yep, I have never even visited Williamsburg," I admitted in embarrassment.

* * *

"How unpatriotic!" His mocked gasp caused me to giggle.

"Yeah, well, what can I say? The need has never arisen," I teased as I stood, wiggling and dusting off my backside.

For the next hour, all we did was walk on the soft, sandy beach, asking each other the little questions you do when you want to get to know someone. We covered everything from favorite colors to what we were going to study next year when we both started college.

It did not surprise me that he wanted to be a financial analyst. He did seem surprised to hear I wanted to be horticulturist. The way the world was going green, it seemed like a smart choice. It was something I could do with my life that would mean saving the planet. Ambitious, I know, but it's what I wanted to do.

Together we watched the red-and-orange sun set on the horizon. It was truly a spectacular sight. It was not something I had taken the time to stop and enjoy over the last few years. Somewhere in the middle of seeing it on a daily basis, the beauty had been lost on me, until now.

"Are you ready to grab a bite?" His radiant smile started the butterflies in my stomach fluttering in triple time as he extended his hand to me.

"Sure, what did," I gasped as I touched his hand, "you have in mind?" I quickly darted my eyes away, but didn't let go of his firm grasping hand.

"How about burgers?" It was the first time I'd noticed he had a slight European accent.

I smiled. That I could afford, I thought. "Okay, sounds great."

● ● ●

Surprisingly, instead of letting go of my hand, he intertwined our fingers and led the way back up the sand dunes.

With our hands locked as one, we dashed through the oncoming traffic, laughing. There was something about the way he laughed that made me want to laugh with him. He seemed to just exude happiness.

Our chat continued as we ate, but more and more, I found myself watching the way his mouth moved. It didn't matter if he was eating or talking, his enticing lips amazed me. I thought I might have died and gone to heaven when his tongue darted out and licked off a smudge of ketchup from the corner of his mouth. What was it about him that forced my mind to contemplate these new thoughts?

"Wow, it's getting late. I have to be back before curfew. Can I drive you home?" he asked as he checked his watch.

"Oh. . .I, um. . .well," I stuttered as I racked my brain for a good excuse why he couldn't. I really didn't want him to see the rundown house where I lived with my family.

By family, I meant me, my mom, my nana, and my sister. Did you notice there are no men in our house? Yeah, that would have to do with the fact that every man my family has had a relationship with has left us.

"Stella, don't," he begged as he reached out, grabbing my hand again. "I don't care what your house looks like." His smile disarmed me yet again.

"Okay, but only if you want to. I don't want you to do it because you feel obligated," I whispered, feeling insecure.

"I want to." The way he smiled and gazed into my eyes when he said it told me he was telling the truth.

It was the first time I had been in a classic car. The Mustang he drove wasn't something you saw a lot of these days. Turns out, it wasn't his at all, but his brother Michael's. Michael was two years older than Stefan. He had been in South Carolina going to college for the last two years.

I cringed when I pointed out my house on the little dead-end street not far from the strip. I glanced up to see Stefan staring at me, not the house.

"Can I see you again tomorrow?" he asked. I bit my lip and debated the logic of seeing him again.

"Sure, six again?" What was it about him that had me willing to endure the pain of being walked out on again?

At first, I thought he was stretching, but then he started playing with my hair and twisting it in his fingers. I shivered and looked up in time to see he was leaning toward me. I found myself breathless when his glorious mouth was only an inch from my desperate lips. Was I really going to have my first kiss?

With soft and sweet brushes, his lips ghosted against mine, causing my eyes to flutter shut. My heart raced when he kissed me two more times before pulling back. Yep, there went the rest of the ice around my heart.

I opened my eyes to see Stefan grinning at me. "That was the first time I've ever kissed anyone," he breathed across my face.

"Me, too," I panted.

* * *

22

"I'll pick you up after work tomorrow," he said as he traced my cheek with his fingertips.

"Okay." I giggled, fumbling for the door handle.

I quickly jumped out and ran for my front door before I lost the willpower to leave him.

The rest of my night seemed to crawl by as I thought about what I was getting myself into. No good could come from this situation. He would leave, and I would be left behind again. Why had I opened up to him in the first place? There was no logical reason for me to allow this to continue; I knew better.

Work flew by as I waited for six o'clock to arrive. Before I knew it, it was time to cash out. Stefan still hadn't shown up. Unhappily, I headed out the door only to walk into a wall of flesh. I looked up to see Stefan smiling at me.

"Sorry I'm late; traffic." He shrugged, still smiling.

"Oh, that's okay," I replied, relieved.

"So, do you want to come to the base and walk around there?" He grinned.

"Sure, why not." I bit my upper lip to keep from saying that I was afraid of the base. That place was the source of my family's pain.

Once we were back in his brother's car, we headed toward Fort Story. The guards looked menacing as we approached them. Still, Stefan waved at them, relaxed, and handed over his ID'. Thanks to some quick thinking on my part, I wedged my hands under my thighs so Stefan wouldn't see them trembling. When the M.P. leaned

* * *

into the car, I held my breath and waited.

"Have a nice night, guys." He chuckled.

Relieved, I slowly exhaled. We made our way to our first stop; it was a small cul-de-sac with five houses lining only one side of the road, which ended sharply at the water's edge. The buildings had once housed the personnel who were stationed here; now they were rented as bungalows for visiting and retired military.

The view was breathtaking, to say the least. He showed me to an outcrop that had been built so everyone could enjoy a view of the water below. When he slipped his arms around my waist, I flinched. However, he only chuckled and continued holding me.

The chilled air blew against my exposed flesh, causing me to shiver. Pulling me closer into his embrace, I reveled in the warmth of his skin against mine. His heated breath tickled me as he lowered his face into the crook of my neck and held me tighter. Our bodies molded together becoming seamless and I couldn't help but feel safe there. Safe with him. Inhaling as deep as I could, I absorbed the scent of his cologne. It was such a unique smell, sweet and musky at the same time. No amount of time could erase that scent from my memory.

By the time the sun illuminated the skyline in a rainbow of dusky hues, we were on the main beach of the base. There were no lifeguards, just a plenitude of people who were strolling along the sand. The setting was so serene; I couldn't help but think how worried I had been about being here on the base. Each couple or family was lost in their own little world, so no one noticed the two teenagers sitting side by side, talking and watching the family of dolphins swimming through the shallow water. I had never seen so

● ● ●

many dolphins up close. They were such a magical species.

"Stella, when is your birthday?" He reclined back onto his elbows, grinning.

Rolling onto my stomach, I laughed at ease. "I turn eighteen on August twenty-third. How about you?"

After several failed attempts to speak, he blurted, "Are you serious?" He looked bewildered.

"What?" I was suddenly intrigued by what could have had him so confounded.

"I turn eighteen on August twenty-third, too!" He laughed loud enough to scare off a flock of seagulls.

"Wow, that's weird." I giggled.

"I have never, ever met anyone with the same birthday as me. Maybe that means something." I fought the idea of rolling my eyes at him.

Hidden in the darkness, we made our way back to his car in the parking lot. It was already well after ten o'clock, and he needed enough time to get me back to the strip before his mandated curfew. As he had last night, he parked in front of my house. With a new confidence, he leaned in with hooded eyes and peppered my awaiting lips with sweet kisses. There was no resistance when he pulled me closer to his lap. Of course, the gearshift dug into my hip, but I didn't care about being comfortable. I just wanted to get as close to him as possible. By the time he was done paying his tribute to my swollen lips, I was panting like a dog on a blazing afternoon, then again, so was he.

* * *

"I want to see you tomorrow," he whined, resting his forehead against mine.

"Yes, but I don't have to work," I whimpered, trying to catch my breath.

"Good, then we have all day." He cupped my face in his hands and kissed me again. This time, I was the one trying to wiggle closer to him. We moved our lips against each other's in a slow, synchronized ballet. When we broke apart for the last time, I found I was staring at him breathless; all conscious thought had escaped me.

"Goodnight, Stella." I nodded when my speech still failed me.

I had just reached my door when I turned to see him pulling away. Tonight my mom was not at work, so I was basically busted. I didn't have to see her disapproving expression to know what was coming.

"Who was that young man?" she inquired, no doubt puzzled.

"Stefan. His father is headed for D.C. for a new posting." I tried to sound nonchalant.

She sighed. "Just don't get hurt, baby. Boys from the base only want one thing from the locals. I don't think I need to tell you what that is." I nodded, running for the safety my room.

As usual, my sister Brianna was out with her friends, so I had the room to myself. Sitting on my desk was an ominous symbol of my fate in the form of a large envelope addressed to me. No amount of self-control would cease the trembling that rocked my body as I reached out and grasped the seemingly innocent-looking white rectangle. Clutching the high grade parchment, I slid onto the edge of

● ● ●

my bed. It took more than a few deep gasps for air before I could tear it open.

One word leapt off the paper. Accepted.

It was a letter of notification stating that I had been accepted to Worchester State in Massachusetts. I screamed, jumping up and down like I was on a trampoline.

"Oh. My. God!" I screeched.

"What? What happened?" My mom dashed in scanning the room.

"I got my first letter!"

She looked incredibly proud as she grabbed me into a celebratory hug. "That's awesome, baby!" She grinned, but I knew what she was thinking.

"Don't Mom," I stopped her before she could speak. "I can always get financial aid and student loans to cover it."

She did look more relaxed when I let her go. She smiled, leading me to the bed to sit with her. "I know how you've prayed for this day. Just because it wasn't something I wanted for myself, doesn't mean I don't want it for you. I always knew what I wanted to be, and so have you. I just want you to be happy. Whatever you do, don't lose track of that. Your dreams will never come true if you follow the same path I did."

"No offense, but I don't want to be like you." I chuckled.

"None taken. But I can't help but wonder what's happening. Where did you meet Stefan?" She air quoted his name, making me

* * *

laugh.

"I meet him on the beach. He's different; I can't explain it." I huffed.

"Just don't do anything stupid. Okay?" With quick kiss, she left me stunned. Really? That was the extent to her sex talk? Good thing they covered it in school.

I had no problem falling asleep now that I knew I had at least one school that wanted me. Slowly, I slipped into the dream I'd had for years. This time next year, I would be in college.

● ● ●

Chapter Two

Stella's doing the forbidden

THE SOUND OF A CAR HORN BEEPING FROM THE FRONT yard had me scrambling to the closest window to see who it was. To my delight, it was Stefan. He was just walking up the stairs when I peeked out the living room bay window. Giggling my way, I opened the door and proceeded to throw myself at him. Thankfully, he caught me.

"You're not going to believe it; I received my first acceptance letter!" I shrieked.

"That's awesome! So where is it from?" He laughed, placing me back on my feet with his hands gripping my waist.

● ● ●

29

"Worchester State! They have an awesome horticulture program," I sang like a songbird.

"Congratulations," he breathed as he pulled me further into his embrace.

This time when he kissed me, I automatically threaded my fingers in his black, wispy hair. The soft strands felt like silk between my fingers. His soft lips molded to mine and set off a reaction deep in my chest. Rising up on my tip toes, I pressed in closer to his broad chest. He seemed to really enjoy it, judging by the way he grabbed my hips and pulled them flush to his body. I moaned when he licked my lower lip, which seemed to be an invitation for him to invade my mouth like a marching Army Band.

Slowly, he explored every inch of my mouth with his tantalizing tongue before he backed out and let me do the same. I'll admit, I had no idea what to expect when I slipped in the tip of my tongue. It was single-handedly the best feeling in the world, all slippery and smooth. With hunger, my tongue dove straight in search of more. The taste of his spearmint toothpaste teased my taste buds. There was no way to describe the tingling sensation that ran through my body. Even if the kiss was messy, I didn't care. It was the first time either of us had ever put our tongues in someone else's mouth, and it felt more magical than my wildest fantasy.

We were both panting when we looked into each other's eyes. He seemed just as surprised by what happened between us. We both stepped back, looking around to see if anyone else witnessed our intimate moment.

Looking guilty, he cleared his throat and muttered, "I . . . um . . . sorry. I didn't plan that. It sort of just happened." He ducked his

● ● ●

head, but his blushed cheeks were easily visible.

"Yeah, totally, heat of the moment kind of thing." Stuttering and shuffling my feet seemed to be the new norm for me. Why did he make me so nervous?

"So, we should go and do something to celebrate. Any ideas? Would you like to come back to the base to meet my family?" His eyes danced at the idea of taking me back there.

"I don't know about that." I gnawed my lip nervously.

"Don't be so bashful; they're not so bad." He smiled, looking all too cute to be legal.

"Okay, but if they don't like me, you're bringing me back. Right?" I pleaded.

"Deal! Grab your bag, and let's go." He nudged me with his hip.

I was a wreck the whole way to his townhouse. I had avoided the base for so long, since both of the men who had left my mom pregnant were from there. When I was young and naive, I actually thought they would come back for us. Yeah, stupid, I know. This would be the second time in two days I had visited the taboo location.

Though thinking about it, I realized it wasn't the base that freaked me out. It was that his family would be there. There was no way to know what their expectations were. Did they even know about us hanging out? What did Stefan tell them about me? Or did he tell them anything?

Stefan grabbed my hand firmly and just about dragged me out

* * *

of the car. Seeing him grinning at me left me breathless. The first member of his family we encountered was his brother Michael. He was outside, stretching for a run.

They shared the same physique. Their legs were long and muscular, and both boys were lean with taut, broad shoulders. Together, they had the perfect runner's bodies. I noticed Michael had a tiny amount of hair peeking out from the V-neck of his dark blue T-shirt.

"Michael, this is Stella. Stella, this is my older brother Michael." He placed his arm around my shoulder with pride. Michael looked a lot like Stefan, except his eyes were a blue-grey.

"Nice to meet you, Stella. So you're the one that he can't stop talking about," laughed Michael. This time Stefan looked unabashed.

"I guess." I laughed, ducking my head, smiling.

"Don't pay him any mind, he's just ticked that I keep borrowing his car." Stefan chuckled.

"Just make sure to put gas in her when you bring her back," Michael called out over his shoulder as he took off running down the asphalt. When he referred to his car as a "her," I wondered if he was the type of guy that named his car. Probably, I thought.

A short distance away, we spotted an older couple watching the ships cruising by. From their looks, I guessed they were Stefan's parents. As we approached, I could see more and more how closely he resembled his parents. His mom had short, red hair, and her light-grey eyes were like Stefan's. His dad had the standard military crew cut, and like Stefan's, it was pitch black.

● ● ●

"Mom, Dad, this is Stella. Stella, these are Maurice and Shirley Sterling, my parents." He smiled broadly, but his parents didn't seem so thrilled to meet me.

"Hello," I squawked nervously.

"It's a pleasure to meet you," they said in unison.

Even though they each shook my hand, it felt stiff and hasty. From the way his mother looked at my washed-out jeans and pastel pink T-shirt, I'd say she didn't think much of them or me. Maurice just avoided looking at me entirely. Stefan seemed ignorant of the behavior of his parents, but I wasn't. They were less than thrilled by my presence. There was no pretense in the way they looked down upon me. For Stefan's sake, I made no fuss about leaving. I could endure this for him.

For the next two hours, we sat around on the picnic benches outside, trying to make idle chitchat, but it was strained at best. Once Michael returned from his run and took a shower, it was a lot easier. He seemed so much friendlier than his parents.

Shirley showed me to the bathroom when she retreated inside to prepare dinner. When I returned from the bathroom, Shirley was in the kitchen cooking dinner, but Stefan and his dad were nowhere to be found. I decided to take a walk to the car. That's when I heard their raised voices.

"So that's the little trollop you've been spending your time with?" Maurice sneered.

"Dad, don't! You don't have the right to call her that. You don't even know her." Stefan fought back.

* * *

"I don't have to know her, I know her kind. She will just try to trap you. I bet she spread her legs for you the night you met her!" I winced at his words.

"No, she hasn't! She's not like that!" When he glanced around, I ducked back behind a set of stairs so they wouldn't see me.

"Take her back to whatever hole she crawled out of. I don't want you to see her again!" His tone reflected his authoritative Sergeant Major tone. Stefan had told me his father didn't hide the fact that he had achieved the highest enlisted rank possible.

My stomach clenched at the thought; Stefan was no longer allowed to see me. I had been called worse things than his malicious slurs, so they really didn't bother me. However, hearing him forbidding Stefan from seeing me, felt like he had stabbed me in the heart with a bayonet. My labored breathing caused my chest to heave, and a lone tear slid unprotested down my cheek.

"No, Dad, I can't obey you this time." When Stefan spun around on his heels, Maurice grabbed his shoulder in his attempt to stop him, but he shrugged it away and headed for the car.

I raced back to the Mustang, praying to get there before Stefan. Luck was on my side, and I arrived there first. Pretending to pick at my fingernails, I looked up when he stalked over. Stefan had no idea I'd heard anything, and I wanted to keep it that way. The ride to my house was quiet since we were both lost in our own thoughts. Once he parked, he turned to me with a distressed expression.

"Stella, I am sorry my parents were not nicer to you." I leaned into his hand when he stroked my cheek.

"It's okay, I understand. Thank you, and I wish you the best

• • •

in D.C." I swallowed the lump in my throat.

"Stella, I don't understand. Are you breaking up with me?" he snipped.

"Stefan, first, I didn't know we were together. Second, your family doesn't approve," I mumbled the end and locked my eyes on my hands so he wouldn't see the tears that refused to stay in my eyes.

"I thought you understood. Do you think I would kiss you like I did if you were just my friend? Is that how you kiss your friends? Because I distinctly remember you saying you'd never kissed anyone before me. So tell me now if I am just another guy to you!" His eyes, now sad, mirrored the same aching I felt in my chest.

"No, there's never been anyone else for me, just you. But, you never said anything. I hoped . . . I mean."

Stefan paused before leaning over, trapping my lips in a passionate kiss. He held nothing back. Our lips moved together with so much vigor, I could feel all of his feelings flow into me.

"I don't care what the old fool has to say. I plan to come back to you on my birthday. We can go to the same college. I will go wherever you go. I just want to be with you," he implored as I stared into his steel-grey eyes.

I believed him. "I want that, too. But. . ."

He shushed me by placing his fingers over my lips. "We have a week and a half before I leave. We'll write, email, text and call each other after that. At least until I can come back." He grinned, excited with his ideas.

"Everyone says that; then they forget about me," I

● ● ●

whimpered, clutching onto my black hoodie.

"I'm not everyone. I promise I will come back," he mumbled, peppering my wanting lips again.

The night after his father banned us from seeing each other, he came back, thanks to Michael. We were careful enough to stay away from the base after the disastrous first meeting with his parents. If I wasn't working, I was with him. Sometimes Michael had to drop Stefan off and drive around the beach while we hung out. His parents were still being difficult. He insisted that he didn't care, that he wanted to see me, and that was all that mattered. I prayed to God he was right. It was torturous whenever he left my side.

Michael was being great with the whole scenario. He snuck Stefan out every day to see me. Stefan was creative with the things we did. One night we went bowling; he won, of course. Another night we went miniature golfing, and it was my turn to gloat. Hey, I live in a tourist town; we golf all the time.

It was hard to believe it'd been only a week since I met Stefan. I wouldn't admit it to him, but I had some seriously deep feelings for him. He was different from everyone else I'd met on the beach. Then again, I'd avoided meeting anyone on the beach for years. After my disastrous first summer of playing on the beach alone, I'd refused to get to know anyone, and not just the tourists. The pain of people walking away wasn't worth the short comfort an outsider would bring, or anyone else for that matter. Something about Stefan had suddenly changed that, and I was at a loss to explain why.

"Stella!" Stefan called me out to the yard. When I ran straight into his arms, he chuckled and wrapped himself around me.

"Hey, beautiful," he breathed into my hair.

● ● ●

"Hey, good looking," I cooed at his intense gaze.

"I've missed you. Michael wants to drive us to the Drive-In to see a movie. Do you like that idea?" he purred in my ear, making my knees weak.

"Sure, let me just get my stuff." I quickly scrambled inside to retrieve my bag from the couch.

"Hey, Michael." I giggled as he let me into the backseat.

"Hey, Stella. Kiss this kid already, he's been driving me nuts all day to come see you." He laughed.

I didn't have to kiss him; he beat me to it. There was no better feeling in the world than the way he set my heart ablaze. Never would I deny him the right to devour me from the inside out.

"Hey, Michael, crank up the radio." Stefan chuckled.

"Did you miss me?" he purred in my ear.

"Uh-huh." I bit my lip to keep it from quivering.

"I missed you, too. How was school?" He plucked my lip free from my teeth.

"Boring; it would have been more fun being with you." I giggled.

"Our mail caught up to us. My aunt said I received a letter from Norfolk State."

"Really? Have you decided where you're going yet?"

"Yes. Have you?"

● ● ●

"Yes, Norfolk State."

"Then it's a good thing that's where I want to go, too."

I tried my best not to giggle as Stefan ghosted his fingertips along the hem of my sweatshirt. It tickled in a heated way. The desire he invoked was a new feeling for me. In fact, every feeling with Stefan was a new feeling from the beginning. The way he spun my world on its axis the moment he touched me was still mind-boggling.

After a breathtaking kiss, he moaned, "Stella," his voice raspy as his breath fanned out across my neck and chest.

I screeched when Stefan was suddenly ripped from my embrace and out of the car. Maurice, his dad, stood with a struggling Stefan by his throat just feet from where I sat in the backseat. From Maurice's expression, I would say he was past the point of being pissed off. With one shove, Maurice threw Stefan against the side of the car. Michael, who had stepped out to use the restroom, came running back to defend his younger brother from their burly father. I had the distinct impression this was not the first time he'd needed to do that.

"What did I tell you about seeing her?" Maurice looked like rabid coyote, ready to foam at the mouth.

"I will see anyone I choose to!" Stefan struggled to stay in his path, attempting to keep him from approaching me.

"Not when you are living under my roof, you won't!"

"Dad, stop!" Michael tried to situate himself between them when his dad stalked forward, trying to grab Stefan.

Climbing out, I tried to stop the madness. However, Stefan

● ● ●

had other ideas.

"You can't stop me!" Stefan snickered, incensing his father further.

I grabbed Stefan by the arm to pull him to his senses, but he yanked his arm away.

"Oh, yes, I can!" Maurice seethed. "Get the hell in the car!"

"No!" He leered back.

I screamed again when Maurice backhanded Stefan across his right cheek. Stefan crumpled to his knees, holding his slacken jaw. Michael finally managed to shove Maurice backward. Maurice was stunned, to say the least. Rushing to Stefan's side, I tried to calm him, but it didn't work.

"Michael, I would suggest you stay out of this, if you know what's good for you." While Maurice read him the riot act, Michael stealthily slipped the car key behind him and motioned to us to take his car.

Before either of us could blink, Michael spun around. "Run kid!" he grunted as he twisted back and wrestled his father to the ground.

Stefan grabbed my hand and shoved me into the car. Before Maurice could break free from Michael's hold, Stefan started and floored the car. Thank God, we were in the back row, so there weren't many cars to avoid. His hands were shaking when he reached out and latched onto my hand.

"Are you all right?" his voice quivered.

* * *

"Yes. Are you?" My hands started shaking too as the adrenaline rush hit me.

"Yeah, I'll be fine. It's Michael I'm worried about. My dad has a bit of a temper," he said, letting go of my hand to rub his cheek.

"I noticed. Will he really hurt him?"

"No, he's probably already in his car speeding our way." He grimaced at the thought.

"What are we going to do? Maybe you should go back? I don't want to tear your family apart," I pleaded, looking through the back window.

"No, I love you!" he blurted.

I looked at him with my mouth agape.

"Oh, I see. You — you don't love me back." He mistook my shocked expression for rejection.

"No, I do love you. I just didn't think you loved me, too." A smile crept across my cheeks.

"Don't scare me like that! I think my heart skipped a few beats." His infectious laugh vibrated through the car.

"What now?"

"Well, I'm not going back to the base, that's for sure."

"We can't go to my house. My mom would throw a hissy fit." I could just see her face if I strolled in with Stefan. It was not a pretty thought.

● ● ●

"We can find a motel away from the beach. I can drive you to school in the morning." I nodded apprehensively.

Together, we scraped up enough money to rent a room at a dive motel off the strip. The Mayflower Motel was used by the locals. It was frill-less and had no amenities. They didn't even have a pool. I followed him to the room, feeling a little more than anxious. He must have sensed my apprehension, because he hugged the stuffing out of me and stroked my rumpled hair. The fact that there was only one bed did not escape me, which meant we would have to share. I called my mom from Stefan's phone and left her a message that I would be staying at a friend's house to study. Now, if I had friends, that would have been believable.

In the end, he was a perfect gentleman. We cuddled and kissed, but nothing more. True to his word, in the morning he drove me to school and promised to pick me up when I got out. Watching him drive away made me feel like I was suffocating.

The day crawled by as I watched the clock on the wall tick by at a snail's pace. I willed it to move faster; of course, it didn't work. Instead of paying attention to the lessons, I counted down the minutes until the final bell. At three o'clock, I was waiting outside school. My school bus drove past as I shifted between my feet, waiting. At half past three, I sighed heavily and started the two-mile walk home, crying the whole way. My heart was officially broken again. Maybe broken was not the right word; obliterated sounded more like it.

When I reached my house an hour later, the house was empty. I tried to call Stefan's cell, but it went straight to his voicemail. Allowing myself to wallow in loneliness, without even doing my homework, I fell asleep miserable and alone.

* * *

Chapter Three

Stefan's soul stirring awake

AFTER TEN YEARS OF LIVING ABROAD, MY DAD received his orders to ship back to the States. It was the best news I'd heard in two years. Two years ago, my older brother Michael had moved to South Carolina to go to college. Michael was more than my older brother; he was my best friend. When he left, I totally shut myself off from everyone. Using the internet, we talked every chance available to us. Just knowing I would be in the same country lifted my spirits.

Michael was ecstatic when he heard we would be living in Washington, D.C. Even though it would be a long ride, it would be feasible in the classic, faded, green Mustang my grandfather left to

* * *

Michael when he turned sixteen.

The last time we were in the States was four years ago in Miami for my grandfather's funeral. I missed the old coot. He just couldn't live without my grandmother. When she passed a few months before him, she took his heart with her. He told us the story of how they met and how he instantly fell head over heels in love with her. She, of course, said the same thing. What a pair they were. Never have I ever seen two people more in love than the two of them.

I always laughed off the idea of falling for someone so fast until the day I saw her. Even in a white, logo T-shirt and black, washed-out, skinny jeans, she was beautiful beyond compare.

What had started out as me buying a simple chocolate ice cream turned into the awakening of my soul. Sure, I had friends and family that I loved, but I'd never been in love. First off, never knowing when you would be moved to a new base made getting close to people tricky. Kids living on the bases understood this fact. We were friends, but we were ready to move on or say goodbye at a moment's notice.

Looking into Stella's eyes for the first time, they enchanted me. They shimmered in the sunshine like pools of honey. I was so fixated on them that I forgot what I wanted to order. When she bit her pouty bottom lip, my knees started to buckle beneath me. I would have fallen if I hadn't been holding onto the white Formica countertop.

The sudden attraction was all so new to me. I was at a loss for words, so I did the only thing I could do, I left. Of course, I kicked myself in the pants for not talking to her more than about the weather. The girl seriously left me speechless. It took a full night of

● ● ●

my brother heckling me until I promised to try again the next day.

"Are you serious? The weather? That was the best you could come up with?" Michael chuckled at my embarrassment.

"What can I say? I was distracted," I defended myself.

"Dude, you need to go back and woo her." He laughed when my jaw hung open.

"How do I do that?"

"For starters, treat her like a lady. She sounds inexperienced, so take it slow. Don't push her unless you see her hesitating. There is probably a reason for it. Maybe she was hurt by someone." That thought made my stomach churn.

The last thing I wanted was someone to have hurt her. Taking mental notes, I tried to remember everything he suggested. The basics he provided would help; at least that was the hope I clung to.

I counted my lucky stars when I showed up and business was slow. To my amazement, she remembered my order and, before I could ask, she handed me my chocolate cone. This time, I took the initiative and spoke to her in earnest. She was so adorable the way she gawked and stuttered her name. I just wanted to grab her and whisk her away before anyone could distract her. I wanted her undivided attention.

It appeared that I wasn't the only one having problems with concentration when I caught her watching me seductively lick my ice cream. I chuckled when she blushed in embarrassment. I'll be honest; my intention was to keep doing it just so she'd kept watching.

This was new for me, too. I'd never liked when someone's

* * *

attention was focused on me. I'd always avoided girls who were pushy. Something about Stella screamed that she was not that type.

The snappiness of her tone alerted me that I had inadvertently insulted her when I suggested she should go to Italy. It was the last thing I wanted to do. All I wanted to say was that she was stunning, but she didn't take it that way. After a heartfelt apology, she forgave me. It was a mistake I would not soon be repeating.

Trying to be sincere, I reached out and grasped her tiny hand in mine. It was so soft and warm; I never wanted to let it go. She seemed shocked by my touch, as if she had never been touched before. The downfall to borrowing Michael's car was that I needed to get back before he banned me from ever driving it again, and I needed it to see her again.

Holding my breath, I asked her if she would let me come back and see her again. Seeing her nod and whisper, "Six," relaxed me as I exhaled. I wanted nothing more than to stay there and stare at her with her lip locked between her teeth again. Obviously she was as nervous as me. The best I could manage was a sharp nod. When the hairs on the back of my neck stood on end, I knew she was watching me make my way to the Mustang.

The elated feeling started my insides quivering with excitement. Thoughts of running back, pulling her close, and kissing her fogged my brain further. The ride back to the base, hanging by the pool, and the ride back were a blur. All I could think about was the girl that drew me in like a bee to pollen.

I must have surprised her when I arrived back at the stand. Her cute gasp tickled my eardrums as if it were the sweetest music they'd ever heard. The way she crept out the door to meet me had my

● ● ●

stomach doing flip-flops. Stella was even shyer than I had expected.

Our first date went perfectly, until I needed to bring her home. The worry etched on her face announced her fear of me knowing where she lived. I guessed right, but after a little reassurance, she relaxed. She was indeed embarrassed when we pulled up, not that I really noticed the house. I was too busy memorizing her perfect, angelic features. A new blush colored her cheeks a beautiful shade of rose.

Softly, I begged to see her again the next day. Her hesitation caused my heart to race. It raced even faster when she agreed.

Fearing she'd run away, I stretched out and twirled my fingers into her silky, auburn locks. She shivered when I made my first move, leaning in to kiss her. From the first brush to the last, my lips begged for more. The gentleness of her lips against mine made me physically ache. It was difficult not to move past chaste kisses, but I managed. When her eyes fluttered shut, I let mine do the same. When mine opened, hers were still shut. I couldn't help but tell her, "That was the first time I ever kissed anyone," I confessed, amazed that my lips tingled, her taste still lingering on them.

"Me too," she breathed.

"I'll pick you up after work tomorrow," I said and outlined her sleek jawbone with my fingertips.

"Okay," she giggled when she reached for the door handle without looking. Now it was my turn to gawk as she ran for the house. The way her body swayed was poetry in motion.

Michael was out walking the beach when I returned to the base, so I jogged up to join him. "Hey kid, how did your date go?"

● ● ●

"Really great! There is something about that girl that just turns me into a puddle of mush. Have you ever felt that way?"

"Once." He looked away and refused to elaborate any further.

"I had my first kiss," I chuckled.

"And Stella?"

"Yeah, her first, too." I grinned, thrilled by that fact.

"That's awesome. I'm so happy for you." He clapped me on the back.

"Can I borrow the car tomorrow to take her out again?"

"Sure, why not."

Not wanting to rush back, we walked the beach for another hour before heading back to the townhouse. I was surprised at how much Michael knew about dating. He had never even mentioned a girl before, and whenever I asked, he'd look off into the distance, leaving my questions unanswered. I knew my brother well enough to know that there was something he didn't want anyone to know, but I didn't know what it was. Maybe he had been hurt by someone at school and it still smarted?

By the grace of God, my parents were asleep when we slipped in. Stifling our laughs, we tip-toed in and dashed for our room before our parents had a chance to hear us.

As a family, we spent the day on the beach swimming, playing volleyball, and tossing the pigskin around. With dinnertime quickly approaching, I knew I needed to tell my mom why I wouldn't be there.

● ● ●

"Hey Mom, I have plans, so don't make me any dinner." I kept my eyes trained on the sand at my feet.

"Really? What are you doing?"

"I have a date," I mumbled.

"With who? Did you meet someone here on the base?"

"She's not from the base. I met her on the boardwalk when Michael and I went there yesterday." I glanced up to see she wasn't as happy about it as I was.

"Stefan, I don't think that's a good idea." Her voice sounded edgy as she stared out at the water.

"Mom, please don't act like that. This is the first girl I have wanted to get to know better." Okay, so 'better' didn't sum it up entirely.

"We leave in two weeks. Then what?"

"I don't know. We'll see how it goes. Maybe we could do the long distance thing." I was willing to give it a shot if Stella felt the same way about me.

She blew out a deep breath. "I guess I don't have a say in this. Do I?"

"No, not really. See you tonight, Mom," I chuckled and kissed her on the cheek before running off to get ready.

Thanks to a minor fender bender, I was five minutes late getting to Jerry's. Talk about road rage; I wanted to get out and push the piece of junk out of my way. Relief washed over me when I saw that she hadn't left yet. Stella seemed apprehensive when I asked her

● ● ●

to join me on the base, but I wanted us away from the tourist thing so getting to know her better would be easier. Really, what did she have to be afraid of?

Stella didn't fool me; I saw her sitting on her hands. The girl was petrified, and I couldn't figure out why. Once we'd passed through the checkpoints, I took the second right off the main road. It was a dead end that ended sharply at the water. My dad had given us a tour the day we arrived. He had been here before for training. We'd been in Italy for the summer visiting my aunt, so he had come solo. I was only a toddler at the time, so I don't remember him even being here.

I led her on a tiny tour. "See those houses? They used to be houses for the families stationed here. Now they rent them out for bungalows." I pointed out the five houses that lined the street.

Grabbing her hand, I dragged her to the overlook. She gasped when she looked over the railing. Below us, the water crashed into the rocks. Moving backward, she found herself moving right to where I wanted her to be. The cool night air whipped through her T-shirt, causing her flesh to break out into goose bumps. Encircling her, I shared my body heat to keep her warm. Every time I touched her, it wasn't enough; I needed more. Breathing into the crook of her neck, I watched as the tiny hairs there shivered. The scent of her perfume tickled my nostrils when I inhaled deeply against her neck. Oh, she smelled so good, so sweet.

"We should go to the main beach; it will be warmer there." I hated the thought of unwinding myself and letting her go.

Holding hands, we strolled our way back to the car. The main beach was only a five minute ride from where we were. When the

● ● ●

wooden walkway ended, we stripped off our sneakers and socks and strolled the sandy beach, talking. Stella was in awe of the mated dolphin school making their way to feed only thirty feet from the shore.

There was just so much about her I wanted to know. To my amazement, we learned that we shared the same birthday. Just about everything about her fascinated me, even the fact that pink was her favorite color. The conversation just flowed effortlessly as the sun set and darkness engulfed the sky.

The details of her family dynamics explained so much about her fears of me and the base. I finally understood why Stella was standoffish about us. She'd been hurt in a way no one who didn't live it could understand. What she needed to learn from me was that I wasn't like everyone who had hurt her and her family.

With my curfew quickly approaching, I was forced to drive her home. Tonight when I kissed her, I wasn't nervous at all. The downfall to that was that I could feel my hormones surging when our lips danced together. I never wanted to stop, and the way her lips caressed mine was like heaven.

Unlike last night, she seemed to hesitate when she slipped in through her door.

I felt like I was dancing on clouds when I bounced into the townhouse. Michael chuckled when he glanced up to see me grinning from ear to ear.

"I'd ask how it went, but from that grin, I don't think I need to."

"Stefan?" My dad interrupted.

* * *

"Yeah, Dad, I'm home on time." I plopped down on the sofa next to Michael.

"Don't be up all night." Michael growled a retort under his breath.

Stifling a laugh, I answered, "Okay."

"So kid, tell me about your girl." He smirked, amused.

"She's perfect. I cannot explain it, but deep down I know I was just waiting for her. It's like Grampy used to say; it was just there."

"Ah, the infamous love at first sight?"

"Yeah. I never believed in it either, but now I'm a believer," I chuckled and nodded.

"I believe him, too." He looked somewhat sad when he said it.

My parents didn't say much on the subject of Stella and me for the first few dates. It wasn't until I brought her back to the base to meet them that my dad made his opinion known.

"Stefan, I want to talk to you while Stella is in the bathroom."

"Sure, Dad. What's up?"

I could see the disgust in his features as he went off on his tirade. When he called Stella a trollop, I wanted nothing more than to deck him right then and there. Who did he think he was? She was the furthest thing from a trollop, and I knew this first hand, not him.

Balling up my fists, I flat out denied his orders to stay away

● ● ●

from Stella. As the words slipped out of my mouth, a plan formed in my mind. I would continue to see her; moreover, once I was done with high school, I would be by her side if she wanted me. I had known the moment I'd laid eyes on her that I loved her. Now I needed to know if she felt the same. Before he could lash out further, possibly being overheard, I stomped off.

Stella was sitting on the hood of the car, looking gorgeous as always, when I approached. "Ready to go?"

"Sure," she simply replied.

Stella was too quiet as we drove back to her house. The fidgeting with her black hoodie told me that she wanted to say something, but was holding back. However, nothing prepared me for her statement when we parked out front of her house.

"Stella, I am sorry my parents weren't nicer to you." Her flushed cheek molded to my hand as I caressed it.

"It's okay, I understand. Thank you, and I wish you the best in D.C.," she whispered, so soft and unsure.

I was flabbergasted. The best I could manage was a croaked, "Stella, I don't understand. Are you breaking up with me?"

Looking like an idiot, I kept trying to stop her as she explained that she didn't know we were a couple. How could she not know? Did she think I walked around locking lips with everyone I met? When she paused to breathe, I set her straight on my thinking. Laying my heart on the line, I told her what I had planned for my birthday. Making it clear, I told her how we could do this. Even if we couldn't see each other, there were plenty of other ways to keep in touch. It broke my heart when she thought I would forget her. That

● ● ●

was no longer a possibility for me. She owned my heart, and she always would.

Making the most of the time we had, I made sure to do all the things that would remind her of me. She wouldn't be able to walk by the bowling alley, mini golf, or the beach without seeing me there. At Michael's suggestion, I asked Stella to go to the Drive-In. Like me, she never even asked what we would be seeing.

The slow, relaxed ride to the Drive-In was spent in each other's arms as we chatted about the stupid things we did that day. Michael cranked up the radio when I asked, so it was like being alone as we cuddled in the backseat. I surprised Stella when I told her I had also received a letter of acceptance to Norfolk. Stella had actually received three acceptance letters since our first date, but this was the only school we had both applied to.

Without a word, she latched her lips onto mine and did her best to suffocate me. If I had to die, that would definitely be my choice of infliction.

Once the movie started, Michael slipped out to use the men's room. Taking advantage of the alone time, I pulled Stella into a searing kiss. Without thinking, my fingers found their way to her hips, then the border of her jeggings and white hoodie. The feel of her soft skin under my hand had my hormones surging.

"Stella," I moaned, letting the emotions I was feeling show through.

She groaned in my ear, not that I minded. But apparently my father did, because suddenly the car door flew open and he dragged me out. For the second time on this vacation, I found myself defying my dad. Why is it parents do not understand their children? When

● ● ●

you find love, you cannot control it. They think because I fell for Stella so fast that it was a fleeting emotion. It was far from that.

This time when we fought, Michael jumped in the middle. It didn't stop my father from striking me. I'll be the first to admit it, it hurt like hell. Michael and my dad have never seen eye to eye on anything. He always defended me when my father would lash out at us.

When Michael threw the keys and yelled, "Run, kid!" I did without hesitation, pulling Stella along with me. It was a massive adrenalin rush when we sped away in search of freedom. Not knowing what else to do, we headed for the cheapest motel we could find, The Mayflower Motel. Neither of us had much money in our pockets, but we did have enough for one room.

With only one full-sized bed in the room, Stella and I needed to share it. "Stella, come here." I patted the spot beside me on the bed.

Stella looked petrified, but she crept over anyway. "Don't be afraid of me. You have nothing to be worried about."

"I've never stayed in a motel before." She blushed, showing her innocence.

"I have, but never like this. You know, with a girlfriend. I really need to hold you right now. Normally, after a fight with my dad, me and Michael are there to keep each other company." Nodding, she slipped down and wrapped her small arms around me.

I almost laughed after we both sighed at the time. There was something about the way our bodies molded together as one. With her touch came comfort and acceptance, something I had never felt

● ● ●

before with anyone outside my family.

I have never spent a better night than that one, laying there holding and kissing her. She felt so right cradled in my arms. It was like she belonged there. With her face in the crook of my neck, she softly panted, drifting off to sleep.

In the morning, I drove her to school and promised to be back at three o'clock to pick her up. It was a promise I wouldn't be able to keep.

• • •

Chapter Four

Stella's goodbyes and letting go

AFTER STEFAN NEVER CAME TO PICK ME UP FROM school, I spent the next two days attending school and sulking around the house. I went through the motions of doing homework, attending classes, and doing my chores, but that was about it. I was too miserable to do anything else. The feeling of having my heart torn out lingered and tortured me. I had known better, but still I'd let him in where he could shred my soul without even trying. I should have listened to my brain when it had screamed for me to run. I had run, but in the wrong direction. I should have dashed away the second he introduced himself.

Stefan was still not answering his cell phone or returning my

* * *

messages. The best I could come up with was he went back to his family at the base. They must have convinced him that I couldn't be good for him. I didn't want to admit it, but deep down, I knew they were right. Being with me only promised both of us pain. His leaving was now the only guarantee he could give me.

When I disembarked the school bus, I was stunned to see Michael sitting on my doorstep with a long-stemmed, red rose in his hands. His face also sported a new blackened eye, no doubt compliments of his dad.

"Hey, Stella. Stefan wanted me to bring you this." He held up the rose.

"I don't understand." I tilted my head questioningly.

"Yeah, well, he's being kept under lock and key, thanks to my very overbearing dad. He sent you a note with it explaining everything." He shrugged and stood to leave.

"Is he okay?" I whispered, staring at the rose in my shaky hands. If he'd hit Michael, had he also hit Stefan? The thought caused a new fear to well up in my chest.

He sighed and hung his head low. "Yeah, but he misses you something fierce. I'm sorry things turned out this way."

"Thanks, Michael. Will you tell him I miss him, too?"

"Will do. See you around."

I wanted to say, "I doubt it" but it seemed a moot point.

"Michael, would you do me a favor?"

"Sure, Stella. What can I do?"

● ● ●

58

"Would you bring him a letter back from me?"

"Yeah, I can do that." He chuckled at my ridiculous question.

I dashed into the house and ran to my cluttered desk, stumbling over the vacuum cleaner in my haste and retrieving the needed supplies. In less than perfect penmanship, I scribbled down a quick note on my initialed stationary I'd had printed the year before.

S.R.A.

Dear Stefan,

Thank you for the rose, even though I am sure Michael picked it up for you. It's beautiful. I miss you. The pain of being separated is unbearable.

I will love you always and dream of you every night hoping you'll return. The thought of never seeing you again is tearing me apart, but I will survive if I know you're happy. So be happy, safe, and content in life.

If you never come back, remember one thing, I will forever remember you and the time we spent together. Please don't forget me; it would kill me if you did.

You are the only man I have ever loved,

Stella

● ● ●

I added half of the strip of photos we had taken in one of those automatic photo booths that littered the beach front before sealing it shut. I added one squirt of my favorite perfume, *Pink Sugar*. It was a simple gesture I hoped he would appreciate. I raised the envelope to my lips and placed a small kiss on the seal, leaving a slight trace of my pink lip gloss on it. My rattled nerves made my hands shake as I looked at what could be my last correspondence with Stefan.

Before I could change my mind or lose the courage to follow through, I raced back to Michael delivering my note and pictures.

"He'll love this. He has been out of his mind worrying about you," Michael snickered, waving the envelope and fanning himself. The scent of my perfume had him grinning when he sniffed the small gift.

"I hope so. I miss him something terrible," I muttered.

"If it's destined to be, it will." He smirked, shrugging his shoulders before turning and walking away.

Leaning against the green siding, I slid down the wall, dropping to the porch flooring. From my squatted position, I watched him climb back into the faded Mustang. Once he was gone, I pushed myself up, moved inside, and plopped down on the decrepit, black suede couch in the living room. With trembling hands, I opened the expensive-looking envelope and began reading. Stefan's script was very elegant for a man's, but I guessed it had something to do with living abroad.

Dear Stella,

* * *

I am so sorry I could not pick you up that day. The M.P.s caught sight of my car and they dragged me back to my parents.

I miss you. If I get an opportunity, I will try to see you before we leave. If I can't, I will call you or send you a letter once we settle. I will do everything in my power to see you before I leave. You cannot reach me by cell phone right now, my dad confiscated it.

I love you! Never doubt that. Trust me, I would rather be in your arms than here missing you.

You own my heart and soul,

Stefan

A tear slipped down my cheek onto the paper. Somehow, I found the strength to drag myself to my room, and I flopped onto my bed with the note in one hand and the rose in the other.

❖◇❖

In my dark bedroom, I reveled in the thought that he still loved me. My mind spun as I replayed every moment of our short time together. It had been the best week of my lonely life.

My life was lonely for a reason. I had made it that way. The summer I turned ten, I'd learned one important lesson: never let anyone in where they could hurt you. Annie was a prime example. She was my first and last best friend. The two weeks we spent together playing in the sand were the best two weeks of my life, until she left. Annie promised I'd hear from her once she went back to

Boston, but it never happened. Lesson learned.

After making five more friends that summer, I had shut everyone out, not just the outsiders. The outsiders, or tourists, were users. They invaded our territory and pillaged the area, leaving it battered and scarred from their abuse. The residents who catered to them were no better, in my eyes. I knew it made me a hypocrite for working at the ice cream stand, but I needed the money.

◊◊◊

Two more days passed. Stefan would be leaving the next day. As per my usual, I was lying in bed, curled up into a tight ball, staring at the wall. It was one of those rare days when it was raining.

Suddenly, I heard someone outside my window screaming. I rushed over and threw it open to see Stefan standing in the rain, soaked from head to toe.

"STELLA!" he bellowed. It was just like my mother's favorite movie. The same movie she picked my name from, *A Streetcar Named Desire*.

I rushed down the stairs to the back door. I didn't care that it was raining; I ran straight out and leaped into his waiting arms.

"Oh God, I've missed you!" he mumbled against my lips between kisses. His voice echoed the desperation I felt.

"I missed you so much." I openly sobbed as he started kissing me again. "How?" I gasped.

● ● ●

"Michael," he panted, his kiss deep. Stefan's tongue danced with mine, our kiss deepening even further.

The sheer force of the desire that swelled deep in my chest was mind-boggling. There had never been another man who could penetrate the defensive walls I placed around my heart over the years. In just under two weeks, he had obliterated those walls to a fine powder.

I'm not sure how long we stood there brushing our lips against one another's and caressing each other's faces. I did know, by the time we reached my house, we were both soaked to the bone. With shivers wracking our bodies, we tried our best to towel dry each other off. The water pooling at our feet was proof that the towels weren't going to be enough.

"Stella, I leave tomorrow, but we still have tonight. Please, let's spend our last few hours alone?" he pleaded, his hair still dripping, the droplets glimmering as they rolled down his cheeks.

"I would like that," I admitted, breathless. My body tingled as he stroked my arms.

He didn't hesitate to drag me through the house and upstairs. I pointed out the door to my room with my trembling hand. With our hands clutched together, he spun to face me and kissed me desperately until I felt like I would pass out from oxygen deprivation.

"Stella," he moaned, cupping my face in his hands. "I've never felt like this before with anybody. I need you in a way I've never needed anyone," he whimpered into my mouth.

Stefan started rubbing his cold hands across my wet clothes. His clothes clung to his firm physique, making him look even more

* * *

defined. His chest heaved against mine, making me want to be as close to him as possible. Our shared body heat started to warm our cool, damp skin. No amount of denial could hide the effect our closeness caused.

"Stefan, this isn't a good idea. I don't want to be like my mom." My mind said no, but my body was screaming yes.

"I promise I'm not like your dad. I'll be back on August twenty-third, when my parents can't stop us from being together," he vowed with total confidence.

"I love you. Can't we wait until then?" I chewed my lip, nervous.

"I love so much, I feel like my heart will explode. I want to show you by giving you the one thing they can't stop me from giving you: me!"

There was no fighting it anymore. He wanted it, I wanted it, and that was the moment my dreams died. Whether I knew it or not at the time was irrelevant. At that moment I sealed my fate.

Lying in his warm embrace, I never wanted that moment to end. But you know what they say, everything ends. Promises were made, declarations declared, and prayers spoken that come August, we'd be together again.

With heavy hearts, we kissed one last time. His kiss sealed the vow of his return. We clutched each other close on the porch before he made himself leave to join Michael in the car. I watched them drive down the road and out of my life.

It was the longest night of my short life. From beneath my

● ● ●

sheets, I stifled my sobs when my family started arriving home. I didn't want anyone to know I had done the unthinkable; I had let an outsider in.

I winced and whimpered as I hopped into my jeans the next morning. The night before had felt so right at the time, but it had left me sore - not just in the physical sense, either. I knew Stefan was already gone, torn away and dragged to a distant state where I couldn't follow him. His father planned to leave after his five o'clock morning run. That had been two hours ago.

Begrudgingly, I made my way to school for the usual onslaught of the weekend's conquests. The barbaric ritual of girlfriend dumping after the ultimate goal was achieved was running rampant like the swine flu. It was something I had never taken part in, so I just ignored the rumors of who dumped whom and started dating whom. It didn't matter to me; Stefan was the only thing that did.

I know they say misery loves company, but there was no one I wanted to spill my guts to about the loss of my first love. Through the years, I had succeeded in alienating myself from everyone. I was a loner by choice; it was not something I would be changing now. I wanted to be left alone.

◈◇◈

The lunchroom was filled to the brim with happy couples who'd obviously hooked up over the weekend. Every table had at least one couple holding hands or snuggling. The other occupants seemed not to notice what was going on. However, I did from my seat in the corner. The table in the furthest corner has been my corner since the first day of high school. That was where I did my homework or read. No one attempted to invite me to sit with them anymore. They had quickly learned after the first week of sophomore year that I wanted nothing from anyone there.

Glancing around the room again, it saddened me to see that I wasn't the only one alone. Several girls who had been replaced over the weekend looked devastated at seeing their ex-boyfriends with someone new already.

Even sadder was the lone table in the opposite corner of the cafeteria where the outcasts sat. By outcasts, I mean the unfortunate ladies who found themselves pregnant before graduation. Typically, once their boyfriends found out about their "condition," they couldn't reach the door quick enough. There were also a few that had found themselves shoved aside because the fathers of their unborn children were on vacation and long gone before the rabbit died.

The only exception to that scenario was Danielle Atkins. Her boyfriend Christian Mathers had stayed with her, and together they intended to raise their child. It was endearing to see them so in love. Christian was constantly caressing or kissing her bulging belly. Their small clique of friends didn't seem bothered by their affections toward one another.

By the time the final bell rang, I was aching to see Stefan again, even though I knew it might not happen again until August. We'd made a date for our birthdays to meet at the lighthouse at dusk. We would try to see each other before then, but in the event his parents didn't allow it to happen, that was the plan.

● ● ●

We'd spent the last night locked in each other's embrace for hours, deciding since we were both accepted to Norfolk State, we would attend together. After that, we had no idea, but that was enough. He promised to write every week until he got his cell phone back. I agreed to do the same since I couldn't afford a cell phone. The plans did nothing to erase my agony or despair.

The first week passed slowly. Every day I'd run home and check the mailbox. Each day I sunk deeper into despair when there would be no letter from Stefan. How did military families survive the torture of being away from their loved ones? Waiting was all I could do as the week crawled by. What I wouldn't do for any sign from him, anything to say "I'm alive" or "I miss you."

The last letter from Stefan was secured safely in my wallet with the only memory I had of my heritage, a single wallet sized photo of my father and the half picture strip of Stefan and I. Each night, I'd slip them out and trace the handwritten script of his note. Just seeing his features in the tiny photos made me tear up. I missed him.

◊ ◊ ◊

By the first weekend, no letter arrived. Without school to distract me, the loneliness spread like a wildfire through my chest. My heart physically ached to be with him, even for just a moment. Working at Jerry's part-time didn't help either. Everywhere I looked, I would see someone who reminded me of him. Each time, my chest would tighten, and my heart pounded. Without Stefan, I had no life worth living.

The next week dragged by with still no word from Stefan. My reality now was that I might have to face the fact that he might not come back. Had I been like my mother? Deep down, I knew that wasn't true, but it didn't stop me from dwelling on it.

◊ ◊ ◊

April

"April showers bring May flowers" is a way of saying that, if you get through the bad parts, you will be rewarded with something beautiful. I could say that was a good summary of my life. If the beautiful part would arrive, I'd be ecstatic.

Trying my best to look inconspicuous, hidden beneath my straw sun hat and shades, I did my best to try to look touristy. I strolled through an unknown pharmacy on the other side of the beach. It took a mere trolleybus ride to get me across the two-mile stretch of the strip. It was a long trip, but my hope was that no one from school would see me. If anyone in school even knew why I was there, my life would have been a living hell. Oh wait, it already was. Well, it would only get worse if the word spread.

Standing at the end cap of the aisle, I pretended to be completely enthralled by a trashy tabloid, but the truth was I was deciding from a distance which box I wanted to buy. With my brow furrowed, and my lips pursed, I darted down the aisle grabbing the desired box stealthily. Without trying to look like a shoplifter, I hurried to the counter and placed down the exact amount that was due. The cashier — who seemed uninterested in my purchase — just

● ● ●

bagged the box and passed it back without ever taking her eyes off the cheap magazine she was reading. It seemed God was not in a cruel mood after all.

A month to the day after Stefan left, my world came crumbling down. Not only had I not received word from Stefan, it seemed my period had gone missing with him.

It was hard to ignore the obvious signs, like the pain in my breasts when I showered, the fact that I was throwing up every day, and the aforementioned lack of my period, which should have arrived two weeks after he left.

On Easter Sunday, I was sitting on the tub wall staring at the blue plus sign when my mom busted through the door. I didn't even have time to hide the stick. The look on her face said it all. She was hurt, furious, disappointed, and ready to kill. I'm sure it was the same reaction Nana had had when she found out about my mom since, like my mom, she had been an unwed, teenage mother. Great, three generations had made the same mistake! When would we learn?

There was no stopping the salty tears that slipped down my cheeks as I whimpered, "Mom?" My lip quivered as I fell apart. My mom sobbed when she grabbed and hugged me tightly.

She stroked my hair, whispering, "It will be okay; we'll fix this."

My mom must have showed Nana the stick when she passed by, because next thing I knew, the three of us were clutching onto each other, crying. Three generations of tears for the loss of our dreams. When we had collected ourselves enough to separate, we took the conversation to Nana's room.

* * *

"We can get rid of it. No harm, no foul."

I gaped at my mom. "Mom, I still love Stefan. I cannot kill his baby without at least knowing he doesn't want it. And even then, I don't think I can." I was flabbergasted she would even think about such a thing.

"Baby? He walked out on you and left you here pregnant without a word. Do you seriously think he's going to show up here and marry you? Stefan is not coming back! Face it! You meant one thing to him. You're of no use to him now."

I cringed, sick to my stomach. I sucked in a deep breath before releasing it. "Mom, would you have killed me? Or Brianna?"

With a snap of her wrist, she slapped my cheek. I held my face in my hands, willing the sting away. She sneered. "That was different; I didn't have a future; you do!"

Her smack across my cheek shocked me, but I wouldn't let it end the fight. "Well, futures change! I won't kill my baby, and that's final!"

I wasn't even aware I'd made a decision until it spilled out of my mouth. Once it had, I wasn't taking it back. It was how I felt, pure and simple.

"I can't do this again, I won't!" She stormed out the door — slamming it so hard it rattled — leaving me and Nana staring at each other in disbelief. Where did she think she was going?

I caressed my still-stinging, flushed cheek and looked to Nana for understanding. With gentle eyes, she nodded. "It will be okay, Stella. We'll figure something out," Nana cooed as she cradled me.

● ◉ ●

"So, what now?" I implored.

"We'll call a doctor and confirm the test result. They have been known to be wrong from time to time." Her voice held more hope than I felt.

"I wish Stefan was here. He always made me feel like everything would be all right," I muttered.

Mom never came back that night, and Brianna just laughed when we told her about the possible baby.

"Great, just what we need: another mouth to feed," she snickered and pranced upstairs.

"That's not fair, Brianna," I called up after her.

"Fair or not, it's a fact." With that, she slammed our bedroom door.

● ● ●

Chapter Five

Stella's confirmation

NANA WAS NICE ENOUGH TO SCHEDULE AN appointment with her gynecologist. Therefore, two days after the scene in the bathroom, we were in Doctor Marcus' office waiting for the official results. The secretary stared at me like I was nothing but a stray mutt. I wasn't enjoying her uppity attitude as she looked me over while taking my insurance card.

Once I had done all the paperwork and I'd urinated in the plastic cup, we were ushered into your standard-looking examination room. It was cold, white, and sterile. Not the comfiest of places in the world, I thought. Without having seen the doctor, I was ready to leave.

I knew the moment he walked in shaking his head, it was not going to end the way Nana had hoped. With my trembling hands

* * *

covering my face, I sobbed into my grandmother's shoulder as the gray-haired doctor informed me of the results that would alter the rest of my life.

"Stella, it's indeed positive." He was very apologetic about my situation, but there was no hiding the concerned look on his wrinkled face. "Are you sure you want to keep it? There are other options for you. You're young and healthy; you can have a baby when you're more ready for it," he said while patting my knee, trying unsuccessfully to soothe me. If anything, it made me want to cringe away from the unwanted physical contact.

"No, I'm keeping it." I sniffed.

With a sharp nod, he started typing on his laptop, printing out things I would need to know. The only option I found acceptable was keeping it. Abortion and adoption left me feeling as if my stomach was locked in a vice grip. Those choices just weren't for me. With or without Stefan, I would be a mother in eight months.

Nana and I rode home in silence. We both were at a loss for words. Without bothering to eat, I retreated to my room, seeking the solace it provided. It was official; I was now a statistic. My name could be added to the list of those who hadn't listened to their parents. I'd listened, but foolishly fell in love anyway.

When my mom finally showed up a week later, she acted as if I was invisible. She completely shut me out of her life. I never told her I tried again to reach Stefan's cell phone. Now instead of his voice mail, I got a recording saying the number I had dialed had been disconnected or was no longer a working number. Well, that was a rude awakening.

There was no denying the facts that were as plain as the nose

* * *

on my face. He'd done everything he could to leave me in his past.

One last time, I allowed myself to come undone. My body shook uncontrollably when the gut-wrenching screams erupted from my heaving chest. I stopped fighting the tears and allowed them to fall freely until there was nothing left. It felt freeing to let it all out. At the same time, it was too painful for words.

The sting from my mother's avoidance was far worse than the slap I'd received when she'd first discovered my condition. I felt like an outsider in my own home. After several tries to talk to her, I gave up. If she wanted to live in a world where I'd never existed, so be it.

School was horrendous after getting my test results. The only thing people talked about was prom. A stray guy here and there asked me to attend with him, but there was only one person I wanted to take me to the prom and he wasn't around to ask. The lunchroom was the worst place on the planet. Every day, a new girl was spotted running out in tears. The hell of high school couldn't end fast enough for me.

My grades were starting to show my lack of enthusiasm. More than one teacher pulled me aside to tell me my once-perfect grade point average was slipping. I knew my grades were suffering; I did not need someone else telling me the obvious.

With prom and graduation just two weeks away, I took a chance and mailed Stefan an invitation to my prom with the hope he'd at least call so I could tell him about our child. It was a long shot, and I knew it. It was a P.O. Box that belonged to his parent's. I had to at least try to reach him, even if he didn't want to hear from me. The Internet was no help. I searched every engine I could; he wasn't out there. How it is someone could literally drop off the

* * *

planet?

May

The night of prom came and went without any word from Stefan. I had held out hope that he would answer the invite I sent in my letter. I actually mailed him four letters over the last few weeks. I even went as far as to mail it myself, just in case Nana wasn't sending them correctly. Still, my letters went unanswered. I'd long given up on him. In the end, I never bothered going to the prom. There was no point. I hoped to never see any of my classmates again after graduation anyway.

"STELLA! Get your skinny butt down here!" Her joke did not go unnoticed.

"Yeah, Nana, I'm coming already!" I wanted to add ready or not, but I held that back.

With one last peek in the mirror, I made sure my auburn hair was tucked neatly in a ponytail, and my black eyeliner precisely lined my light-brown eyes. Considering I was a mess on the inside, the outside didn't look half bad. I blamed my looks on my genes. I had my father to thank for my looks, of which my mother had reminded me daily as a child. I scurried down the stairs and joined Nana in the kitchen.

"It took you long enough. Now, let's leave or you'll be late for your big day." She smiled, making me wonder how she could be so happy.

The fifteen minute car ride passed quickly with us bopping and singing along to the music on the radio. For an old lady, Nana was pretty cool. After closing my eyes, I took a few calming breaths before getting out of the car. I really wasn't ready for what was about to happen.

When we reached Dr. Marcus's office, I sighed when the receptionist glared at me, her disparagement clear on her makeup-caked face. This wasn't new; in fact, it had been becoming routine with every visit.

"Stella, are you ready?" I heard from the next door.

Reluctantly, I followed the technician into the tiny ultrasound room. Nana followed close behind us. Since my mom refused to come or have anything to do with me, everything fell into Nana's lap. Again, my mother's behavior was no surprise. Being in the same room with her was the same as being alone. Brianna was indifferent to anything regarding my pregnancy, or me for that matter. Her world revolved around her friends, and I wasn't one of them.

The technician left just long enough for me to remove my clothes and slip into a gown.

When she reentered the room, she chirped, "Hop up on the bed and let's have a look, shall we?" The paper-covered table was cold and unforgiving, just like my mother. My butt hanging out didn't feel that great, either.

"Is this going to hurt?" I asked with fear lacing my voice.

"No, sweetie. It's painless, I promise." She patted my arm in her feeble attempt to soothe me.

Susan, as I learned from her name tag, smiled warmly as she readied the machine. For someone who was only almost three months along; I already had an itty-bitty, tiny bump. It was enough to make my already-tight skinny jeans uncomfortable. Stretchy pants were going to become my favorite pants soon enough.

I wiggled when she squirted the cold gel onto my stomach. The room filled with a quick thumping sound the second she started rubbing the wand across my skin. She didn't say anything at first, but kept doing the examination. When she pulled out a plastic sleeve, covered another wand, and handed it to me, I gawked at her.

"You need to insert it." She looked at me, expecting me to know that. Yeah, I didn't know that.

Totally repulsed, I inserted the device for her. A hiss slipped through my lips as the wand filled me. Nana smiled as the black screen showed different variants of black, grey, and white. The images on the screen really made no sense to me. Susan's fingers flew over the keys of the ultrasound machine. She tapped and clicked the buttons vigorously.

Finally, she withdrew the offending machine's appendage, stepped out, and came back moments later with the doctor.

"Let's see how it looks. Hmm . . . interesting. Yes, I see them. Well, Miss Richards, it would appear you are having twins. Those

* * *

sounds you are hearing are their heartbeats. They sound nice and strong."

"Twins?" I croaked, feeling faint. I could barely process I was having one child, never mind two.

"By your measurements and the dates you gave me, I put your due date at December twenty-fifth, just in time for Christmas." Dr. Marcus smiled, slipped out of the room, and returned to his other patients.

"How nice, Christmas presents. Sorry sweetie, these aren't the kind you can return. And don't even think about putting them under the tree tagged for Santa." Nana smirked, looking quite pleased with herself.

Did I wrong someone in another life or something? This situation was getting worse by the minute. Nana being Nana, she patted my hand and smiled reassuringly. Well, I'm glad she was reassured, since I was a mess. At this rate, I was going to have a heart attack before I ever delivered. Was it hot in here, or was I having a hot flash? From the clamminess of my skin, I was going with a hot flash.

On the ride home, it was time to face the facts. "Nana, I am not going to college. I'll have to take care of two babies. I don't have enough money saved to take care of myself, let alone three people. Loans are out of the question; if I could get one, I would never be able to pay it back," I whined.

"Stella, I'm begging you to rethink your decision about going to college. The babies will be here before the start of the second semester. Please?" My heart broke seeing Nana beg.

* * *

I sighed, irritated. "It's not that I don't want to, because I do. I just don't see how it will be possible!" I broke down and sobbed on her shoulder, which caused her to change lanes a little too quickly. Guess we can thank the driver of the tow truck for only honking his horn and not plowing into us. When she snapped her jaw shut three times, I thought she was fighting the urge to yell at me for trying to wreck her car.

"What if it was possible? What if you had enough money to attend an affordable college?" Eyeing her, I could tell she was hiding something.

"But, I don't have enough money. Were you not paying attention to what I just said?" I huffed.

"Look, I'm going to tell you a secret and I expect you to keep your trap shut." She squared her jaw, trying to look tough. It was almost funny. "When your mother came along, I started saving for her to go to college. When she got pregnant with you, she informed me she had no intentions of going to college. She wanted to be a hairdresser, and that was that. So I left the money in the account, hoping that when you grew up, you would want to go to college. It's still there, and I'm still putting more in each week." I gasped at her admission.

Sniffling, I asked, "So, you're saying, I can have it to go to school?"

"Of course, that's what I'm sayin', but, you only get half. The other half goes to Brianna should she want to go to school, too." I bounced up and hugged the stuffing out of her. She almost wrecked the car again.

"Now that that's decided, where should I send the check?"

● ● ●

Smiling, I clued her in. "Norfolk State." There was no hesitation in my reply; I knew where I wanted to go.

I tried to show my mom the pictures from the ultrasound when we got home, but she wouldn't even look at me. "Mom, do you want to see the sonogram pictures?"

"I'm having twins, Mom." She looked away again. "You can shut me out, but can you shut them out?" I grumbled, storming off to the kitchen.

In the end, I put the pictures on the fridge for Brianna to see. Not that she gave a hoot; I guess I was just hopeful. Damn Stefan! I was never one to hope. I knew what I wanted, and this wasn't it.

The mail held some good news, at least. I had received a few scholarships that would help me afford the tuition. It was not a huge amount, but mixed into what I had, it would help nicely. Financial aid also sent me notification that I qualified for assistance. The week could have only been better if I had heard from Stefan, but that dream was dead, too.

I took a few moments to fill out all the needed forms that Norfolk State sent with my acceptance letter. Even if Stefan wouldn't be there with me, it was close enough that I could commute. That thought also reminded me that I needed to get my license and buy a cheap junk box to commute with.

My days working at Jerry's Ice Cream continued as if nothing had changed. If only that were really the case. There was one instance when I thought I saw Michael driving down the strip, but I knew it was the sun glaring in my eyes. The car was long gone before I turned back around.

* * *

◈◇◈

When graduation day arrived, I was thrilled that no one in my class had figured out I was pregnant. I'd made it through four years of high school without my name hitting the rumor mill. I wanted to keep it that way.

Dressed in a white, flowing satin gown and cap, I crossed the stage and received my diploma. Amazingly, my mom attended. She still refused to acknowledge me. However, it was something that she attended at all. Brianna hooted and hollered with Nana; they were my official cheering squad.

Nana sprung for dinner at a nice seafood restaurant. We didn't do that often, or ever. A few others from my class ate at the same restaurant, but I was never friendly with them. Being cordial, we nodded at each other.

"So, Stella, what's your grade point average?" Brianna asked in between mouthfuls of her broiled scallops.

"Um, 3.6. It could have been better if I hadn't been so distracted," I answered while I rubbed my tiny belly under my simple white sundress.

"That's cool. I'm not as smart as you, though. Don't get me wrong, I'm smart enough. I just don't see the point in it. I'll probably just end up like the rest of you. If I find anyone who can hold my attention for more than five minutes," she cackled, causing me to nearly choke on my Cobb salad.

From the expression on our faces as we openly gawked at her, I'm sure she knew we weren't happy with that idea.

● ● ●

"Don't even think about it. You don't want to go through this; you deserve more." I chided, my sincerity shining through.

"I never said I was planning on it, but in this family it seems like destiny."

For the first time in months, we all laughed. She was right; it did seem like we were all destined to be unwed mothers. It seemed as if destiny was mocking us at every turn. Maybe it was more of a curse.

By the end of dinner, I was exhausted and ready for my welcoming bed.

As a graduation present, Nana bought me my first cell phone. It was a prepaid one, loaded with plenty of minutes. She insisted I needed to have it for when the twins came or if I was at school and the twins were at the sitter's. Her logic had merit. My mom's gift was a used desktop computer. The fact that she bought me anything astonished me.

● ● ●

Chapter Six

Stella's time rolls on

June

"OKAY, STELLA, TAKE A FEW DEEP BREATHS AND PUSH."
How Nana was staying so calm I will never know; I was a nervous
wreck.

On my last exhale, I pushed. "Like this?" I grunted.

"Not so hard!" she screeched in my ear. "Push the other one
now!" She panted almost as hard as I was. "Too hard," she groaned,
her face gaunt from the strain.

"Stop yelling at me; I'm trying!" I growled, my face flushed
and coated in sweat.

"Don't shut your eyes!" she screeched in my ear again.

• • •

"No more! I can't do this, it's too hard!" I puffed as I buckled under the pressure.

"Yes, you can. Just remember what I told you. Now try again."

Slowly, I pushed down again. We were thrown back into our seats again when the car jerked forward. As before when I hit the brakes, we were thrown into the dashboard.

"Maybe that's enough for one day. We should stop before I have a heart attack." She smiled at me with a pat to my knee.

"Oh, come on, Nana, I'm not that bad. Mom survived my earlier attempts," I teased.

"Did you ever ask yourself why she stopped trying to teach you?" She grinned.

"I thought it was because I don't exist anymore," I muttered, looking out the windshield. It still smarted that she wouldn't acknowledge me.

"For someone who doesn't exist to her, she sure can't pry her eyes off the pictures on the fridge," Nana pointed out.

"She's not looking at me. She's looking at her grandchildren. There is a difference, you know." I huffed rather un-dignifiedly.

"Not really. She'll come around, Stella."

I nodded, unconvinced.

This was our second attempt at teaching me how to drive. Last weekend had ended the same way. We would have bruises on our shoulders from the seatbelts and matching whiplash. Great, we

● ● ●

could be twins, too. I just couldn't get the hang of slow. The car leaped forward and came to a screeching halt every time I tried. It was very frustrating.

"Stella!" Nana's blood curdling scream forced me to snap my head to the left just in time to see a red SUV flying into the parking lot entrance. There was no time to react before it slammed into the driver's side of Nana's Gray Ford Taurus.

Screeching tires, shattering glass, and crunching metal echoed throughout the small lot. I shrieked in horror when the SUV plowed into the driver's side, setting off the airbags. The impact was only inches from me. My seatbelt kept me mostly in place, but I was tossed a bit. I knew from the instant pain in my skull that I had hit my head on the window. The metal of the vehicles groaned around us as it settled into position. When my vision cleared, I could see the slivers of glass covering my baby blue tank top. Several fragments cut into my head, neck, and arm deep enough for the gashes to start bleeding.

"Oh no, Stella, don't move! I'll call 911." Nana's frantic callings caused me to realize the warm liquid running down my cheek was blood — my blood.

When I looked up, Nana seemed frazzled and concerned. At least she looked unharmed, which was a good thing. Scrunching my eyes shut, I tried to move my left arm only to discover it was ensnared by the rumpled driver's side door. My head wound was the least of my concerns. I rubbed my belly with my free hand. There wasn't any blood, but I knew that meant very little in this situation. A sudden realization occurred to me: the lives of my children were the only things that mattered to me. It didn't matter anymore about my mother's avoidance, Brianna's constant ribbing about my pregnancy,

● ● ●

or even Stefan's absence. It all seemed irrelevant. The twins had to be okay; they just had to be.

Nana's panicked ramblings on her cell phone became muffled as the blood seeping from my head slid into my ear. The pain in my trapped arm started to throb harder as I tried to move it again. Finally, I gave up, the pain too much to do anything else but wait for someone to pull me out of the mangled mess.

"Are you all right?" asked the elderly man from the other vehicle.

"Does she look all right to you? She's pregnant!" Nana growled back.

"Did you call an ambulance?" he croaked, putting his handkerchief against my hairline.

"Of course I did. They're on their way." Nana patted my tummy.

"Don't worry, Stella, we'll get you out of here. Everything will be fine," she cooed to me like she had done when I was a small child.

There was no mistaking the panic that spread across the wrinkled features of the other driver. "I am so sorry. I didn't see you until it was too late. I hear the sirens, they're almost here."

My body started shaking. The flashing lights filled the parking lot, the shrill sound of the sirens blaring in my ears. I don't know how many responders there were, but it was definitely more than one. The other driver was pulled away just in time for a chocolate brown, curly-haired paramedic to slide between the two

● ● ●

rumpled cars.

"Don't move. I've got ya now. Can you tell me your name?"

"Stella Richards," I uttered.

"Okay, Stella, my name is Joe. I need you to relax while I take your vitals." He didn't wait for a reply; he just set to work. His eyes had a gentleness to them when he smiled at me. For the first time in a long time, they weren't judging me.

"Pete, get in on the other side. There is not enough room over here," Joe called out.

A blond, lanky paramedic slid into Nana's newly-vacated seat. "Hi, Stella. Your grandmother says you're fourteen weeks pregnant with twins?"

"Yeah," I grunted when Joe attempted to move my left arm.

"Well, this is what we need to do: first, I'm going to get in the backseat and try to get the seat to recline. If that works, then we'll slide you onto a board and out the door. If that fails, then we'll have those nice firefighters use the Jaws of Life to pry off the door." As Pete walked me through everything, Joe started slipping on a neck brace. I groaned as Pete climbed in behind me.

Pete's breath fanned across my neck when he struggled to reach the leaver. "Cam, see if you can reach it from under her feet." Another blond EMT crawled into the car head first.

It took every ounce of control I had not to flinch when his hands touched my legs. With the exception of my elderly doctor, no man has touched my legs besides Stefan. From the strangled sounds he was making; I guessed it wasn't going very well. When he popped

● ● ●

back up, he shook his head.

"Okay, Stella, we're going to have to tear off the door. Those protectors Joe is putting on you will keep you from being burned by the sparks and any flying debris," Pete explained.

I started to panic when the motor started. My body shivered from the anxiety welling up inside me. My eyes bulged and my heartbeat shot up as the machine started biting into the twisted metal.

Joe and Pete both held the seat still while Cam slipped back in on the passenger's side. Sitting in the darkness, I could barely hear Joe telling me comforting thoughts as he tried to relax me. For the next five minutes, the only other sound I could hear was the shredding metal giving way under the pressure of the hydraulic machine. I had never been so afraid in my life than at that moment.

The unmistakable, deafening pop of the door springing loose was a relief. I would be free soon. The second the shields were removed, I struggled to look around, but the brace made that impossible. Through the cracked windshield, I could see Nana crying on her phone. I wondered if she was calling my mom.

"All right, Stella. It's time. Now, don't try to move. Cam is already getting the board. As soon as it's in place, we're taking you out." Joe's smooth voice penetrated the rushing sounds of the rescue crew.

"Cam, drop the seat on the count of three." Pete, Joe, and Cam slowly slid the seat back so I could see Joe's face again.

His smile was gentle and reassuring as he gazed down at me with his ocean-blue eyes. "See, smooth sailing." He grinned. "This part is going to hurt a little, but we'll be as gentle as possible." I

● ● ●

grunted my understanding.

In his eyes, I could see my own reflection. Boy, did I look roughed up. Not that I cared about my appearance, but you could already see where I was bruising and bleeding. I looked like I had gone ten rounds with a heavyweight boxer and lost.

Once the board was slipped in, I heard the count off: "One, two, three." A gurgled howl escaped my parted lips when my body was suddenly lifted onto the plywood plank.

Every part of my body hurt. The pain was unbearable when they shifted me into place. I hurt in places I hadn't known existed. This time when I felt the liquid on my cheeks, I knew it was tears, not blood.

Four loud grunts sounded in the car when the men lifted me out of what was left of the driver's side door. I winced as they lowered me onto the gurney. That was just what I needed, more pain. Glancing up, I could see at least six rescuers rushing me to the ambulance. Somewhere in the bustle of movements, I lost track of where Joe had disappeared to.

"Did you miss me?" He smiled, poking his head through the arms of everyone surrounding me.

With one last jostle, they lifted me into the ambulance. After Joe, Nana climbed in and cradled my hand. Nana tried to smile, but it didn't quite reach her eyes. She was worried like I was.

I yelped, alerting Joe that I didn't appreciate the needle for the IV pricking the back of my hand. "Sorry about that, but you need the fluids."

● ● ●

That was my first time in an ambulance, and the only thing I could think was that it would be nice if they'd shut off the blaring sirens and flashing lights. They were giving me a migraine. Once, I thought I might fly off the stretcher when we banked a corner going faster than I'd ever driven before.

The chaos continued when minutes later, we made an abrupt halt outside the Emergency Room. I watched as the iridescent lights overhead flashed quickly by. Joe's rushed ramblings must have made sense to the doctor when they rolled me down the narrow hallway. My vision finally faded to a foggy gray. Soon, the voices of the nurses replaced Joe's.

"They'll take very good care of you," he whispered before he left.

"Time to wake up, sweetie," an unfamiliar female voice startled me.

"The doctor will be right in. How are you feeling?"

"Like I was hit by a truck. Oh, that's right; I was," I said through gritted teeth, my voice hoarse from the trauma.

"Yes, well, that is true," she chirped, strutting out of the room.

The first thing I noticed upon looking around was that I was alone. Shutting my eyes, I tried to remember what had happened after Joe had left. All I could remember were fragments and flashes of rooms and people's faces, my most pronounced memory being of Joe. His genuine smile when he looked at me made me feel like I mattered. The caring and soothing way he spoke calmed me before he slipped away. The memory of him fading into the darkness

● ● ●

brought one thought to the front of my mind.

There was only one thing I wanted to know: were my babies okay? From the weightiness of my left arm, I knew I had broken it and was wearing a splint. Letting out a deep breath, I surveyed the damage. Gingerly, I caressed my tiny baby bump with my good hand; the fact that I still had a bump gave me hope. Sitting up a little, I glanced at my toes, wiggling them. They still worked.

"Stella Richards?" a caramel-skinned doctor called out.

"Yes," I croaked.

"It's nice to see you awake. My name is Doctor McKenzie. You're probably wondering about your twins?"

"Yes, please!"

"They're fine. We'll watch them, but for now everything seems to be just fine. You do have two fractures in your left arm, one above the wrist on your radius bone and one just above the elbow on your humerus bone. You also have a concussion from the impact of your heading hitting the car window." I smiled and relaxed against the stiff sheets. "We're keeping you overnight for observation, and if all goes well, you can be released tomorrow." I nodded while he made notes on my chart.

"Is my grandmother here?"

"Yes, she's in the waiting room. I'll let her in once I'm done examining you."

True to his word, once he had done the usual pupil check and all his questions were answered, he departed. Moments later, Nana burst through the door carrying an adorable floral arrangement. As

⬤ ⬤ ⬤

soon as she saw me, her face split into a huge smile.

"Thank God, you're all right!" she gushed, rushing up to hug me.

"How's the other driver?"

"Oh, Calvin is fine. He's been sitting with me for hours. I think he's smitten with me." She fluttered her eyelashes.

"Nana, please! Too much information!" I gasped in mock disgust.

"Oh, sweetie! I'm a grandmother, not dead." Yeah, I gaped like a fish out of water. "They did another ultrasound while you were out. The babies look real good, honey." She didn't seem the least bit worried.

"Did you call Mom or Brianna?"

"Yeah, I just hung up with them." When she turned away to put the flowers in the windowsill, I knew she wasn't going to elaborate.

"That's good," I said, trying to sound unaffected, but the truth was it hurt to hear.

"You should rest. I'll be back in the morning to take you home." I smiled when she kissed my cheek.

"Night, Nana." I looked out the window just in time to see the sun setting. Dusk was always the hardest time of day. It reminded me of Stefan and the date that would never happen.

It was lonely being in the hospital. There were too many noises. The TV was useless since I didn't like the new trend in TV

● ● ●

shows. My life was a reality show; who needed to see any more of it?

"Knock, knock. Hey you, how are you?"

"Hi, Joe! I'm okay. They're watching the babies for now." I shrugged and fiddled with the hem of my sheet.

Looking around, he seemed surprised. "What? No doting father-to-be?" Not knowing what else to do, I just broke down and started weeping.

"Nope, he's long gone." I sniffed.

He sat on the edge of the bed looking quite distraught. "I'm so sorry, I didn't know." I sighed when he grabbed my hand.

"It's been a while since anyone's touched me," I whispered while withdrawing my hand.

"I can't understand why; you're a very beautiful, young woman." I peeked up to see him watching for my reaction.

"Not beautiful enough, apparently."

"Was the father blind?" I giggled. He was being so sweet.

I sighed. "No, he just moved on to greener pastures."

After patting my leg, he grinned and stood up. "Then he's grazing in the wrong ones."

"If I ever hear from him again, I'll make sure to tell him you said so." I snorted.

"I have to get home, but I'll stop by and see you tomorrow." He paused when he reached the door. After blowing out a deep

* * *

breath, he looked back with a look of concern etched on his face. "Stella, destiny has a plan for everyone. Even if it feels like destiny is mocking us, everything works out the way it's meant to." He lowered his head and departed my room.

For the next few hours, his words bounced around in my mind. Just a few weeks ago, Brianna had said similar words at my graduation dinner. And before that, Michael had said something comparable to that. Did destiny really have a plan for us? If so, what was my destiny?

Somewhere in the quiet of the night, I slipped off to sleep, dreaming of a life in which Stefan didn't leave.

Much to my displeasure, I woke to a very perky nurse named Liz grinning at me. "Good news. The doctor has started your release forms. We already called your grandmother, and she is one her way."

"Great. Is this breakfast?" Liz gave me a sympathetic glance.

"Sorry, hospital food is never the greatest, but, you should try to eat it." She turned, heading out the door.

Pushing the nasty food around with my fork didn't improve the taste. The runny, scrambled eggs looked disgusting. I think there might have been bacon, but I could be wrong. The toast did make an awesome hockey stick to shoot the white chunky stuff around; my guess they were trying to pass them off for potatoes.

● ● ●

"I hear you've got your walking papers." Joe popped his head in the door. From his uniform, I surmised he was working.

"Yes, once my grandmother springs me, I am a free woman." I laughed at my own joke. I would never be free; my heart belonged to a man who didn't want it, and my children would always need my love and affection.

"Hey, I have to get to work. But here . . ." He passed me a folded piece of paper. "It's my phone number. Call me when you get over Mr. Wrong." He winked with a warm smile.

"Thank you for everything, Joe. And if I ever get over him, I'll call you." My cheeks burned.

"See you around, Stella." Joe waved over his shoulder as he left.

I was released as promised a few hours after Joe's impromptu visit. The house was empty and uninviting when I limped my ravaged body up the stairs to my bed. The hospital had sent me home with no pain medication because of the pregnancy; I doubt I would have taken them even if they had. The lives of my children were more important than the pain. For them, I could suffer through anything.

Nana spent the next week catering to me and looking for a new used car. Brianna did ask how I was doing when I saw her, which wasn't often. My mom never stopped in on her way to her room. After a week, the doctor okayed my release from bed rest, but I was forbidden to work anymore. Now the hard work began.

I started to apply for every public assistance there was, from Welfare, W.I.C, and S.N.A.P to Section 8 and childcare vouchers.

* * *

Nana drove me to the appointments in her rental car since she hadn't found anything she liked yet. They all said it could take months; some would be approved sooner than others. However, I wanted everything ready before the tiny beings in my belly arrived.

• • •

Michele Richard

Chapter Seven
Stella's reawakening

THE END OF JUNE APPROACHED FASTER THAN I HAD
thought possible. My life moved on without a word from Stefan. I
knew his school had been let out long ago. In a final effort to reach
him, I called the telephone information line and asked for the phone
number of Maurice Sterling in D.C.

I was amazed when they gave me a number. I didn't want to
call, but in good conscience, I needed to at least try to inform him of
his impending fatherhood. I paced the living room for a good five
minutes, gathering up enough courage to call.

The warring in my head felt like my brain would explode. On
one hand, I wanted to hear his sweet voice. On the other, I feared
he'd be cruel when I told him why I was calling. I took one long,
deep breath to steady my nerves and dialed. It rang once, and I was

* * *

already gasping for air. I froze when the call was answered on the second ring, and I recognized her voice immediately.

"Sterling residence," Shirley answered with a pleasant tone. I hoped her good mood continued.

"Is Stefan home?" I heard her sigh into the receiver.

"Who is calling?" she snipped.

"Stella," I mumbled, already regretting calling.

"No. I'm sorry, he's out. Stella, he's moved on. You should do the same." She sounded so harsh and unfeeling.

"Oh, okay. I — um — I understand. But I really need to talk to him. If you could just tell him I called, and tell him it's important. Please?" My quivering voice sold me out. She knew it hurt to hear it. It all seemed to just spur her on.

"Do you really think he cares what you have to say? You only served one purpose. And I think we both know him calling you is not going to serve anyone's needs. Please don't call us again!" she snarled like a lioness protecting her young.

Fighting back the tears that threatened to slip out of my stinging eyes, I blurted out the reason for my call. "But, he should know I'm pregnant," I whimpered.

"It's not his. Go find whatever hick knocked you up and find a nice trailer park."

"Excuse me?" I gasped.

"You heard me. You are not trapping my son. Don't call here again, or I will call the police and report you for harassment." My

● ● ●

heart dropped into my stomach when she slammed the phone down.

Stunned and hurt, I staggered backward to the wall and slid down. It didn't matter that I had promised myself not to cry over him ever again. This time, the tears I cried were for my children. They'd never know their father. He wouldn't be there to push them on a swing, take them to the park or teach them to ride a bike. They would only have me. Like it not, I would be their mother and father all rolled into one. If my mother and my grandmother could do it, so could I.

I wasn't mad, but I was beyond crushed. The girls at school talked about how the fathers' parents always said crap like Stefan's mother. I'd foolishly believed they were different. Why had I even bothered to try reaching out to them? It's not as if they'd bothered to get to know me before they passed their judgments. Stefan had given me hope that not everyone would act like my father had. He was wrong.

For the next two weeks, I moped around even more than ever before. I told Nana about the phone call and everything that was said. I told Nana everything. She was the only one who'd listen to me. No one else knew, and I liked it that way. I didn't need to hear Brianna reminding me every moment that men were useless, only out for one thing, and not worthy of the air I breathed.

My visit to the doctors this month didn't go as I'd hoped. Dr. Marcus made it clear I should be gaining weight by this point. However, at my weigh-in I'd managed to lose another two pounds. That brought the total weight loss up to five pounds. He also informed me that if by next month my weight remained low, he'd be forced to call in a nutritionist. He wasn't convinced about my excuse of morning sickness causing my weight loss.

● ● ●

The difficulty fell under one category: I was too depressed to eat. I ate when I was hungry, which wasn't often. In my defense, since the accident, I'd been eating more. It just wasn't enough. Doctor Marcus also said the twins hadn't received any ill effects from the accident, so that was a bright spot.

I measured larger than most mothers-to-be at three and a half months, but the fact that I was small statured and carrying twins explained that.

I spent most of my time sitting on the beach where I'd spent so much time with Stefan. He never left my mind, even though his mother had said he had moved on. I would never be able to move on. I'd have two little reminders of the short time we spent together.

I couldn't in good conscience call Joe. The agreement was I'd call when I moved on. That was just not going to happen any time in the near future.

July

"Okay, Stella, you already knew this was going to happen. This is Laura, and she's our nutritionist. She's put together a special diet for you to follow. Right now, your diet is very important. Yes, you gained two pounds and that is better, but it's not good enough."

"What Dr. Marcus is trying to say is that you need to gain at least six pounds a month to catch up to where you should be." Laura smiled.

* * *

I blew out a breath. "I'll try harder." Laura nodded.

She was younger than I thought she'd be. She had the prettiest green eyes I'd ever seen. "I know you will. Call me if you need anything adjusted on your diet. Next month I'll have another diet ready for you."

Once all the usual exams were done, I couldn't get out of there fast enough. With Nana at work, I took the trolleybus home. Staring out the window, I watched all the happy families playing on the beach. Was it too much to ask for the same for my children?

What they needed was a daddy. Any man can be a father, but it takes a real man to be a daddy. A daddy is the kind of man who gets down on his hands and knees and gives his children a pony ride or lifts them onto his shoulders so they can see a parade march by. That's what I wished for my twins.

After my call to Stefan's mother last month, it was official; I'd given up hope of ever seeing him again.

As a family, we sat on the beach watching the Fourth of July fireworks. They were spectacular as always. The sheer fact that my mom showed up wasn't lost on me. Of course, she kept her distance, watching the colorful burst of color above us. Yet again, I sat on the beach thinking about the man who had swept in, stolen my heart, and then run away with it like a thief.

With all my money from financial aid, scholarships, and from the time I spent working at the ice cream stand in the bank, the only thing left to do was wait for September. Nana, true to her word, sent the first check to Norfolk State.

Luck was on my side when I qualified for welfare, food

* * *

stamps, and W.I.C, but there was still no word on the childcare voucher. Section 8 could take years to receive, so I wasn't holding my breath on that one.

Fitting into most of my clothes was no longer an option for me, so it was sweatpants or leggings. At least I could still hide my bulge under my baggy sweatshirts and XXL T-shirts. The morning prayer sessions to the porcelain God finally stopped, so that was one good thing.

All in all, July passed by fairly tamely. I was eating somewhat better and resting a lot. The pain of missing Stefan never faded, but I handled it better. My mom still stayed hushed around me, but she'd glance at me from time to time, which was an improvement. Brianna was missing most of the time since it was summer break.

On the last day of July, the cast on my arm came off, and all evidence of the car accident was gone. The only scars that remained were the ones on my heart.

◊ ◇ ◊

August

Standing on the dunes of Virginia Beach, staring off watching a destroyer and an aircraft carrier cruising toward Norfolk to dock, I found myself reflecting on the last five months. It was hard to believe I'd turned eighteen today; this was definitely not how I'd expected it to be, but, it was how I planned to spend it. After spring break, I'd really thought my life would change. And boy did it, just not in the way I envisioned.

I spent the last five months preparing for two life-changing events. The first was the two little lives I'd be responsible for, the second being my first year at college. Even though I'd be starting with everyone else, I was ready to take a medical leave if I needed it. The twins were due during Christmas break; if all went well, the timing would be perfect. I hoped that I would be ready to return to school in January. It just seemed so far away.

I glanced around but didn't notice anyone in particular. It confused me, I could have sworn I'd heard my name. Then something caught my eye. Was that Stefan? But that wasn't possible. I squinted my eyes. It couldn't be; he'd moved on and forgotten me.

When he started running my way, illusion or not, I had to smile. Even after all those months apart, I'd never stopped loving him. A realization hit me as the mirage drew closer: it was him. He was really here!

Haphazardly, I tried to move closer. With my hands protecting the twins, I struggled to close the gap. Even if he was only there to tell me he was over me, I didn't care. I wanted one more chance to see him and memorize his glorious face.

The second his hand touched me, I wanted to melt into a puddle of goo. There was a desperation that I didn't understand when he pulled me into a crushing embrace. At that moment, I didn't care why he wanted to hug me; I just never wanted him to let go. With my head to his chest, I soaked up the scent of his cologne. I'd really missed the way he smelled. Like me, his heart was hammering in his chest.

With his arms wrapped around my enlarged waist, he leaned

* * *

105

in and captured my lips in a searing kiss like no other we'd experienced. Maybe it was my imagination, but at that moment, I just let every emotion from the last five months flow from my deprived lips, hoping he would feel them too. Tears threaten to spring forth when he pulled back to gaze at me.

"Stella, please say it's mine." His smooth voice rang out in my ears.

"Yes, they're yours." I flushed, gnawing on my lip.

"They?" His shocked face was too cute; I couldn't help but giggle and nod.

"Twins." His hands suddenly reached down and caressed them through my skin. It was like they knew it was their father's touch. They started wiggling and vying for his attention.

Then he dropped to his knees, placed his cheek against my baby belly, and told them, "Daddy's home." I thought I must have heard him wrong.

I forced myself to choke back a sob as my eyes filled with tears. Blinking quickly, I refused to let him see me fall apart.

After he placed a sweet kiss on my bump, he stood up and pulled me back into his arms, where I stayed silent and watched the tide come in as the sunset turned the sky every hue of the rainbow. Without a word, he nudged me down the dunes to where I could already see the Mustang parked.

A sigh escaped my lips when he released my hand after I was in the passenger seat. Hopping in, he started the car. The familiar purr of the engine sounded so good to my ears.

● ● ●

106

"Stefan, we should talk about this," I mumbled, nervous about what needed to be said. I really didn't want to have this conversation. However, I had to let him off the hook so he could go home and back to the new life he had made for himself.

"Wait. Let's go get something to eat first. Then we can talk over dinner." The best I could muster was a nod, because deep down, I knew that it would be the last night I'd spend with him.

I didn't want him to know it was eating me from the inside out. I knew the only reason he was there was out of obligation, and I wasn't about to let him hurt himself to do the 'right' thing. He didn't have to stay with me, even if that's really what I wanted.

My thoughts held me hostage the whole ride to the restaurant. Every time I looked at him, I would get so brain scrambled that I'd have to start again. It wasn't an easy feat, planning out how to tell someone that he didn't have to do something he was only doing out of guilt.

He'd be starting school somewhere in a week; he needed to concentrate on that. No doubt, that's what he had come to tell me anyway. I just needed to find a way to make it easier.

He chose a great restaurant, but a little pricey for my budget. I did try not to fidget when he led the way inside the trendy establishment.

Once we were seated at a quaint, little booth, I looked over the menu. There was very little I could afford on it.

"Stella, anything you want on the menu is fine. I'm buying." His adorable smile managed to disarm me, again.

* * *

I sighed. "You don't have to."

"No, I don't have to, but I'm going to." Crap! How did he do that?

When the waitress left with our orders, I couldn't take it anymore. The stress was killing me. I just had to get it out in the open and be done with it, like a Band-Aid, quick and painful.

"Stefan, I know what your mom told you, but it's not true," I softly blurted out without looking up at him.

"What's not true? And, when did you talk to my mom?" My face snapped up to see his shocked expression.

"When I called to tell you, she told me you'd moved on and that you didn't care about the baby. She also told me to find the hick that knocked me up and look for a nice trailer park," I rambled, unable to stop myself.

"You called? When?" The realization hit me. She'd never told him that I had called.

"She didn't tell you, did she?" I knew she didn't like me, but really?

"No, I came here for you like I promised. I never gave up on you." How could I not believe him? His sincerity said it all.

My thoughts were a jumbled mess as I tried to figure out what he meant. His mother had said he'd moved on. Was that a lie, too? Could he still care about me as I did for him? Was this only about the guilt?

There was only way to find out what was going on in his

● ● ●

head. I had to suck it up and ask. "So you didn't come here because you felt guilty?" I mumbled.

"Oh, I felt guilty, but not about this. I felt guilty because I couldn't contact you, with the exception of Michael's notes." He cocked his head to the side confused, only to see the confusion on my face too.

"What notes?" I gasped.

"You didn't get the notes Michael taped to your front door? Or the phone message he left?" he growled in disbelief.

"No. Then who did?" My brow furrowed as I thought about it. Who in my family would do such a thing? We all knew what it was like to grow up without a father. Why would someone want my kids to have the same fate?

"I don't know, but I do know why your letters never reached me. I found them in my dad's desk drawer this morning. They were a welcome relief," he chuckled, his nervousness apparent.

"That's why you never answered." I sighed in relief. It wasn't him who had ignored me. You can't ignore something you'd never received, but it didn't explain why he hadn't tried to write me.

"Yeah, well, considering my dad dropped me off at military school on our way to D.C., I had no way to communicate with you. So someone on both sides of our families is conspiring to keep us apart."

"Wait! He sent you to military school?" I felt my chest constricting, knowing that I had been the reason they'd sent him there.

* * *

"Yeah, but I don't care. You're worth it." Just hearing those words made me feel all squishy inside. I knew I was grinning. For that moment, he was the only thing I could think about.

"I'm still sorry you had to go through that. I really thought when you shut off your phone and never wrote that you'd moved on, like your mother said." Saying it meant I had to think about it, and that's not always a good thing.

"No, I never shut my phone off; that was my dad's doing. I would have written if I'd had a way to mail it. They watched my every move, and poor Michael — they even restricted his movements, probably because they knew he'd mail things for me or lend me his phone. Michael was my only resource. He did what he could, considering the scrutiny he was under."

"Even Michael had to pay the price for us being together?" Great, I needed more guilt! Let's just pile it all on my shoulders.

"Stella, it didn't bother me, or him for that matter. I counted down the days until I could leave, and they couldn't do anything about it. What did you do when you found out about the twins?" He reminded me that they were what really mattered, not this petty squabbling.

"It's water under the bridge. I can't change how our families feel about us. I have to worry about these tiny critters," I said, totally changing the subject.

"I almost lost the chance to be with you and my children!" He glared.

"But you didn't. We're here. And we have a lot to figure out. For starters, are we together?" I couldn't look him in the eyes; my

● ● ●

110

insecurities were getting the better of me.

"You can't be serious! Of course we are! We never broke up. Please tell me you didn't think otherwise. You didn't date someone else, did you?"

"Yeah, there's a long line of boys waiting to date a pregnant girl." I laughed.

"Don't even joke about that! If someone else touched you, it would kill me," he retorted.

"No one could replace you. Are you sure you don't want to run, now that you know?"

"I'm not going anywhere. I love you." When he leaned in and locked his lips against mine with a new passion, I might have inadvertently whimpered.

"I love you, too. So, do you want the twins?" I whispered while protecting the twins with my hands in case he said no.

"As much as I want you." There he went again, turning my insides into Jell-O while grinning. How did he do that?

"Are you going to go to Norfolk? School starts in a week." I didn't know if his parents had changed his mind or forced him to go somewhere else.

"We agreed on Norfolk, and my dad already sent in this year's tuition payment. I have the rest of my college money; we could get a place closer to school. And maybe if we're lucky, the school will give me back the part of the tuition that covered housing." I shook my head.

* * *

"That's for school." With my chin in his grasp he led my eyes to his.

"No, it's for my future. You and those two are my future."

• • •

Chapter Eight

Stefan's whereabouts

THE MOMENT I LEFT HER ARMS ON OUR LAST NIGHT together, I felt like my dad had stabbed me in the chest with his survival knife.

Stella wore the same pained expression as I kissed her one last time before forcing myself to join Michael in the car. Watching her stand on her porch with tears in her eyes tore me apart.

I tried not to let Michael see the tear that slid down my cheek, but he saw it anyway.

"You okay, kid?" His voice echoed my pain.

"Nope," I mumbled, staring out the window.

Everything in my life seemed to lose its beauty. I thought of

* * *

Stella when we drove by the beach. The times we shared there were precious to me, but watching the people mill around there, laughing at one another, sounded more like heckling and taunts in my head. I hated it. I felt I was being robbed.

"Stefan, call me when you get to D.C. Try to sleep on the ride; you look exhausted." Michael huffed, knowing full well I'd barely slept the night before.

"Yeah, I'll try," I grumbled, hugging him solidly.

When we left Fort Story before dawn, I expected we'd go directly to D.C. I was so wrong. My dad exited the highway in Maryland. When we reached the front gates of what looked like a fortress, I read the sign and groaned. Jonathan Edward Bentley Academy. My father had threatened to send me to the J.E.B. whenever I wouldn't follow his rules. Even though Michael was the one closest to being sent there, it turned out it was me that had ended up actually making it there.

My father deemed it necessary for me to finish high school in a military academy; however, not just any academy. He sent me to the toughest one out there. My dad's friend Jurgen Scott was the Commandant. Since he ran it, I was allowed late entry. Boy, wasn't I lucky? No, not really.

The school was worse than a prison. No cell phones, no calls of any kind, no Internet or emails, and our regular mail was monitored. They read everything that came in and went out. The campus was even guarded by sentries and surrounded by fencing standing fifteen feet high. The barbed wire twirls on the top made me cringe.

"Don't fight me, boy. Walk in there like a man." My dad's

● ● ●

features had never looked so stern.

"Can I call Michael before I go?" I sighed.

"I suppose so. Here's your phone." I nodded and stepped away so they wouldn't hear me. When I powered up the phone, it said I had fourteen messages and twenty missed calls, no doubt all from Stella. I fought the temptation to call Stella instead and forced myself to dial Michael's cell number.

"Stefan, you good? Dad gave you back your phone?" I cringed. He wasn't going to be happy.

"No, dude, it's just to call you and tell you I'll be at the J.E.B until June." He hissed at my statement.

"You cannot be serious! What is he thinking? Run, Stefan. Don't let him get you inside the gates," he seethed.

"Michael, it's too late. I'm already inside. It's only two months. I can do this, if I know Stella is okay. Can you check on her whenever you get the chance? I know it's a six hour drive each way, but I'd do it for you."

He breathed heavy into the phone. "Yeah, no guarantees on how often, but I'll try to go by and see her."

"Thanks, Michael. Write me, but remember they watch everything." I knew he'd remember the strict rules.

"Will do. Love you, kid." He cursed before he hung up.

My dad's hand was out expectantly when I walked back. My mom tried to hug me, but I stepped back shaking my head. She could have stopped him from doing it, but knowing her, she'd helped him.

● ● ●

He ran her life the way he ran ours. Iron-fisted didn't even cover it.

What she didn't realize was that she had lost her youngest son that day, and maybe her oldest, too. Even if Stella wasn't waiting for me, I would never go back after my eighteenth birthday. I'd endure the summer, setting everything up for my escape.

I missed Stella so much it physically hurt to think about her, but I knew there was no way for me to reach her. My only hope was that Michael might see her and tell her where I'd ended up. I hoped that he could explain my inability to see or contact her, and with any luck, she would wait for me.

Seeing how chummy my dad was with the Commandant spurred on my anger. There was nothing I wanted more than to wipe the smug grin off his face when he pulled away. My mother looked blissfully naive as they left the gates. Well, she was in for a rude awakening.

Walking the halls of the academy only served to sour my mood further. Keeping my reactions to myself, I simply walked in and dropped my bag on the immaculate floor. When my escort departed, I set off to make the room as bearable as possible. It was no easy feat.

Every night for the first two weeks, I woke up sweating from nightmares of Stella finding love with someone new. Were her feelings for me as fleeting as my parents seemed to think? I didn't think so, but only time would tell.

Being at the academy wasn't easy. We were required to wear uniforms and follow all the usual protocols. Still, it didn't matter what they did to me; they could never remove my memories of her angelic face, the feel of her skin against mine when I held her, or the

● ● ●

last night we had been together. I had given her a piece of myself that night; my virginity. There was no mistaking the fact that she also had given me hers. I was connected to her forever, and I knew it. I only hoped she felt it, too.

I'll admit, I'd lied to my dad. When I'd told him I wanted to go to Norfolk State, he'd accused me of wanting to be near Stella. He had been right. I did want to go there for her, but that was only a small part of the lie. I'd proceeded to tell him about Stella's letter from Worchester State. Yeah, he thought she'd be in Boston while I went to Virginia. That's the beauty of it; he thought he'd be sending me someplace where she wouldn't be.

◊ ◊ ◊

April

Everyone was forced to study every minute that they weren't in class. Since I'd studied in Germany, I had one up on them. That paid off when I would stare out the window and wonder where Stella was and what she was doing. Stella was the only thing that could make the torture worth it.

Each night before bed, I would hide under my covers and look at the strip of photos I had in my wallet. Stella and I had used one of those photo machines to take our pictures. It was my lifeline to her. When Michael delivered them to me, I nearly jumped up and hugged him. The pictures and her letter kept me going, even when it was at its darkest for me.

At first, I was overjoyed when Michael's letter arrived. It was the first one I had received since being there. I sat in my room to read it. It wasn't good news.

Dear Stefan,

I miss you and can't wait for summer break. I miss our times at the beach.

Things at school aren't that great. I don't have a schedule for my exams yet. I keep missing them. I'll try to do better. I've written myself little reminders, so that should help.

I'm going to visit the beach on the way home for the summer. I'll try to bring you a souvenir.

I'm trying bro! Don't hate me if I fail.

Your brother,

Michael

I sighed and I let it sink in. He had gone to the beach and couldn't find her. However, he did leave her notes, so that was something, at least. He would attempt another visit on his way to D.C. If he could find her, he'd try to get her to write me something to bring back. I prayed she hadn't forgotten me or, worse, thought I'd stopped caring.

◊ ◇ ◊

May

I couldn't stop the aching in my chest every time I thought about Stella. The pain of missing her hadn't gotten any better. I tried not to worry about it, but it became increasingly harder. I received my second letter since being here, this time from my mother.

Dearest Stefan,

You're going to love D.C. There are a lot of cute girls here that would love to date you. My new friends all have daughters your age and have agreed to set up some dates for you after you graduate. We'll be down to get you on June 3rd. Your dad is pleased by your easy adjustment to his way of life. I hope you're eating well.

See you soon,

Mom

Was she kidding? Did she really believe I'd adjusted easily? There wasn't a snowball's chance in Hell I'd date her friends' daughters, not even for the summer. The only woman I wanted was Stella, and my mother couldn't change that.

In the end, I crumpled up the note and threw it like a basketball into the trash barrel. Swoosh, two points! She still didn't realize I'd have nothing to do with her once I moved to Norfolk.

A few days later, I received Michael's second letter.

● ● ●

119

Mocked By Destiny

Hey little brother,

I made it to D.C. Mom is off on a tirade about finding you a girlfriend here. Thankfully, she is giving me a pass. There's no one here I want to date.

My side trip to the beach was a total bust. Sure, the sun, sand, and water were beautiful, but it missed the spark to make it worth it.

Sorry, no souvenir this time. I waited by the beach hoping to spot a dolphin so I would at least have a photo for you, but I couldn't find any. Visiting the lighthouse was very lonely. Sorry again.

This is going to be a long summer, and I can't wait for you to come home.

Your very sorry brother,

Michael

For an umpteen amount of time, I let the tears roll down my cheeks. I missed the girl who held my heart hostage. I decided to write to Michael, but not my mother. I had no interest in conversing with her in any way whatsoever.

Hey Michael,

Thanks for trying. The few pictures of dolphins I have will have to do. Maybe you could take me to see one for my birthday.

I hope your little reminders worked for the exams. It's the best I can hope for.

Could you tell Mom I said, "No thanks," on her offer. I'm really not

● ● ●

interested in her playing matchmaker. It won't matter; they won't be my type.

Maybe we can get away for a day trip or two to pass the summer quicker?

See you soon,

Stefan

June

I was in high spirits during the last two days of school; well, until my parents arrived. The only bright spot was that they brought my brother. I kept my distance from them when they tried to hug me but wholeheartedly wrapped my arms around Michael. You could see my mother's disappointment, but honestly, I didn't care.

"You look real good, son. This place did wonders for you." My father tried to look positive, but even I knew I'd lost weight and my eyes were dark from lack of sleep.

"So, Michael, how did you do?" I tried to deflect the fact that I hadn't answered him.

"Good, I made it another year," he laughed.

I flinched away when my mom tried to grab my arm. "Stefan, would you like to take a walk? We'd love to see the campus." She smiled sweetly, making me want to gag.

"Whatever," I grumbled and led the way with Michael by my

● ● ●

side.

I knew when I got home, I would get my butt kicked for not treating my mother better, but I refused to fake the lovey-dovey crap. She had sealed her fate the day she'd let my father leave me here.

"Stefan, I took care of all your paperwork for Norfolk. Your mom has all the dates you'll need when you get there."

I couldn't risk him taking it away from me. "Thanks, Dad," I said in a non-emotional tone as politely as possible.

We quietly walked the pristine, antique halls I hated with a passion. The rest of the campus was no better, if you'd asked me. Sure, it was a beautiful day for a walk — if I'd been with Stella, I would have enjoyed it. Once my tour finished, they left with the rest of the parents. With the exception of Michael, I was pleased when they left.

The next morning, I was ready in my dress uniform and prepared for it to be over, when Michael arrived solo.

"Hey, kid. Mom and Dad ran into some old friends, so we have a minute to talk." He shut the door behind him.

"I miss her, Michael. How am I going to make it another two months before I get to see her?"

"I don't know. Clearly, you found something special. I really did try to find her. She wasn't at home, and she wasn't at work every time I went. I even drove the strip looking for her." He looked as sad and heartbroken as I felt.

"I know you did. What did you tell her in the notes?"

● ● ●

122

"The truth; that our dad — the jackass — shipped you off here, that you missed her, and that you would see her in August."

"Where did you leave them?"

"Taped to her front door." He smiled finally. "So she wouldn't miss them."

"Thanks, Michael. I just hope it's enough." I sighed.

"I left her a message on her answering machine once, too." He grinned.

"Really?"

"Yeah, it was the least I could do. I called a few times, but only left the one message. I told her you couldn't make her prom, even though you wanted to."

Just then, we heard the unmistakable sound of a woman's shoes clicking down the hall's polished marble floor. We were silent when my parents walked in. Smartly, my mother didn't try to hug me this time. I think she knew she wasn't forgiven for her part in the betrayal.

Michael grabbed my duffel bag on the way out the door. I think he was safeguarding it for me, and for that, I was grateful, since it held my prized possession: the photos of my angel: Stella. Everyone walked ahead while I lined up with my classmates. Unlike regular high schools, military graduations are more solemn and formal. No one made a peep until we had been dismissed for the last time. When everyone else threw their caps in the air cheering, I just stood there staring at mine in disgust until I limply dropped it to the ground.

* * *

I turned and stalked away, making a beeline for the car. I wanted to be off the property as fast as humanly possible.

"Stefan, don't you want to say goodbye to your friends?" My mom looked shocked.

"What friends? Did you really think I would make new friends after coming in at the end of the year? They had four years to become friends. I was here for two months. Now, I would like to go home. I have a lot to get ready before college starts in the fall," I seethed and crawled in the backseat with Michael.

The two-hour ride passed quickly because I slept through it. It seemed like the best idea to avoid them. We weren't living on base in D.C., which we had never done before. Of course, the minute we arrived, the neighbors came out to say "Hello." I couldn't run into the house fast enough.

Michael led me to my room. He must have set it up, because he knew how I liked things. It resembled all my other rooms. The furniture from Germany gave it a homey quality, but that was irrelevant to me. The white walls looked barren and unwelcoming. Even with all the things I had collected over the years scattered around me, it wasn't my home.

Little did they know that this would be my one and only summer there. My plan was a simple one: the day I turned eighteen, I'd take all my paperwork and find Stella. If she'd have me, that's where I would stay. I had no plan if she hadn't waited for me. She'd promised, and I held on to that.

I hoped to be able to slip away for at least a visit to see Stella, if possible. But knowing my dad, he'd never let that happen. One could always hope, though.

● ● ●

July

June slipped by without a chance to see Stella, and my dad refused to let me get a new phone until I left for school. My parents made sure to never leave me alone, even in the house. If I made one move, they were there to counter it. I'd hoped for a moment alone when I called Norfolk to ensure everything was all set. I wanted to ask if Stella had enrolled, but my dad sat right next to me during the entire phone call. Even Michael was watched closely.

The furthest they allowed me from the house was the driveway to play basketball with Michael, but still someone would sit there and watch us. The house became a prison, and we were the prisoners, even if there weren't the telltale bars on display.

"Stefan, there is someone here to see you," my mother called up the stairs on the last Saturday in July.

I had no idea who could have possibly come by to see me, so I made my way downstairs slowly. "Yeah, Mom?" I asked, trying to sound uninterested.

I wasn't expecting to see a girl standing in my living room. She had shoulder length blond hair and light green eyes. I guess to most men she would be considered cute.

"Hi, I'm Cassie. Our moms are friends." She extended her hand.

I shook her hand. "Hello, I'm Stefan."

"I was wondering, since you're new around here, if maybe you'd like to hang out?"

"Oh, doesn't that sound nice, Stefan?" My mother grinned, pleased with her handy work.

She didn't fool me. I knew what she'd planned to happen. I wouldn't let her win, so I played as dirty as she did.

"Thanks for the offer, but I think my boyfriend might get jealous." She gasped when I winked at her.

"Oh, I . . . um . . . right, well I have to go." I snickered when she bolted out the door.

"Stefan, go to your room!"

Laughing, I took the stairs two at a time.

When my father arrived home at six sharp, a screaming match ensued. I heard his angry steps when he rushed up the stairs and barreled into my room. With one punch, I landed on the floor, bleeding from my now-fattened lip.

"Do you realize what you've done?"

It hurt like hell, but I laughed at him anyway. "Do I look like I care?" I chuckled, trying to infuriate him further.

"Well, you should. That girl has probably called everyone she knows and told them you're gay!"

"I don't care if they think I'm gay or green with yellow polka dots!" I staggered to get back up only to have my legs kicked back

● ● ●

out from under me.

"I DO!" he leered.

"I guess that's too bad," I laughed.

"Dad! What the hell are you doing?" Michael rushed up the stairs and into my room.

"Michael, I swear if you don't stay out of this," my dad growled.

"You'll what? The only reason I'm here is for Stefan. It's not for your cheery disposition," Michael snarled.

"You just condemned yourself to the same fate. Neither of you will leave your rooms until you leave for school. Is that understood?"

"Yes, Sir!" I snapped to attention and saluted, thinking just three more weeks and I'd be gone.

Michael didn't bother answering him. The door practically shook off its hinges when he slammed it shut.

I didn't blame his actions on the military life we were raised in. In fact, I thought it was the complete opposite. I thought it would have been a lot worse if he hadn't been in the military. The service did not turn him into a monster; it kept him from becoming a bigger monster. His training and command structure kept him in check. Thank God for that.

◊◊◊

● ● ●

August

After being locked in my room for three weeks, my birthday finally arrived. I was ecstatic when I woke up at 4:30 a.m. One way or another, I'd get out of this house. I waited until my dad left for his five o'clock run. I crept out into the hall and down the stairs while my mom started his breakfast in the kitchen. Mom never heard me when I slipped into the old man's office and shut the door.

Stealthily, I headed straight for his desk. I knew that was where he kept our manila envelopes filled with our important papers. We each had one, filled with everything from our birth certificates to our 529 college funds. Using his precious engraved envelope opener, I jimmied the draw open and grabbed my paperwork. Just below mine, sat a stack of unopened letters addressed to me and postmarked from Virginia Beach.

She had written to me!

I grabbed the letters and headed for the window. Checking the door, I slid the window open enough for me to slip out. I almost jumped out of my skin when, there under the window, I found Michael waiting for me. Without a word, he pointed to the manila envelope and then to himself. He wanted me to grab his too, so I did.

Without a sound, I slipped out and followed him to his car, which to my surprise wasn't in the driveway, but two houses down the street. Like me, he had planned this.

Once in the car, he started it up and headed away from my dad's running route. I couldn't help but stare out the back window as we drove away. The fear of being caught caused my heart to race.

* * *

Once we hit the highway, he laughed.

"Wow, what a rush!" Michael's adrenaline rush was evident in his exclamation.

"He's going to kill you; you know that, right?"

"What can he do to me now? You have all my papers, and my tuition is paid for already." He cocked his eyebrow, challenging me.

"Did we really just do that?" I asked in disbelief.

"Yeah, kid, we did," he chortled, rolling down the window. "Next stop, South Carolina!" he shouted out the window.

"Wait, you need to drop me off in Virginia first." He just shook his head.

"No, Stefan. You need to drop me off, and then you can take the car to Virginia Beach," he corrected with a smile.

"Are you saying you're giving me your car?" I gaped at him.

He grinned. "Happy Birthday, Stefan."

We didn't talk for the next hour. Michael seemed too deep in thought. He looked like he wanted to say something but kept snapping his jaw shut. Finally, he found the courage he needed to open up. His next question floored me.

"Stefan, did you mean what you said about being gay?"

"I am racing off to see the woman of my dreams, and you're asking if I'm gay?

"No, I'm asking if you would care if I was." The gears in my

* * *

brain started working overtime, things clicked together, and I understood.

Shaking my head, "No, I don't care, but I think I always knew. Girls never did draw your attention." I smiled at him.

"I met someone at school. I think you'd like him." The gleam in his eyes told me he had found love, too.

I clapped his shoulder. "Michael, I'm sure I will, but I can't meet him today. I'm just going to have enough time to meet Stella on the beach at dusk. I need to turn and burn."

"Stefan, if she's moved on, you can join me in South Carolina. Eddie and I moved off campus last May."

"I know, and don't take this the wrong way, but I'm praying she hasn't moved on."

"That makes two of us." He smiled back.

We spent the rest of the ride talking about his boyfriend and new townhouse. He even called Eddie from his cell to tell him we had left already. He sounded so happy for a change. I was happy for him. He shut off the phone when my parents started calling it. They knew we were gone.

I tried a couple of times to call Stella's house, but the machine answered. I didn't bother with a message, since I planned to go straight there anyway. More than once, I prayed she'd be waiting at the lighthouse. If she wasn't, my heart would be obliterated.

Speeding off the minute he exited the car, I watched Michael run up to a waiting young man. I waved to them both as I sped by. From Eddie's smile, he'd really missed Michael. They'd endured the

● ● ●

same separation I had. My world would be righted if Stella met me on the beach with open arms.

I made the ride back to Virginia Beach in record time. Hell yeah, I broke the speed limit, but I was a man on a mission. Nothing would stop me from finding her.

A stunning sight stood in front of me as I climbed out of the car. Even though she faced away from me, I knew it had to be her. Her auburn hair blew in the light breeze, and she was wearing a white flowing sundress with a matching white straw hat. The sunset shining in her hair made it shimmer a golden red. She stood there, as beautiful as I remembered.

A gasp escaped my lips when she turned her slight form to the side and I saw her enlarged belly. I knew the moment I saw it. It had to be mine. It had to be, for the sake of my heart.

Rushing forward, I raced up the dunes screaming her name. At first, she acted as if she couldn't see me. Then her face lit up, and she cradled her belly and tried to trudge through the sand to meet me.

I pushed forward harder, not wanting her to strain herself. As soon as she was in reach, I grabbed her and pulled her against my chest. For a moment, we didn't say anything. We just let ourselves feel each other. After waiting all those months to see her, I kissed her with every ounce of the love I felt for her. Slowly, I caressed her tender lips until she opened up and let me lead our tongues in a heated tango. In return, she did the same. My body reacted to her closeness in its usual way. The surging of hormones was a wonderful sensation. Apparently, my body had missed her, too. It was a breathtaking experience; one I wanted to repeat every day of my life.

Thankfully, when I begged, she complied and told me they

● ● ●

were mine. By "they," she meant twins. We were having twins! I'd never pictured our reunion ending with me becoming a father, but I couldn't find it in me to be mad. Stella would never have done that on purpose, not after her life.

I dropped to my knees, placed my cheek against her tummy, and told them, "Daddy's home."

● ● ●

Chapter Nine

Finding out about the parents

Stella

THE MEAL, OF COURSE, WAS DELICIOUS. YOU CAN NEVER go wrong with chicken and broccoli over ziti. I selected it because of my recommended diet. We decided since someone in my family was also working against us that we would stay at the Mayflower Motel again. This time, our stay would be completely different. He wouldn't admit it, but deep down, I knew he'd used his school money.

I did manage to get him to stop at the local Food Lion supermarket on the way to the motel. Today, after all, was both our eighteenth birthdays. Waddling along, I made my way through the

* * *

aisles in search of the one thing dinner didn't cover. At the bakery, I found a chocolate cake with chocolate frosting: Stefan's favorite. On the way to the registers, I grabbed a few other things to snack on and some sodas to wash them down with. As usual, the cashier, who seemed to be about forty, gave me a disapproving look when I pulled out my food stamps EBT card. The card was a dead giveaway, announcing to everyone that I was a single woman having a child with no one to support me. Avoiding her glare, I rushed and grabbed my bags from the bagger, scooting out the door without looking back.

Stefan's glowing smile greeted me when I came out. Seeing him leaning against the faded Mustang and grinning was more than my poor heart could stand. He was so sweet to meet me halfway and to help me carry my bags before he put them in the backseat and got in. I let him carry everything except for one bag. I didn't want him to see the cake just yet. After he placed a soft kiss on my lips, we drove to the motel.

My nerves were starting to get the better of me. The last time we'd rented a room there, he had been a perfect gentleman, but now that we had done the deed, would he want more? Was I ready to give him more?

The wounds were still so fresh. I wanted to believe everything he'd said at dinner, but the fear was ingrained too deep into my soul.

As soon as he went inside to rent the room, I called the house phone, knowing everyone would be out. Mom and Nana would be at work, and Brianna would be at one of her friend's houses.

"Hi, Nana, it's Stella. I'm crashing at Danielle's house; you

* * *

know, celebrating my birthday and all. See you tomorrow." They knew about Danielle being pregnant, too, so they wouldn't suspect anything out of the ordinary, even if I didn't usually hang out with her.

I took a deep breath before following him into room seventeen; we'd rented this one last time, too. I wondered if he did it on purpose or if it was one of those kismet things. When I sat on the edge of the bed, I sat on my hands to hide the fact they were shaking. Stefan could tell I was out of sorts when he sat down and hugged me.

"What is it, Stella? I'm missing something here. What are you hiding?" he pleaded.

"I just never pictured my life turning out like this. I don't mean the falling in love part. I thought I'd be different from Nana and my mom." A strangled whimper escaped me as my eyes filled with tears.

With his thumb, he caught a lone tear that had managed to escape and slip down my cheek. With each vow he uttered, he calmed each of my worries. Even the financial ones weren't embarrassing any more.

"Stella, I'm not here because I have to be. I'm here because I want to be. You know that, right?" he implored with worry etched on his sharp features.

"I guess I just needed to hear it. I'm sorry I don't have more to contribute."

"It doesn't matter. I haven't looked through my envelope yet, but I'm sure I can skimp on a few things so I can use some of the money for a place." I hated the thought that he might have to go

* * *

without the things he wanted or needed.

In yet another attempt to stop him from worrying too much, I hopped up and went to retrieve his mini-present. I fumbled pulling it out and opened the white, cardboard cake box. Using my tummy as coverage, I moved closer and whispered, "Happy birthday."

He grinned when I pulled out the cake to show him. "Get over here, and bring the cake," he laughed.

My eyes widened when he grabbed a handful of cake with his fingers. I'd forgotten the silverware. "It's your birthday, too. Happy birthday, Stella."

He was so adorable feeding me the cake from his fingers. I returned the favor, so when we were done we were both covered in chocolate. Together we laughed, licked each other's fingers, and snuggled. All those long-forgotten joys came back, and it felt like when we'd first met. The thrill of being so close hummed between us. You could feel the electricity in the air.

"Don't worry; we'll figure it all out. You look exhausted. Close your eyes, and we'll start sorting everything out tomorrow," he cooed when my brow furrowed.

I didn't want it to end, but I couldn't guess how we were going to be able to be together when I couldn't take him home. After a few relaxing breaths, I slipped off to sleep in his arms.

I was jarred awake by a sudden, loud slamming against the room door.

Stefan leapt out of bed and flung the door open. "Dad, stop!" he roared.

● ◉ ●

"What the hell were you thinking? I told you to stay away from her!" Maurice snarled like a lion on a rampage. Shirley scowled from behind him. There was no stopping my heart; it tried to hammer its way out of my chest. His parents had come here to steal him away again.

"You can't tell me what to do anymore! I'm eighteen, so get over it. I will see her as much as I want. I can tell you now, it will be every minute of every day," he seethed at his father.

With his arms protectively wrapped around me, he moved me forward so they would see my baby bump.

"She's . . . she's pregnant!" his dad gasped in shock.

The expression on his mother's face was priceless. She couldn't hide the fact that she knew all along. Maurice didn't miss it, either. It was there for all to see.

"Yes, and we're having twins." Stefan stroked my bulging belly with love.

"Let's take this inside," Maurice sneered at his wife.

Stefan and I backed up to sit on the bed while Maurice paced the room, shooting daggers at this wife. He was scaring the hell out of me. Stefan reached out, grabbed my hands, and held them.

"Stefan, you don't really know if they're yours. She is awful big for someone only five months along. I wouldn't doubt it if she had already been pregnant when she seduced you," his mother grumbled, trying to deflect the blame. Instead, she looked guiltier.

"You don't know anything! She was a virgin when I seduced her. She was the one who wanted to wait until I came back for our

* * *

137

birthdays." Shirley stood there gaping until Maurice cut her off.

"This is easily fixed. We'll put them up for adoption. That's all." The twins churned in my stomach as if they'd heard him.

"I am not putting my children up for adoption! That is the end of that subject!" Stefan shouted, losing his calm exterior.

"Stefan, you're not thinking clearly. You are going to college! You can't take care of two infants. And what about Stella? Doesn't she deserve the right to go to college?" Stefan sighed before gazing into my eyes.

"We'll both go. We just have to be creative. Our schedules will alternate so that one of us can be with the babies while the other is in class. We can also find someone who's willing to watch them if we are both required to take a class at the same time." I smiled, realizing he'd given this a lot of thought.

"Stella, you've been quiet on this. What were your plans if Stefan didn't come back?" Maurice grilled me.

Looking down at our intertwined fingers, I answered, "I planned on going to Norfolk with the help of my nana and the public assistance I'm receiving. I hope it will get me through until I can work for myself. I'm taking the minimum number of courses I can for the first year," I stammered, unable to keep my voice smooth.

"Do you two realize how hard this is going to be?" Maurice asked, exasperated.

"We don't care. They're worth it. She didn't want this, but like her, I agree that now that they are here, we're going to love them and raise them as a family."

● ● ●

"I'm not going to lie about how I feel. This is the biggest mistake of your lives. I also can't stop you from doing it. You are my son, and I only want to see you succeed. So, I will tell you what: when your grandfather died, he left a small amount of money that has been sitting in a trust fund. I'm sure you found the checkbook by now. Let's go find her an apartment closer to the school, and you can visit her when you're not studying or in class." From Stefan's smug expression, he knew about the money.

"Can I talk this over with Stella for a moment?" Stefan stroked my arm, calming me.

"Sure, we'll go to the breakfast place across the street — Pop's Place. Join us when you're done, and we'll talk some more." There was no mistaking the fact the Maurice was less than pleased with his wife when he stomped out of the room.

"Stella, are you all right?" Stefan whispered as the door clicked shut behind them.

"Yeah, I'm fine. Are you sure you want to do this?" I breathed.

"Yes, I am. I love you. And, if he's willing to give us the rent money from my trust fund, I say we go for it. But please don't mention my plan about the housing money." He grinned as he leaned in to kiss me.

"So, you're not planning on staying on campus?" I held my breath and waited.

"Hell, no. I'll be wherever you are. That's the only place I've ever wanted to be. There's no way I'm going to promise him that I won't stay with you. If he tries, it'll be the deal breaker, and we'll

* * *

leave." I reveled in the feeling of his hands on my cheeks. There was just something about his touch that assured comfort.

"I'm starving; we should get this over with," I said, hoping to end this faster.

"Just remember, he has to be back in D.C. by tomorrow night, so they can't stay forever," he murmured against my lips as he placed a sweet kiss on them.

"Okay, but we're going to have to tell my family about everything today," I implored, hoping he would agree.

"Don't worry about that. I'll be right by your side when we do." If only he knew the ramifications of what he'd just said.

Together, we crossed the street, holding hands. The smell of pancakes on the griddle was the first thing that caught my attention. Scanning the room, there before us sat a very unhappy Shirley as Maurice was undoubtedly laying into her. Of course, that all ceased when they saw us approaching the table. Stefan pulled out my battered, red, metal chair before sitting next to me.

"Stella, first, I would like to say I'm sorry about not telling Stefan about your call, and also for the way I treated you on the phone." *Geez, could she be any less sincere?*

"Thank you, Mrs. Sterling," I replied with a smile, more for Stefan's sake than hers.

"So, we called a real estate agent in Norfolk. They have a few listings for families, not students. As the agent put it, 'they never said the family couldn't be going to school'." Maurice chuckled at the agent's cunningness.

* * *

"Fine, after breakfast we'll follow you there, but the choice is ours. You will not be deciding which place, if any, we agree to. We will, however, take your observations and opinion on the place under consideration." Stefan spoke so self-assuredly.

"Good; sounds like a solid plan. Have you spoken with Michael?" *Change the subject much there, Maurice?*

"Yeah, Dad. I called him last night when we got to the motel." I peeked up to see Stefan smiling at me. He'd never told me he had called his brother.

"So, he went back to school?" Shirley inquired.

"Of course, Mom. Why wouldn't he?" Stefan gasped, taken back.

"She's referring to him moving off campus," Maurice retorted.

"And?" Stefan played coy.

"He never told us," his mom huffed, pouting.

"Well, he's twenty-one now. He has the right to choose where he lives, and according to Michael, student housing isn't all it's cracked up to be."

Following Stefan's lead, I ordered the pancakes. All through breakfast, I had little to say, mostly because no one except Stefan really wanted me there. I latched onto his hand and refused to let go. Even once the food arrived, he never tried to free himself from my grasp. This promised to be a very long day.

● ● ●

Mocked By Destiny

Stefan

Stella and I spent the hour after our reunion in silence, watching the tide rise and the sun set. Holding her in my arms with my hands resting on her belly that housed my children brought me the serenity I'd desired for so long. With my arms still around her from behind, we made our way back to the Mustang. I could tell something was on her mind, but I didn't want to push her just yet. I was just happy to be with her again. After enduring being separated for five months, I was apprehensive about letting go of her, even after I'd helped her into my car. For the short ride, we both remained quiet, no doubt thinking about the upcoming conversation. She did try once to start the dreaded conversation, but I wasn't ready quite yet.

I kept catching her peeking up at me. What I wouldn't pay to know what she was thinking at that moment. The thought that she might not want anything to do with me made my chest ache all over again. Keeping a cool exterior did nothing to keep my insides from quaking.

We found a quiet little surf-and-turf restaurant named Benny's off 21st Street. The hostess showed us to a tiny booth in the back and left the menus on the table. Once we had taken our seats, we quickly looked over the menus. She had a habit of making this adorable worried frown every time we went out for meals, the same one she'd made on the beach during our first date.

In a firm voice, I made sure she knew I was buying her dinner. Money was no object tonight. She deserved only the best, in my eyes. When she blurted out that she had called and spoken with my mother, I was fuming. Not because she had called, but because my mother had never told me. I knew she had been trying to keep me away from Stella, but at the cost of my children and her grandchildren? What was she thinking?

The mystery about who in her family would have taken Michael's notes lingered in my mind. Who would be so cruel to hurt my twins intentionally?

My heart hammered in my chest when she asked if we were still together. With my voice raised, I made it crystal clear that we had been together all along. Still she held back, telling me what she was thinking. It was beyond infuriating. When she spoke her words of love for me, I finally smiled in relief. That was the only thing I needed to hear.

As the conversation continued, I started to pick up on what Stella was thinking. She was afraid that I didn't feel the same as she did. Keeping my resolve to keep her in my life, I squelched every one of her fears down. Such a beautiful woman should never have to fear being unloved. Stella was loved — by me. She just needed to hear it.

We both wanted to be together, we both wanted the twins in her womb, and we'd have it. If it cost me every penny I'd saved for college, I would pay it.

For the next few minutes, we just ate and eyed each other with caution. When the bill arrived, I used the preloaded credit card my parents had filled with the money from my savings account. I didn't tell her it was intended for my school expenses. Once the bill had been settled, it was time to get a room for the night. We needed

* * *

to figure out what to do next.

Stella wanted to stop at the supermarket on the way to the motel we had stayed in last time. She ran in to grab a few things for us to snack on. Mesmerized by the sight of her walking into the store, the memory of the night we conceived the twins re-invaded my mind. It also gave me a few minutes to try to figure out why she was apprehensive. I came up empty.

With a slight waddle, she started back for the car. That wouldn't do. One thing my parents had taught me was that you always assist a woman in need. I rushed up, and Stella allowed me to carry all of her bags save one. She flat-out refused to hand that one over. It looked light enough, so I didn't push her. With her bags in the back seat, we headed off to the motel. In minutes, we were parking in the adjacent lot. The Mayflower Motel was not my idea of a suitable place to stay, but we needed to watch every penny.

While I went in and rented the room, she phoned home to leave a message that she was staying at a girlfriend's house for the night. We had so much to discuss and thought it best that she not tell them about me just yet. I laughed when the manager handed me the key to the same room we had stayed in last time. Again, I used the credit card from home.

Stella seemed as bashful as the last time we'd rented a room. Reverting back to her shy ways, she sat on the edge of the bed and sighed. It took a little coaxing, but she did open up and tell me her fears. Making sure to reassure her, I soothed her worries with gentle words.

Inwardly, I cringed when she revealed she'd had to rely on government aid. It should have been my responsibility to provide for

● ● ●

144

her, something I would have done without any qualms.

We both scooted up the bed and leaned against the pillows. Feeling Stella's body pressed flush against mine was where I always wanted her to be. There in her embrace, I felt at home. The thought that I might be forced to stay in student housing while she stayed at home wasn't something I wanted to entertain, but we might have to.

I waited until she drifted off before I reached over and grabbed my envelope from the nightstand. Most of it I had seen before — my passport, 529 fund statement, birth certificate — but surprisingly, there was a bank statement for a checking account and a checkbook with my name and my dad's name on it. Where had that come from?

The last thing I found was a letter that I'd never seen before from my grandfather. The envelope was old and faded, but I easily remembered his elegant script.

He had died just mere months after my grandmother had lost her fight with breast cancer. My dad had said he'd died of a broken heart, but the doctors had said he'd had a heart attack. If you ask me, I think that was just two ways to say the same thing.

Dearest Stefan,

I asked your father to give this to you the day you turned twenty-one. I wanted you to know from me that I love you.

When Grammy died, I knew my days were numbered. She was my life and without her, I'm lost.

One day, I hope you find someone who is your life. The love

● ● ●

of a woman is not something you should throw away. It should be nourished and cared for.

I have moved one third of my money into an account for you, Michael gets a third, and your parents will get whatever is left. Use it wisely. It's all I have left to give to you.

Your loving Grampy

Now, I just had to get to the bank before my father had a chance to empty it out. I rushed, using Stella's cell phone to call Michael.

"Michael, it's Stefan."

"So was she there?"

"Yes, she was there, and she's pregnant. I'm going to be the father of twins." At first, he didn't say anything.

"Are you happy about it?" Michael sounded cautious, that was evident.

"Yeah, I truly am. It's not what I wanted for us, but I can't seem to be upset about it." Looking down at the sleeping angel on my chest, I spoke from the bottom of my heart. I could always tell Michael everything.

"Well, if you're both okay with it, then congratulations!" he chortled.

"Thanks. Hey, when you turned twenty-one, did you get a letter from Grampy?"

● ● ●

"Yeah, so you found yours?"

"Yes. Why didn't you say anything about it?" I asked.

"Dad wanted to surprise you with it," he muttered.

"So, it's real?" I probed.

"Yeah, it's real. Unfortunately, you don't get it until you're twenty-one. That is, unless Dad agrees to take it out for you."

"I doubt that, not after the stunt we pulled today. You don't think he'll empty it out before I turn twenty-one, do you?"

"No, he's not that cruel. Besides, you have the checkbook. Without that, he can't access it, either," he sniggered.

"I didn't think about that. Are there any other stipulations to the trust fund?" I couldn't help, but hope for a loophole.

"No, just twenty-one or the day you get married."

"Are you serious? So, if I marry Stella, I can use the money to get us a place?" I knew one day I wanted to marry her, maybe sooner would be better.

"Stefan, don't marry her for the money. Marry her because you love her." His voice was stern, but not harsh.

"I do love her, with every fiber in my being. I just want to give her more than a trashy studio apartment to raise my kids in." I knew I sounded whiny, but it was the complete truth.

"Look around for a place, and I'll lend you the money until you get yours."

* * *

"You'd really do that?" I queried.

"Hey, those are my nieces or nephews, and I don't want them living in a dumpy apartment either. How can I say no to them?" It lifted my spirits to hear him claiming my children as family.

"Thanks, Michael. I'll call you tomorrow. Save this number; it's Stella's cell phone."

"I will. Take care of those three, and we'll work this out. Oh, Eddie says hello."

"Tell him I said hi back." I hung up, feeling ten times better about our situation. With some of the weight lifted off us, I drifted off to sleep in Stella's loving arms.

For the first time in months, I awoke rested and happy. It definitely had something to do with the girl of my dreams being in my arms. After being separated for five months, it felt like it had been only yesterday that I had been dragged away from her.

Just as I was about to kiss her awake, my father started banging on the door. His obnoxious ranting even woke Stella. The poor thing almost fell out of bed. I whipped open the door to come face to face with my parents. I almost smacked my head against the door. How had I been so stupid? He had tracked my purchases on the credit card!

He screamed his usual jargon until he saw it: the belly that had me unable to leave her, ever. Not because I had to, but because I wanted to be there for them. My dad played every card he could think of to get me to leave her, even that it would be better for Stella card. But when he suggested we give them up, I was about knock his head off his shoulders.

● ● ●

When he mentioned the trust fund, I knew he was caving. He knew I had him over a barrel. You bet I gloated.

After ushering them back out the door, Stella and I talked privately while my parents went out to the breakfast joint across the street. There was no hiding that she didn't want to go, but I convinced her otherwise.

By the hand, I led her across the street to the restaurant. My parents were quietly arguing, and I could see my dad's anger. He was furious with my mother. Their bitter banter ceased when we approached and took seats opposite them.

After accepting my mother's half-hearted apology, Stella never said another word at breakfast. Under the table, she clung to my hand as if it were a life preserver. I'd be that for her, and anything else she needed.

I grinned, watching Stella devour her chocolate chip pancakes. Stifling back a groan, I watched her lick a chocolate smudge off her upper lip. God, that woman was stunning.

* * *

Mocked By Destiny

Chapter Ten

Stefan's making a house a home

THE RIDE TO NORFOLK TOOK OVER AN HOUR. DRIVING separately from my parents gave Stella a much-needed chance to relax. To keep her that way, I went into the office with my dad to discuss what we needed from the realtor. There were three possibilities, but one stood out the most. We decided to save it for last.

The first stop was like something out of a cheap horror movie. It was so bad; we didn't even bother getting out of the car, fearing we wouldn't make it back alive. The brown, triple-decker needed to be torn down, not rented. Glancing up through the windshield, I half expected to see the dangling siding drop down

● ● ●

around us. The house even came with its own gang of thugs hanging on the corner. Scenic view near a park was right; we did have a perfect view of a pack of wild teenagers, blaring hip hop music and smashing beer bottles against the jungle gym. That sight alone sent us scrambling in search of the next address.

At least when we reached the next address, it was safe to get out of the car. Stella huffed and puffed her way up the two flights of stairs. I cringed when the realtor slipped the flimsy door open. If the peeling wallpaper, chipping paint, and cockroaches didn't seal the deal, the large, red bloodstain in the middle of the disgusting, yellow carpeting sure would have. Dragging her by the arm, I couldn't get Stella to waddle down the stairs fast enough.

Feeling defeated, we headed for the last place on the list. Fifteen minutes from the realtor's office and the school we'd be attending, we found a very cute, white cottage with matching picket fence. An elderly woman stood in the one-car driveway waiting for us. She reminded me so much of my grandmother before she passed away.

When we got out, she eyed Stella cautiously until she saw me rubbing Stella's baby bump. She started grinning. "C'mon in, folks." She waved us toward the tiny house.

"It's a pleasure to meet you, Mrs. Keenan. We're the Sterling's, Maurice and Shirley." My dad shook the hand she extended. "That's my son Stefan and the expectant mother Stella." He pointed us out one at a time.

"Nice to meet ya'll. Just call me Gloria. Well, let's take this party inside." With Stella glued to my side, we entered the quaint, two bedroom cottage.

● ● ●

152

Stella sighed, looking at ease there. There was some leftover furniture, a recliner, two end tables, a bureau, and a tiny roll-up desk from her last tenants. All the walls had a fresh coat of white paint, making the rooms look clean and well cared-for. The floors were covered in clean, plush carpeting. The kitchen was small and the appliances were somewhat worn, but it would do just fine. There was even a fenced in, well-manicured yard where the twins could play.

After a thorough tour, Stella and I stepped out into the yard to talk in private. "Stella, what do you think?"

I smiled when she began shifting between her feet. "I like it, Stefan. Do you?"

"Yes, and it's only a few minutes from school," I whispered in her ear, my breath causing her to shiver.

"So, this is the one?" There was a glimmer in her eye that said she wanted it.

"Okay, this is the one." With a sharp nod, I signaled for my dad to begin the negotiations.

We listened in as my father discussed that he would be paying the rent - which included everything but a phone and cable - for Stella. Thanks to my dad's quick thinking and inquiring about the furniture left behind, Gloria agreed we could have anything. We offered to pay for it, but my dad let it slip that we didn't have much in the way of furniture with us just starting out and all.

Only an hour after we arrived, the lease was signed, and we were headed to the Goodwill store down the road with the keys to our cottage.

* * *

I wished I could have given her a beautiful new home filled with new expensive furnishings, but this was the best we could've hoped for. One day, I'd get her the house of her dreams. She'd have everything she deserved and more. I was surprised when Stella seemed to know her way around the store.

My parents were handling it better than I'd hoped — well, more my dad than my mom, which was somewhat shocking. With the exception of a few glares from my mom, in the end, we managed to find everything we needed to start off with. Of course, there were a few exceptions, like linens and a TV. My mother originally wanted us to buy them there but I wanted Stella to have a few things that were new and my dad agreed with me. More than once, he shook his head when I'd pick up something.

It took two trips to get everything to the cottage. The couch and loveseat were delivered by the Goodwill — for a small fee, of course.

My dad even insisted on us buying a new, full-sized mattress for the cottage at a local same-day delivery place. He pulled me aside and told me that he wasn't having his son sleeping on a used mattress that was from God knows where and with who knew what living in it.

"Stefan, I'm not stupid. You'll be over here every spare moment. I don't want to think about it, so don't share any details with me."

"Okay, Dad. Let's consider this a black op, and you're on a needs to know basis," I snickered.

"I'm going to need a list of things you want sent down from your room. All your stuff is packed for school, so I'll send that first,"

● ● ●

he muttered.

"Thanks, Dad. I'd appreciated that. Once we unpack, I'll make that list for you."

"I know I don't say it enough, but you know I love you, right?" he said, uncomfortable expressing his affection.

"Yeah, I do. I love you, too; even when we fight. But it might take a while before I forgive you for putting me in the J.E.B." I laughed.

"We thought we were doing the right thing. Now, I see all it served to do was to hurt everyone involved. I thought I could save you from making a mess of your life. Turns out: it was already too late." He huffed.

"I guess we'll never see eye to eye on that. I love her, Dad. You can't change that, so stop trying."

He nodded, grabbing another arm load of bags from his trunk.

After noticing Stella's fatigue, I insisted she lay on the couch while we waited for pizza to arrive for lunch. My dad managed to keep my mom away from Stella. Thank heavens for that. She didn't need to be any more stressed than she already was with all that'd happened in the past two days.

My mother complained non-stop until my father finally snapped at her. "You're one to talk! Leave it be, or we'll never see our grandchildren!" After that outburst, we only had to deal with her dirty looks.

My dad helped me set everything up, including the bed that we'd use tonight if all went as planned. We needed to get

* * *

reacquainted, after all. It had taken sleeping next to her last night for my body to show it missed her, though I'd never let her know that; it would have been too embarrassing.

Whispering in her ear, I woke her. "Rise and shine, baby. The food is here. My children must be starving by now."

"Mommy is, too," she chuckled when her stomach called out, agreeing with her.

She was so cute, stuffing her face with pepperoni pizza. She ate as much as I did. Well, she was eating for three. Right before we finished, the mattress arrived. Seeing the expression on my mother's face when they dragged it through the house was priceless. She looked green, as if she wanted to throw up her lunch.

Once we cleaned up the trash, we headed out to get the last few things we needed. Again, we took separate cars. I didn't want my mother too close to Stella. Nothing good would come from her taunting us.

A trip to Walmart took care of those needs that couldn't be met at the Goodwill store. Like with the mattress, my dad and I insisted we needed new bedding, towels, and odds and ends. Throughout the entire shopping experience, Stella had been a little timid about selecting things. My personal thought was she didn't want to spend too much. I ended up having to pull her aside and talk to her.

"Stella, what's wrong? Don't you like anything?"

"No, I do, but your trust fund was meant for you to have a better life. I can't help feeling like I'm taking something away from your future," she mumbled, wringing her hands.

● ● ●

Grabbing her hands to still them, I made it very clear how I felt about the money subject. "Don't you get it? You are my future, and those babies you're carrying are my future. My grandfather's note said to use it when I found love; well, I have. And if you haven't figured it out, it's you. You will select the things you like and need or I'll do it for you but, one way or the other, you're getting them."

She nodded at my stern tone. "Yes, Sir." She mock-saluted, causing me to laugh at her adorableness.

Of course, Stella still looked to me for approval before she settled on anything, but at least she did what I'd asked. In the bed and bath department, Stella discovered a light green towel set with a matching shower curtain. The mustard yellow kitchen set she found had all the needed towels and pot holders. She even let me splurge on matching placemats. Stella went back to the basics when it came to selecting curtains. She selected all white, claiming they would match everything.

My parents did, however, buy me a new cell phone and enough re-up cards to hold me for a while. The plan had always been for them to buy me a new laptop for school so, while we were shopping from housewares, we also picked up a Hewlett Packard G72 that I could share with Stella. Since all she had at home was a very old Dell desktop, I'd have to teach her how to use it. When all was said and done, we had everything we needed in three shopping carts.

When we checked out, I felt so bad for Stella. She used her food stamps card and W.I.C. vouchers to buy all the food for us. Stella looked mortified when my parents watched her using the government aid. The cashier even seemed a little disgusted by it. What did they expect? Stella needed them to survive.

* * *

After we'd unloaded the cars, Stella set off to setting up her first home. I was surprised when my dad didn't ask for my envelope back.

"Thanks, Dad, for understanding everything." I hugged him for the first time in years.

"Stefan, are you sure about this?"

"Dad, don't ruin the day by pulling this crap. If it were Mom, you'd do the same."

"I did, when she found out she was pregnant with Michael." I looked him in the eye and realized what he'd been hiding.

I sighed. "So you know I can't walk away from her. Even if I didn't love her, which I do, I'd never leave my kids to grow up without me."

"I do know that. That's why I agreed to help you two. Your grandfather did it for me, and his father did it for him."

"So everyone in our family did it, too?" I asked, flabbergasted.

"Yeah, I guess we Sterling's are just very virile men. However, I don't think we'll have that problem with Michael. He won't admit it, but he isn't very interested in the female sector." It took a moment to scrape my jaw off the floor. "Don't look at me like that. I'm not stupid. I tried to toughen him up, but it turned out to be a useless venture. He is who he is. Just don't tell your mother. She still hasn't realized that these might be her only grandchildren." He almost looked sorry for her as he turned, looking back toward the car.

"If she changes her attitude, maybe we could come visit for a

● ● ●

holiday or something," I said unsurely. I doubted that it would happen in the near future.

"Just call me if you need anything. You're right about her. Most girls her age would have run rampant through Walmart, buying everything in sight. She's not out for your money, and that puts me a little more at ease." He clapped my shoulder when we started walking toward his car.

"I will, Dad. I'll call once I have my schedule, so you'll know when to call me."

"Good, and I'll be making a few phone calls to some of my friends down here at the naval station. Maybe one of their wives can take you two into the PX every so often to do some food shopping. It would be much cheaper. Stella needs to eat properly, and she seems the type that would starve herself rather than eat the last carrot stick, making sure you ate it." I couldn't help but laugh, because he was right — she would.

"Thanks again, Dad. We'll talk soon." With a firm handshake, we parted ways, and I felt a little better about our relationship.

My mom didn't bother getting out of the car as she pouted about my life. She shouldn't talk now that I knew she had been in the same boat we were. I couldn't believe she was being such a hypocrite. With time she'd see, like my father had, that it was my life to live, and this was how I chose to live it.

I found Stella in the kitchen hard at work. "Stefan, my grandmother Marie is on her way over. Would you help me put some things away before she gets here?" She looked around quickly. "Where did your parents go?"

* * *

"Home, but I told them we'd call them."

She looked so unhappy. "Oh, okay," she sighed, continuing to putting the dishes away.

"Stella, what's wrong?" I pulled her into my embrace.

"It's nothing. I just wanted to say thank you." When she refused to look at me, I knew she was pouting.

"I thanked them of both of us. My dad's impressed by you." I kissed her pouting, pink lips.

"How so?" She moaned when I nuzzled her ear.

"He said you weren't after my money," I mumbled into the crook of her neck.

"I don't want their money. I just want their second-born son." She giggled, struggling to escape my tickling of her sides.

"You stay here, barefoot and pregnant in the kitchen, and I'll go make the bed up." When I wiggled my eyebrows, she busted out laughing at my little joke.

"You sound like a caveman," she laughed, moving to put the glasses in the cabinet.

I'll admit that I was petrified to meet her grandmother. Could she be the one who had hidden Michael's notes? Maybe she didn't want us to be together? By the time she arrived, most of our stuff was put away, but the house looked naked and impersonal.

Stella, totally at ease with the arrival of the older woman, rushed up to hug her. "Nana!"

● ● ●

160

"Stella, you look so happy!" Marie cooed.

"I am. Come in and meet Stefan," Stella tittered.

I took a deep breath and moved forward. "Don't be shy, boy!" She grabbed and hugged me with the grip of a truck driver.

"It's nice to meet you, too." I gasped, trying to breathe.

"Well, for a while there, I thought you were a dirt bag, but now I see the truth. Stella told me all about your parents, and I'm sorry they did that to you." It was clear that she pulled no punches when she spoke.

"Yeah, well, we're working on them," I chuckled.

"Well, we still have my daughter to deal with. I've arranged a family dinner tomorrow night so we can sit together and hash this out. No worries; I have both your backs when it comes to her." I somehow didn't doubt that for a minute.

"Thanks, Nana. Let me show you around." Stella grabbed her hand and started dragging Marie off.

Stella walked her around the cottage while I went to get the iced tea and glasses to serve. By the time they came back, they were already discussing what Stella could take from Marie's house. I set up the laptop on the tiny desk while they chatted.

Marie stayed for about an hour, and by the time she left, I was totally at ease with her. I doubted she had taken Michael's notes. We agreed to be at her house for dinner at six o'clock in order to explain everything to the rest of the family in person. She also reminded Stella of her doctor's appointment next week, to which I agreed to take her.

* * *

For the rest of the night, I showed Stella how to use the laptop versus a desktop. She was thrilled that we'd received it. I shot Michael an email and told him about our parent's reaction and our father's suspicions about his life choice. In his reply, he told me that he wasn't the least bit phased by it. After reuniting with Eddie, he had decided not to hide it anymore. Michael had known I'd support him; it was his life to live as he saw fit. Who was I to judge?

When I'd shut the laptop down, I headed to the bedroom to change. I had bought a few things to wear at Walmart, but my dad said he'd send the rest of my stuff down. In the end, he figured out that I was going to be here all the time, so it would be the best place to send them.

I gulped when I walked into the bedroom to find Stella standing naked, drying off from her shower. Even pregnant, she was beyond beautiful. I pulled her close, devoured her tasty lips and led her to our bed.

"Stefan," she breathed as I laid her on the bed.

"Stella, you're the most beautiful woman I have seen," I whispered, leaning in and nuzzling her neck.

When I lay next to her, she bit her lip. "How can you say that? Have you seen my stomach lately?" She blushed.

"Your stomach makes you more stunning, Stella." To prove it, I ghosted my fingers over her belly, causing her to sigh.

Seeing her shiver under my touch had my insides quivering. She groaned when I sucked her earlobe into my mouth. With shaking hands, she tugged at my T-shirt. Sitting up, I pulled it off for her without taking my gaze off her eyes. When I lowered myself down to

● ● ●

162

her again, I could see how much adoration and love she held for me in her eyes. I hoped she could see it reflected back at her from my own eyes. Tonight, we made love for the second time.

Waking up with Stella in my arms had to be the best feeling ever. Even in her tousled state, she remained the prettiest woman I'd ever seen. Like a cat, she groaned and stretched herself awake without leaving my embrace. When I looked at the clock, it was my turn to groan. We were going to the school to register for all our classes, and with a little luck, we were deregistering me from the student housing. I hoped to be able to get the money back.

"Baby, we need to get ready, or we'll be late for registration. So move that cute derrière of yours." I hopped out of bed and headed for the shower.

"Five more minutes," she mumbled, throwing the covers over her head.

"Your five minutes are up, my dear," I chuckled, returning from my shower.

"Fine, but I get a nap when we get back," she growled like a furious little kitten.

"Anything you say." I held my hands up and surrendered to her.

By the time she walked out of the bedroom dressed, her breakfast was on the table, and I was on my second cup of coffee. Humming, she devoured the scrambled eggs and toast I had made for her. It didn't last long. She started snarling again when I went to start the car.

* * *

"Let's go, Stella. We still need to hit the bookstore after registration and Walmart for whatever else they say we need."

"Don't forget my nap!" she snapped.

"As if I would deny you your much-needed rest," I said, opening the car door for her.

After a quick trip through Donnie's Donuts, she perked right up. The rest of the ride passed quickly; she didn't have a chance to get any grouchier.

The campus was beautiful, but I had expected no less, although it was a mad house with everyone getting ready for the start of the semester. Every pathway was overcrowded with students either moving in or registering.

Much to my dismay, we were separated in the lines by the alphabet to get our packets. The bright spot was that the line moved quicker than anticipated. Everyone seemed to know what classes they needed for their majors. I reached the front first, and with everything arranged, I joined Stella to wait.

We did manage to arrange our schedules so we were never in class at the same time. The obvious downfall was that it left less time for us to be together. It seemed like a small sacrifice in order to care for the twins when they arrived. With all her classes in order too, we headed to the administration office to discuss my housing change.

That's where our luck ran out. Apparently, my mother had contacted them, telling them in no uncertain terms that I was not to give up my room. Whether I stayed in it or not, she demanded I have it. That ticked me off a little, but what could I do at that point? Next year, I'd just make sure they didn't assign me one. For now, I

● ● ●

possessed the key and room number, so if we ever needed it, we'd have it.

Wall-to-wall people lined the bookstore as we struggled to find the required books. Stella and I bought the bulk of our textbooks 'used,' hoping to save every penny. We even found one we could share. After one too many jostles, Stella took up a defensive posture. She looked ready to tackle the next person who cut in on us in line. We were both relieved when we staggered out of the congested store unharmed.

Stella did her best to make the trip through Walmart as quick as possible; no doubt, so we'd get home for her nap sooner. I did insist on buying her a few bigger outfits. She fought the idea, thinking we should save the money instead. I didn't want to tell her but her clothes were already too tight and soon they would be cutting into her curvy figure.

The moment I opened the door, she dashed for the bed. She looked so cute crawling back under the covers. While she rested, I made myself useful and put everything away for her, even her school supplies.

After spending the rest of the day fixing up the cottage, it was time to head to Marie's for dinner. I had no problem admitting that I was petrified. We still didn't know who had taken Michael's notes. Though we both agreed that her mother looked like the prime suspect, we had no proof.

Stella led me by the hand up the stairs to her childhood home, looking terrified. To calm her, I stroked her cheek, attempting to soothe her rattled nerves as well as my own. With one last peck on the lips, we entered the quiet house.

● ● ●

In the living room waited , Daisy, Nana, and Brianna. With the exception of Marie, we were stared at like criminals. A pin could have dropped in the room, and we all would have heard it. At first, we both froze and looked like a couple of deer caught in headlights. Finally, Stella cleared her throat and introduced me.

"Stefan, this is my mom Daisy and my sister Brianna. Everyone, this is Stefan, my boyfriend and the father of our twins," she rambled out.

"What is he doing here, Stella? Why is he back?" Her mother spoke directly to Stella for the first time in months.

I knew all about the silent treatment Stella had endured from her mother, given her condition and me being gone. It ate at me, knowing I couldn't change our circumstances. We'd both lived in hell for the five months that we had been apart. Nothing would change that.

"I came back to be with Stella." It was my turn to mumble insecurely.

"You left her. She wasn't good enough for you. You couldn't even call or write or anything?" It frightened me to see Daisy sneer just as well as my dad.

"Mom!" Stella huffed, crossing her arms over her chest.

"It's fine, Stella. She's only looking out for you." I caressed her lower back. "My dad stuck me in military school until I graduated. He then locked me up until I escaped on my eighteenth birthday, with the help of my brother. During the time I was in military school, my brother Michael did try to get in contact with Stella to let her know what the situation was, but it seemed his notes

● ● ●

never reached Stella," I challenged.

"So, now what?" she said, getting straight to the point.

"We rented a place in Norfolk near school. We're going to be a family."

Brianna, being the typical teenager, snorted at the thought.

"I'll warn you once; if you hurt them, you'll answer to me. I have no problem telling you how I feel. So, with that being said, I think this is a big mistake on her part. One day you will up and leave her, and we'll be left to pick up the pieces." Yeah, the whole 'telling it like it is' seemed to be a family trait.

"You weren't here the first time around," Stella grumbled, but her statement went unchallenged.

"Ms. Richards, I have no intention of ever leaving Stella or the twins," I vowed.

"Only time will prove if that's true. So let's eat now, and we can talk later." They all rose and moved in unison. Following them into the kitchen, I had to fight back a snicker. I wanted to ask them the name of their unit. Just who had been raised in the military environment? Me or them?

All through dinner, the conversation revolved around school and Stella's upcoming doctor's appointment. Brianna, however, spent her evening shooting daggers at me. Staying mostly quiet, Daisy listened in, only speaking a few words from time to time. Much like breakfast with my parents, Stella clung to my hand under the table. I hated seeing her so anxious.

The food was great. Her grandmother made a mean meatloaf.

* * *

After dinner, Stella went with her mom to her room to pack a few things. She only wanted some clothes and personal stuff like books and photos. Nana, as she now had me calling her, showed me photo albums of when the girls were babies. She was quite proud of them, and it was easy to tell as she turned every page proudly.

When Stella stormed down the stairs with her mother hot on her tail, I instantly thought they must have been fighting. With tears streaming down her cheeks, Stella stormed up to Brianna.

Throwing a hand full of papers at Brianna, she screamed, "How could you! You knew! You hid these from me," she hissed, her face flushed with anger.

"So what! Yeah, I knew. Face the facts, girl, he's just going to leave again. That's what they all do!" Brianna jumped up and moved to lunge at Stella. I leapt between them, managing not to get slapped.

"What is going on?" I roared. Grabbing Stella, I pulled her backward out of harm's way.

"Stefan . . . the notes; she hid them in her dresser," she sobbed into my shoulder.

"Why would you do that?" I barked, my anger now matching Stella's.

"She should face the facts. You'll get bored, and you'll leave like everyone else. Men are only good for one thing, and you've already done that!" She raced off to her room with an exasperated Daisy chasing her.

Stella slumped to the ground, whimpering. It hurt to see her

● ● ●

collecting and reading the notes she'd thrown moments ago. Looking up like a distraught child, she struggled to right herself. I helped Stella up, with her clutching the small, yellow slips of paper. Snuggling into my chest, she allowed me to comfort her. Gently, I wiped away her tears and kissed her on the lips. She looked better already.

"Stella, I'm sorry. We didn't know she had them. We'd have never let her keep them from you." Nana stroked her cheek.

"Stefan, why don't you get her seated on the couch, and then we'll put the stuff I have in the hallway in your car." I did as I was told and then followed Nana.

When I glanced back, Stella had curled up on the couch and had started to read the tiny papers again with a smile on her lips.

After two trips, the trunk and backseat were full. Nana didn't fool me; I saw she'd bought a few things for the house and twins.

We said our goodbyes and left; I had never been more grateful to be going home to our cottage and the solitude it offered. I held out high hopes that all the drama and craziness were behind us now, but I seriously doubted it.

● ● ●

• • •

Chapter Eleven

Stella's   first admission

AGAINST MY BETTER JUDGMENT, I OPENED MY EYES. Blinking away the morning sunshine that poured through the windows, my eyes settled on a grinning Stefan. He was definitely a morning person. Must have been all those years of living on a military base.

"If you want a shower before we leave, you'd better get going." Chuckling at my bewildered expression, he leapt out of bed.

"How about you go without me?" I mumbled while throwing my pillow over my face.

With one quick jerk, he pulled the fluffy heaven away. "I don't think your doctor cares about my health," he guffawed.

● ● ●

Propping myself up on my elbows, I huffed. "Where's the flatbed and winch?"

"Darn! I knew I forgot something!" he chuckled, strolling away to the bathroom to start the shower. "Come on; you'll never need those with me around." He mocked groaning when he pulled me up by my hands.

I think he just liked helping me. Deep down, he knew I liked it, too. He always did little things for me. His upbringing definitely played a role in his strategy in life. Everything needed to be timed, planned, and even prepped. I, on the other hand, was raised by a mother who never planned anything. We did everything by the seats of our pants. We didn't even plan parties. They were something that just happened, and not very often — sort of like my pregnancy.

With Stefan, obsessive didn't cover it. Example in point, my backpack for school has been packed and organized for days. It was the neatest thing I'd ever seen. Everything had been neatly arranged in the pockets with precision. If only he knew that, by this time next week, I'd have it an absolute disaster zone. I think he'd be horrified.

I headed for the steaming hot shower. I snorted when I found my towels and clothes set out on the vanity. It occurred to me that maybe he was more excited about my appointment than I was.

Careful not to slip, I stepped into the hot stream. Looking down, I rubbed my protruding abdomen and sighed. I was huge. However, the fact that all my baby weight rested in my belly made me a little happier. The hot water felt wonderful on my sore back muscles. Carrying around a lot of front weight really tortures a person's back. Maybe tonight he'd give me a back rub? A girl could only hope.

● ● ●

I made a metal note that we'd be forced to make another visit to the store. I hated the idea, but we needed more shampoo. The last time we went shopping, Stefan had insisted on buying me some bigger clothes. Don't get me wrong; the clothes were an absolute must. I couldn't fit into anything I owned. The time before that, we had gone shopping with his parents. It was unnerving how they'd watched my every move. I had felt like I'd been on display. Stefan had made it clear to me that if I didn't help pick out what we needed, he would. Under the glare of his mother's scrutiny, I did select a very pretty midnight-blue bedding set and some plushy, green bath towels.

His mother had literally ground her teeth together when I'd paid for our food with my W.I.C. and food stamps EBT card. Stefan never batted an eyelash at the fact I needed those to pay for my half of our living expenses. Even if it did go against what his parents raised him to believe, I would pay my fair share.

In the end, Stefan said I managed to impress his father when I didn't want their money. Our relationship had never been about money. It would be better if we were on even footing there, but the fact remained that he possessed more than I did. When you grow up with no money, shopping is something you don't have the luxury of doing on a regular basis. Stefan didn't understand that; of course he didn't — he always had money to spend. However, the fact that he didn't care about my lack of money counted as a redeeming quality.

Once I had showered, shampooed, and dressed, I padded off in search of food. One thing about being pregnant, I was hungry a lot. Stefan understood that, and he always carried food with him in case I snapped from food deprivation.

I snickered when I watched him restock the emergency bag of food.

* * *

"You laugh now, but when you're gnawing my left arm off for a granola bar, I'll be the one laughing last, my dear." He cocked his eyebrow, challenging me.

"You won't be laughing when I prefer your arm over the granola bar." I snapped my teeth at him.

"Let's go, my lady," he chortled, bowing and opening the door for me.

It still amazed me that, after everything his parents did to keep us apart, he still loved me. How they had ever thought putting him in military school was a good idea flabbergasted me. I never told him that sometimes when I woke up at night to use the bathroom, another great side effect to being pregnant, I would catch him in the middle of terrible nightmares. There was no mistaking the jerking motions and the mumbling, begging me not to leave him. I hated to see him suffering.

After he joined me in the Mustang, I decided to ask him something that had been playing on my mind for a while now. "Stefan, will you teach me to drive?"

"You don't know how to drive?" he scoffed, then giggled.

"Stefan Sterling, did you just giggle at me?" I covered my mouth with my hand, trying to stifle my own cackle.

"Stella, real men don't giggle. We chuckle." He grinned, showing his pearly whites. "You really don't know how to drive?"

I guffawed, embarrassed. "No one wanted to teach me after my first few attempts behind the wheel. It's a very scary sight, I assure you." With widened eyes and a bobbing head, I emphasized

● ● ●

my point.

"Oh, I'm quite sure I can handle it. Are you sure you want me to be the one?" Seeing his eyes beaming with pride sealed the deal.

"Yes, I'm sure. That's if you're up to the challenge? My mother and Nana have both given up on me." I smirked, taunting him.

"Okay, you're on. I'll teach you to drive next weekend. Do you have a learner's permit?"

"Yes, but I think we might need more than a weekend," I giggled.

"Please, Stella. I learned how to drive on the Audubon." He wiggled his eyebrows.

"Okay, big boy, we shall see if you're all talk." I laughed.

Before I knew it, I'd started giving him directions to the doctor's office. It amazed me that he didn't seem at all nervous about walking into the obstetrician's office. Maybe I was freaking out enough for both of us? At first, the secretary didn't see me and started gawking at Stefan through her glass partition. When I stepped into view and he wrapped his arms around me, I thought her eyes might pop right out of her head. With a smile on his lips, he gave my name and time of our appointment.

Patty just nodded and told us to have a seat in the waiting room. It was satisfying to see her scrambling around her cubicle so she wouldn't have to face us. Stefan intertwined our hands while we waited for my name to be called.

"Stella Richards?"

* * *

"Here," Stefan called back, helping me to my feet. We really needed to get a crane or something.

The nurse stopped off for me to use the bathroom and give her my urine specimen. As soon as I placed the plastic cup on the counter, she fiddled with the awaiting scale. Why did they make us do that? Didn't they understand there was an ongoing war between women and those offending weighting devises? Ask any women about what it feels like to stand on scale, and they'll tell you it makes them want to cry.

Together, we were ushered into the usual examination room. Without a word, I slipped out of my street clothes and into the gown the nurse had left behind. Stefan picked that moment to start pacing. Go figure. After a swift knock, the doctor opened the door and entered. Dr. Marcus seemed quite pleased to see the twin's absentee father present.

"Good afternoon. I'm Dr. Marcus, and you are?" They shook hands.

"Stefan Sterling, the father-to-be." He grinned, squeezing my hand once.

"It's nice to meet you. So, Stella, how are you feeling?" he asked, grabbing the Fetal Doppler.

"Good, a little tired, but nothing unusual." I smiled to assure him.

"Well, let's have a listen." Dr. Marcus placed the monitor on my enlarged belly. "Stefan, the whooshing sound you're hearing is the heartbeats of your children."

● ● ●

Stefan gasped at the sounds reverberated throughout the tiny room. I couldn't help but grin at him.

"That's unbelievable! But shouldn't there be two?" He looked confused.

"No, their heartbeats are beating in sync. There's nothing to worry about. The ultrasound from Stella's last appointment confirmed that everything is fine. The accident left no injures to the fetuses. I do have one concern. Stella, you're still underweight. Are you eating the revised diet from the nutritionist?"

I blew out a deep breath before answering, "Mostly." I cringed at Stefan's glare. Snapping his head between us, he tried to figure out what I meant.

"What do you mean 'mostly?' And what accident?" Stefan sneered.

"Well, I try. But, things have been crazy that's all. The accident? Well, I told you teaching me to drive wouldn't be an easy task," I stammered.

"Dr. Marcus, can I have a copy of what she's supposed to be eating? I'll watch her more closely now that I know she's not doing what she should be. How underweight is she?"

"With her being underweight to begin with, normally by now she should have gained about sixteen pounds. That, however, is not the case. Right now, she's only gained eight pounds in total. That's a third of the normal weight gain for a young woman carrying twins. She should be gaining one to two pounds a week at this point. She is drastically behind. The nutritionist gave her a specific diet in the hopes of getting her up to the normal weight gain range. So, starting

● ● ●

today, you're to get on that diet. No more stalling. The health of your fetuses is on the line now. They need the added nutrition to develop correctly."

Stefan glared at me.

"I'll get right on it," I vowed, afraid to look Stefan in the eyes.

"You bet you will, and I'll make sure of it." Sneering, he looked away unable to hide his disappointment in me. "We'll go shopping right from here. I'll see that she eats when she is supposed to." I nodded, agreeing that I wouldn't fight him.

"That's great. Now, normally, I wouldn't see you for another month, but I need to see an improvement in the next two weeks." The doctor handed Stefan the diet plan I'd received last month.

I knew that the moment we were in the car I was going to get an earful. I guessed right; the minute he entered the car he let loose.

"Stella! What were you thinking? Are you trying to kill the twins? Do you understand that they could come even earlier than expected? Don't even get me started on their chances of low birth weights! In the name of all that is holy, what was going on in that brain of yours? How could you risk them? I thought you loved them, loved me! If your plan was to starve them to death, why didn't you just abort them? It would hurt less!" he growled, leaving me speechless for a second.

I can't say for certain why I fell apart, I just did. Every pent up emotion from the last five and a half months rushed out. His words cut straight through me, so I lashed out in defense.

●　●　●

"Eating was the last thing on my mind when you disappeared. Okay, I admit it, I fell apart. I spent most of my time either crying or sulking. Does that make you happy? Do you want to know how it felt to be used and tossed aside?" I sobbed, my lip quivering. The tears I held back for so long finally fell. "When I did eat, I'd just throw it back up. I was a walking mess. The only thing left of me was a hollow shell!" I screeched, swatting at him with both my hands.

Fighting him off, I continued to resist his efforts to hold me. "Oh, God! Come here!" Grasping me with a firm grip, he managed to pull me close to his chest and rubbed my back. "No, it doesn't make me happy. You'll never have to worry about that again. I'm here to stay. I know what you went through, because I went through it, too. You were all I ever thought about." With tears running down his face, he crushed his lips to mine.

Together we attacked each other's lips as we had the night we conceived the twins. When we finally pulled apart, he rested his forehead on mine, letting our first fight come to a close.

"I'm so sorry. I didn't mean those things I said. Please forgive me?" he begged, holding me tighter.

"I can't forgive you, unless you forgive me, too. I'll do better, I promise." I sighed against his cheek.

"I do forgive you, and I'll help you," he breathed across my face. "Let's go, we need to stock the house with the right stuff. No fighting me when I use my card to make sure we get everything on this list." He tapped my nose with his fingertip.

"No fighting," I exhaled.

With the diet plan in hand, he guided me through the local

● ● ●

179

Food Lion. First stop — the produce section. Together we picked out pounds of fruit: everything from apples and oranges to watermelon and grapes; bags of vegetables including everything from salad to carrots; and my personal favorite, unsalted nuts.

He made shopping fun for some unexplained reason. Before he came back, I'd hated shopping, mostly because of the disparaging looks people shot me. He concentrated on the meat department while I picked out the breakfast cereal and other breakfast selections, and the race to see who could be the first to finish their departments began.

The cart quickly filled up with everything from the list, from peanut butter to navy beans. As a treat, he allowed me to get vanilla ice cream and yogurt so he could make me shakes. It was either that or those gross nutritional drinks. His idea sounded better.

I even explained the accident to him. His brow furrowed, listening to every tiny detail.

"Why didn't you tell me about it?"

"If I told you, would you still want to teach me how to drive?"

"Stella, someone rammed into you, not the other way around. Of course I still want to teach you how to drive." Putting his arm around my shoulder, we headed to the registers.

Deep down, I prayed I'd have enough food stamps to cover the bill. When the register total said $245.96, I knew he'd be pulling out the card. At least my W.I.C vouchers covered all the dairy and cereal, so that helped a little; along with the food stamps, we managed to get the bill down to just over a hundred dollars.

● ● ●

True to my word, I bit my lip when he paid for whatever I couldn't cover. The upside was that we wouldn't have to shop for another two weeks. By then, my new food stamps would be in my account.

Of course, the minute we put away all the food, Stefan started cooking my dinner. While he grilled the chicken outside, I prepared the salad and cooked the carrots. After completing my half of the cooking, I set the table.

I gulped at the amount of food on the plate. How on earth did they think I'd eat all that in one sitting? With a close eye, Stefan surveyed my every bite. Eventually, I managed to eat every last morsel. The downside was that I felt overstuffed, like a Thanksgiving Day turkey.

"See, that wasn't so bad, now was it?"

I leered at his grinning smile. "Speak for yourself. I think if I move I might explode," I whimpered.

"I tell you what — you pick out a movie, and I'll do the dishes. We'll just relax in bed and watch it on the laptop." He smiled and removed the plates from the table.

Looking over the boxes his father had sent, it took a moment to find the right one. After I remembered which box the movies were still packed in, I selected a cute comedy and headed for the bedroom, feeling like the Goodyear blimp. Within minutes, he joined me with the laptop.

That would be our last night to relax, since school would be starting the next day. Once I'd snuggled into his side, he queued up the video. Before I knew it, my eyes had fluttered shut, calling an end

* * *

to our chaotic day.

• • •

Chapter Twelve

Stefan's starting school

I RUSHED TOWARD MY FIRST CLASS FEELING A LITTLE flustered. Stella didn't have a class until the afternoon, but I had a nine o'clock English Lit class. I needed to take twice the classes than Stella. She'd registered for only the essentials.

With one minute to spare, I darted into the room, grabbing a desk and tossing my bag under the seat. At least the professor didn't scowl at my hasty arrival. The one-hour class was a prerequisite. I breathed easier when Professor Hamilton announced that the class would be spent just getting everything set up and recording the expectations of the course. He looked like the stereotypical college professor. I chuckled behind my hand, looking at his red, plaid bow

● ● ●

tie and comb over. Two out of the four books that were required reading, I had already read. That brought a smile to my face. It granted me more time to attend to Stella's physical needs.

After her doctor had filled me in on her neglecting the basics of her dietary needs, I'd promised myself not to let it continue. Since my return, she had been eating, but only when I did. Thinking about it further, I realized that she stopped eating the second I did.

When the nurse originally said she'd gained one pound during our visit, I figured it was normal. Appearances are deceiving. In actuality, she should have gained five to six pounds. Stella had known that she needed to take better care of herself, since the nutritionist had already told her she was in trouble.

Times like that made me regret not breaking away from my parents sooner to be with Stella. I should have known she would've been in bad shape. Stella had always made it clear she feared being left behind. The one thing that had held me back was that I had known my dad would have come looking for me before I'd ever reached her. In addition, he would have held off paying for me to attend Norfolk. I couldn't have risked being away from Stella. I had to go to Norfolk no matter what.

I had just been so happy to be back that I'd never given much thought to how much she'd suffered doing everything alone. When I asked about it after our reunion on our birthday, she had waved me off. It had been very naive of me to think she'd cruised through finding out she was pregnant, learning about the twins, and caring for herself. She must have been devastated. Neither Stella nor I had thought it would happen to us, but it had.

When my finances had been planned out, eating off campus

● ● ●

had never figured into the equation. My preloaded card would need to be replenished more often than originally planned. That meant one thing. I would have to call my dad for money. My children needed me to assure their growth and safe delivery. I could do that for them.

When we were finally released from the class, I headed out into the courtyard. There were a few people I wanted to talk to without Stella overhearing the conversations. I started with calling Michael.

"Hi, Michael, it's Stefan. Do you have a minute to talk?"

"Sure, kid. What's up?" From the sounds of shuffling paper, I had caught him in the middle of something.

"Can you ask Eddie to call me about Stella?"

"Is something wrong?" his panicked voice asked.

"She's hasn't been doing what the doctor instructed her to do. She's not gaining the weight she needs. Apparently, she hasn't been eating enough. Since Eddie is in medical school, I hoped he could tell me what else I can do to improve the twin's chances." I blew out a deep breath.

"He's home; hold on." I could hear Michael telling Eddie everything I'd told him.

"Hey, Stefan. Okay, Michael gave me the rundown. How far behind the eight ball is she?"

"At twenty-two weeks, she's only gained eight pounds." I heard his heavy sigh.

"This is a very crucial time for the fetuses. By the end of her

• • •

twenty-fourth week, she should have gained twenty to twenty-four pounds. Did she see a nutritionist?"

"Yeah, but she never followed the diet the nutritionist gave her. I bought everything on the plan they gave me, and I started cooking her meals. Should I be giving her high-calorie meals or something?"

"That's a double-edged sword. Eating a lot of junk food won't give her body the needed nutrition. It only provides empty calories. Are there any mealtimes she likes better?"

"She only likes to eat when I do," I sighed.

"Then I hope you like to eat. Let me do a little research, and I can shoot you an email tonight. That way you'll have a guide to follow."

"Thanks, Eddie. Hey, would you guys like a visit next month? We have a three day weekend, and I would love to meet you and for you to meet Stella."

"We'd love it. Just call us and let us know when you'll be arriving. Here's Michael." He passed off the phone.

"You're coming for a visit?" Michael asked, surprised.

"Only if you're cool with it," I chuckled.

"I'm always cool with it. We'll talk when it gets closer. Take care of those three." With that, he hung up.

My next call was going to be harder, because I knew my father was going to take the guilt for my mother. Don't get me wrong; a lot of the blame fell squarely on my dad's shoulders, but my

● ● ●

mom was just as guilty, if not more so. My mom had been the only one who had known of Stella's pregnancy. If the rest of us had known, things would have unfolded in a much different scenario — of that I'm positive.

If the news of Stella's pregnancy had been given to me at the time of her phone call, they wouldn't have been able to keep me away, not even my father. After learning my dad had gone through the same thing with my mother, I positively knew he wouldn't have tried to keep us apart.

I wasn't very surprised when he answered on the second ring. "Hey, Stefan. How's the first day going?"

"It's going good so far, but that's not why I'm calling. I need you to increase the money you put on my card each month." I heard his deep exhale.

"Why, may I ask?" He sighed.

"I went to the doctor's yesterday with Stella. She hasn't been eating right." I winced just stuttering it.

"What do you mean?" He gasped.

"She's underweight, by a lot."

"How much is a lot?" His voice showed his strain.

"She's only gained a third of what she needs to. She lost weight — a lot of weight — in the beginning and never gained it back. Dr. Marcus is really worried about it."

"So you want more money to feed her? Is that the question?" He almost sounded amused.

* * *

"Yeah, that's what I'm asking."

"Stefan, I'll take care of the money; you just get her eating right. You might want to do what I did. Go to the library, and get a book on it. When your mother first found out she was expecting, we didn't know anything. Then I was shipped off to Germany, and she couldn't join me until Michael was already three months old. By the time you came along, I knew nothing about what to do."

"I will, right after my next class. Stella will be in class this afternoon, so while I'm waiting for her, I'll head to the library and see what they have. Thanks, Dad."

"Call me if you need me." He ended the call with a click.

After checking my watch, I headed for my next class, but not before I shot Stella a text telling her to eat and that I wanted proof that she had eaten. By the time I'd reached the door to my next class — Statistical Math — I'd received a picture text from Stella: an adorable picture of her with an apple in her mouth, waving. How could I not smile? She was just so damn cute.

Once I'd settled in, I glanced around the room. In the very back corner sat a young woman with long, golden-blond hair. Normally, I wouldn't care, but her devouring eyes never left me. In fact, so were her two friends. I cringed and tried my best not to take notice of her obvious flirting. Please, like some model wannabe batting her icy blue eyes at me could ever take the place of Stella. I breathed easier when the professor and TA walked in.

Unlike my earlier class, Professor Hadley was a no-nonsense teacher. Her uptight and neat-as-a-pin appearance said it all. While her TA Darlyn passed around outlined packets for her class requirements, she jumped right into the textbook we had been

● ● ●

assigned.

Darlyn was the complete opposite of the professor. She sashayed around the room without a care in the world. Her slight smile spoke volumes of her friendliness.

I could feel the blond's eyes still ogling me from behind. I had to fight not to grin from ear to ear when the teacher shot her a dirty look, because she giggled aloud with her friends. The moment the professor said we could leave, I shot out of my seat and headed for the door.

I raced back to my car. The sooner I got home, the sooner I could eat lunch with Stella before her class. The purr of the motor relaxed me. In Germany, most of the girls on the base let me be, but here, they seemed to notice me more. Not that I wanted to be ignored, but I wasn't used to the attention.

Stella must have heard the key in the lock, because she bounced up off the couch and rushed for the door. "Hi. How were your classes?" she twittered.

Pulling her close and purring in her ear, I whispered, "Lonely."

"Me too," her sing-song voice rang. "I have a surprise for you." She grabbed my hand and led me to the kitchen.

"Tah — dah!" She waved her hands at the table.

There on the table sat lunch for two. From the looks of it, she'd copied it right off the diet plan: a turkey sandwich, a homemade fruit salad, and a glass of milk for each of us. Just what the doctor ordered. I kissed her chastely.

* * *

"This is perfect, baby." I pulled out her seat for her.

From her gleaming smile, I'd say she liked the praise. "Thank you," she whispered.

I made sure to take my time, allowing her to eat more. As anticipated, she dropped her folk at the same time I did. Eddie had assumed right; I would be eating more to keep her doing the same. Well, I guessed I'd be gaining back the weight I'd also lost during our months apart.

With everything cleaned up, we headed for school. This time, Stella wouldn't have to rush. I didn't need her to fall and break something — or worse, hurt the twins.

Stella fought me on carrying her bag to class for her, but in the end, I won and did it anyway. Much to my displeasure, the blond from my Math class shared Stella's English class. Stella didn't miss the blond batting her eyelashes at me. I'd be hearing about that when she got out.

Why do women always blame the men when other women flirt with them? It wasn't my fault. I'd rather that the blond ignored me all together. Never taking my eyes off Stella, I kissed her cheek and rubbed her tummy in a show of affection so that the blond would have no more reason to pay any attention to me.

"See you in while." I stroked her cheek.

"I'll be waiting," she gushed and sat in her seat.

With Stella safely in class, I headed to the library to do my research. My dad was right; there was so much I didn't know. The library had a variety of different books on the subject of pregnancy.

● ● ●

190

For the next hour, I read everything I could. Today I concentrated on her diet and why she needed to be gaining the weight for the twins. Their development hinged on that. With a new understanding to why, it made the doing much easier.

Pregnant teenage girls were the most likely to have bad eating habits. The fact that Stella was underweight when she conceived also worked against her. Eddie was proved right yet again; the books said eating junk food would work against her. Things all made more sense after reading the pregnancy guide.

Checking the clock, I put everything away with enough time to get back to her classroom before her teacher let out the class.

When I reached Stella's class, I was horrified to find her sitting in her seat, red faced with tears running down her cheeks. "Stella, what's wrong?" I looked around the empty room for an explanation.

"A few of the girls in class had more than a few negative things to say about me," she sniffled.

I knew which ones she referred to. "Stella, just ignore them. They don't know us or anything about our situation," I pleaded, looking into her eyes for understanding.

"I know that, but it still hurt to hear them saying I'd trapped you," she grumbled.

"Stella, I'm not trapped. You never asked me to do anything but love you. And I do love you with all my heart, no matter what they have to say." I helped her up and wrapped myself around her. "Let's go home." I wiped away her tears with the back of my fingers.

● ● ●

"Can I have ice cream when we get home?" She looked up at me with puppy dog eyes. No man could deny that.

"That you can. Where is everyone?" I chuckled and guided her away.

"Class let out a few minutes early," she uttered.

Once we were driving, she finally relaxed. I knew that some girls could be cruel when they wanted to be. If they approached her again, I'd have to intervene.

As promised, I made her a bowl of vanilla bean ice cream topped off with a scoop of fruit salad leftover from lunch. Of course, I had one, too, so she'd feel more comfortable.

By dinner, Eddie's email arrived. It outlined everything for the next three months. When Michael had said he was in medical school, I didn't realize he was studying to be a pediatric physician. His knowledge would come in handy indeed.

As I cooked dinner, Stella started unpacking the boxes my father had sent earlier in the week. Once dinner sat on the table, we took our seats, eating and discussing what the girls in class actually said to her.

"Well, they said I'm a piece of trash for trapping you like a caged animal and that they wouldn't stoop so low," she stammered.

"What did you tell them?" I squeezed her hand.

"I told them it didn't happen that way. They just laughed and said they didn't believe me, and that if I cared about you at all, I would set you free." She sighed.

● ● ●

"Stella, I am free, that's why I'm here. I want you and my children," I reassured her.

"I know. They were just mean about it. Let's not think about it anymore. There's no denying the blond one has the hots for you," she spat. The look of disgust spoke volumes.

When dinner was done, Stella washed the dishes while I started on my homework. Of course, her prancing around the kitchen with the radio playing was very distracting, so it took forever to get my homework done.

School fell into an easy pattern, and we avoided Savanna whenever possible. If it wasn't for the professor constantly chastising her in class, I wouldn't have known the ogling blond's name. It had gone well for a few weeks, when she suddenly renewed her interest in harassing us.

"Stefan, come have coffee with me. Please?" I looked up from my textbook to see her hovering over my shoulder.

"No, thank you. I need to get home and pick up my girlfriend," I retorted, snapping my book shut.

"What she did to you wasn't fair. You should be living the high life, running around with pretty girls, going to parties, not dragging her fat butt around." With each word from her mouth, I ground my teeth together.

"Savanna, you have no idea what I want, or whom I want it with. Let me make myself perfectly clear here. I'm the one who trapped Stella, not the other way around. As for being with someone who is pretty? Why would I settle for pretty when I can have stunningly beautiful like Stella? And if you call her fat again, I'll see

* * *

193

to it Professor Hadley knows about you cheating on your last test." I reveled in seeing her stunned speechless.

"Well, I'll just tell Stella about you admitting to trapping her." She smirked.

"Do you think she doesn't know the whole thing was my idea?"

"What idea?" I spun on my heels to see Stella walking into the room.

"Nothing, baby, this conversation is over. What are you doing here? I thought I was coming home to get you." I rushed to her side.

"The doctor called and suggested I start walking because my blood pressure is a little high." Stella glanced between us, no doubt trying to figure out what we had been talking about.

"Well, since you're here, let's go grab some lunch," I hoped that treat would appease her.

"Okay." From the way she nibbled on her lip, I knew she was worried about the money.

"Bye, Savanna." I turned and wrapped my arm around Stella. "Let's go, sweetheart."

There was no mistaking the look on Stella's face; she knew something was going on. I knew I'd have to admit to the lie I had told Savanna, but I needed a sure-fire way to deflect her from Stella.

Walking through the empty quad, the smell of today's lunch special — pastrami — wafted our way. The sounds of chatting students filled the cafeteria when we entered through the main door.

* * *

194

Keeping with her norms, Stella kept her choices small. Shaking my head, I laughed. Did she really think that was going to work? To balance us out, I took twice my usual. She looked adorable staring at me in disbelief at my overloaded tray. We snagged the first open table and started dividing up all the food.

"So, Stella, are you excited about this weekend?" She peeked up from her vegetable soup and smiled.

"Yeah, I'm looking forward to seeing Michael and meeting Eddie."

"Good. Me, too. When do we see Dr. Marcus again?" I knew we were scheduled to see him in two weeks, but I also knew Stella had talked to him since we made that appointment.

"Actually, he wants to see me Thursday before we leave." From the way she ducked her head back down, I knew she was holding out.

"Stella, don't make me call him," I chided.

After scanning the room, she huffed. "My blood pressure is becoming an issue. He wants the nutritionist to redo my diet again." She moved on to her Cobb salad.

"How big of an issue?" I think my pressure spiked with her words.

"Big enough that he wants to see me before we leave." I swear she did that just to irk me.

"Stella, you know you can tell me without the doctor being here. Spill it." I was getting more anxious by the minute.

* * *

"He's worried about the chance of preeclampsia." She sighed.

"So, what does he want to do?"

"He's just going to watch it for now. If I get it down and keep it down with no other problems, everything will be fine." She smiled, shrugging.

"I'll call Eddie tonight and see what he can suggest." I grasped her hand and held it through lunch.

There was just something comforting about holding any part of her body close. Even rubbing her feet relaxed me. It's as if touching her made her less likely to slip away again.

With our meal eaten and trash disposed of, we headed to the one class we shared: Computer Science. The professor in that class was a very laid-back ex-hippie. Mr. Kaplan was cool with mine and Stella's relationship. He even pulled us aside at the beginning of classes and told us that if Stella delivered early, I could bring her work to and from school for her, so she wouldn't fail or need to drop the class.

Michael called on the ride home so that Stella and Eddie could discuss Stella's recent phone call from the doctor and the best way to reduce her chances of preeclampsia. Michael and Eddie were really getting excited about becoming uncles. Michael always knew when Stella's appointments were, and if we didn't call him, he called us to find out why. They admitted to being worried, too.

While Stella made dinner to Eddie's specifications, I surfed the web looking for anything helpful. To be honest, everything I read scared the crap out me. There was a risk that we could have the twins earlier than already anticipated, we could lose the babies, or I could

* * *

lose all three of them. None of those were acceptable to me.

During dinner, we decided to walk to and from school together. I drew the line at her walking alone. Too many things could happen to her if she did it alone. Eddie suggested we buy a self-monitoring machine for her blood pressure. Add that one to the shopping list.

My phone went off just as Stella started washing the dishes. At first, I didn't know who it was, but I soon remembered the number and answered it.

"Hi, Anastasia," I breathed out.

"Stefan! My mom just told me. Congratulations!" she screeched in my ear.

"Thanks," I laughed

"Me and mom are planning the shower. Does she know?" Anastasia inquired.

"I haven't told her, and I have no intention of telling her," I groaned feeling hurt about my mom not being the one to plan it.

"Why? Aren't you still coming? Is she nice? Do you know what you're having yet?" Man, did the girl need to breathe?

"The plans haven't changed . . . yes . . . yes . . . no . . . it's too soon," I rambled.

"She's not going to freak out, is she?" she whined.

Sighing, I replied, "No, I don't see her making a fuss over it."

"Can I talk to her?" Her excited voice rattled through the

●　●　●

phone.

"She's done with the dishes; I gotta go," I rushed to get off the phone.

"I miss you; can't wait to see you!" she chirped.

"Yeah, I can't wait to see you, too." Looking around, I made sure I wasn't discovered, and I flipped the phone shut.

● ● ●

Chapter Thirteen

Stella's shocking discovery

STEFAN WAS VERY EXCITED ABOUT OUR TRIP SOUTH. After he had only gotten to talk to Michael via phone or email since August, it didn't surprise me. He entertained me with childhood stories of their lives in Germany. The way he used his voice to animate their adventures left us both in hysterics.

We left the cottage early enough so that traffic wouldn't be problem. South Carolina was a stunning state to see. Driving through the historic city of Charleston astonished me. For blocks, I just stared out the window, soaking up the ambiance. From the intricate arched windows and hand-carved scrollwork adorning the building fronts to the antique street lamps lining the streets, there was no mistaking the

● ● ●

southern charm that seemed to seep out of the city.

Stefan pointed out the townhouse complex where Michael and Eddie lived. That part of town looked more modern. You could see the difference between the new and old architecture.

Stefan chuckled when I gawked out the window at the in-ground pool. "Don't get any ideas. You're not going swimming, chickadee." He wagged his finger at me.

Once he parked, he played forklift and dragged me out of the Mustang. Using my arms, I supported my back, waddling toward the door. Before we could reach it, the door swung open, and Michael rushed out.

"Little brother!" He and Stefan shared a touching, brotherly hug.

When he turned to me, he choked out, "Wow, Stella, you're huge!"

"Thanks, flattery will get you everywhere," I chided, smiling.

"Easy there, dude, you don't want to set off her hormones." Stefan winked at me.

The twin's flipped positions when Michael laid his hands on my stomach. "You know I mean that in a good way." He grinned down at me.

When he stepped back, I saw Eddie standing behind him. Up until then, I had only talked to Eddie on the phone. It was nice to have a face to go with the southern voice. Stefan's description of him fitted him to a T. He had his hair cut in a short, spiked, gelled style. Eddie's skin was tan, which went well with his caramel brown eyes

• • •

that sparkled in the sun.

Michael grinned. "Eddie, this is my brother Stefan and his girlfriend Stella. Guys, this is Eddie Wilkerson."

I'll admit I wished he'd never told us Eddie's last name. It was a name I'd learned to hate early in my childhood. My father's last name was Wilkerson. I once Googled him in a feeble attempt to find my father. It didn't work out so well. However, I refused to hold that against Eddie.

Stefan was the first to extend his hand to shake Eddie's already-extended one. I giggled when, instead of shaking mine, he kissed the back of my hand.

"The pleasure is all mine. C'mon in, guys." Eddie grinned.

Stefan grabbed the overnight bag from the back seat while Michael led me inside. Eddie cackled when I teetered my way into the house.

"Michael will give you a tour while I finish cooking dinner," he said before heading off to the kitchen.

Michael led us through his "humble abode," as he put it. The spacious two-bedroom townhouse was actually quite nice. The cream-colored bedrooms were on the second floor. Trying not to laugh, I couldn't help but notice the two bedrooms were identical. They had pristine wall-to-wall beige carpets, a queen-sized, cherry wood bed, and a flat screen TV on the wall. The bedrooms were separated by a generous-sized, modern, white and gold bathroom.

After dropping our bags in the first bedroom, we headed downstairs to see the rest of the house. Stefan led me down the stairs,

* * *

holding my hand so I wouldn't slip. His newest fear was that I would tumble over something. Ever since I'd slipped down two tiny steps at school, it had become his obsession.

Michael found it quite funny the way Stefan cradled and protected me. It wasn't something that I minded about him. He was protecting the three of us after all; our own private superhero.

Eddie kept busy in the kitchen while Michael popped in to retrieve a pitcher of sweet tea and some glasses. The smell of garlic bread teased my nose as I inhaled it deep into my lungs. Eddie hummed when he drained the penne pasta. It was apparent that he loved cooking. You could see it by the way he shredded the fresh Romano cheese with precision.

Before I started drooling, we moved back to the living room. Michael poured the tea when Stefan sat on the loveseat. Walking around the simple living room, a picture frame on the maple end table drew my attention. The frame itself was just a classic 8x10 silver frame, tarnished minutely by time. But it wasn't the frame that caught my attention — it was the picture inside. Lifting the frame closer, I saw the face that haunted me. My hands started shaking. It couldn't be!

Stefan noticed my distraction and joined me. "What are you looking at, baby?" He gasped when he also recognized the same man I had.

I'd showed him the photo I carry every day in my wallet: the only photo my father had given to my mother. Melvin Wilkerson, the man who had disappeared after my conception. From the closeness of the age, the photograph must have been taken right around the same time he'd been with my mother. My heart was racing. Beads of

* * *

sweat started to break out across my forehead. My hand trembled as I pointed to the face of a man in a Marine's dress blues uniform.

"Stella?" Michael joined us to look at a face I'd seen many times.

"That's Eddie's dad." Michael pointed out. "What?" From the confusion on his face, I knew he couldn't possibly understand why I looked so flabbergasted.

"Have you seen him before?" Stefan and I both nodded when he asked.

"Where?"

Stefan continued to hold the frame while I reached into my bag and pulled out my wallet. "Michael, this is the only picture I have of my father," I whispered. He gasped when he took the tiny picture from my fingers.

He called out without taking his eyes off the wallet photo I showed him. "Eddie, you need to see this."

"See what?" Eddie came in wiping his hands dry.

"This is a picture of Stella's dad." He passed him the photo.

"This . . . I . . . my . . . oh, my God!" Eddie staggered back and sat with a thump in the gray couch. Michael sat next to him, trying to soothe his rattled nerves.

"Stella, where did you get this?" His hands shook, flashing me the picture.

"My mom gave it me when I was ten. I asked her to help me on a school project about our family tree. That picture is the only

* * *

thing she had to share."

Standing and reaching into his pocket, he pulled out his wallet. "I have the exact same one," he mumbled, passing me the two identical photos.

"Do you realize what this means?" His tone screamed out in agony.

"I'm so sorry, Eddie. I didn't know. Stefan, we should go," I pleaded, begging with my eyes.

"No! I'm not mad at you, Stella. I am, however, very pissed at my dad. Well, I guess this makes him our dad." My heart broke for him.

"No, Eddie. He doesn't want me. He's still your dad." I spoke with conviction.

Tears started to stream from his eyes, running down his cheeks. "Stella, does he know about you?" He sniffed.

"No, he was long gone before my mom found out. Eddie, my mom swears he said he wasn't married. I don't think my mom would have slept with him if she'd known." At least, I prayed not.

"Stella, my parents were divorced when I turned two. That means he wasn't still married when he slept with your mother." The sadness in his eyes started to tear at my heart.

"That's good. So, you don't have to be mad at him. Don't you see? He never cheated on your mom, and he never knew about me. Really, he didn't do anything wrong." I tried to soothe him.

He looked up with his toasted almond eyes. "You're right, but

● ● ●

204

it still isn't fair that you were left to grow up alone."

I sighed. "Eddie, it's okay. I'm used to being alone, with the exception of Stefan, that is." Stefan pulled me into his warm embrace.

"But you're not alone now; you have me, too." I yelped when he grabbed me and pulled me into a bear hug.

Being held by him — my brother — overwhelmed me. There was no stopping my tears as they flowed freely. Stefan stepped up and wrapped an arm around each of us. When Michael joined our group hug, we became one family, with the twins at the center.

For a while, no one really knew what to say. It never occurred to me that I might ever find a sibling. In one moment, my family had increased by one. I now had a brother. The question that needed answering was: did he want a sister?

The room erupted in laughter when my stomach howled. Stefan chortled, "I think the twins are hungry." Patting my tummy, he informed the tiny tyrants that food would be arriving soon.

"Yeah, let's eat. That's enough of the heavy stuff." Michael pulled Eddie toward the kitchen.

Eddie was starting to make me nervous. He watched every move Stefan and I made. Nothing went without his notice. I swear he counted the number of noodles I ate.

When he dropped his fork with a clang against his plate, I thought dinner was over and moved to place mine down, but instead, he went to the refrigerator and retrieved more tea. Michael glared at me until I resumed eating with them.

* * *

"Stella," Eddie heaved a deep breath, "I want to call my dad and tell him about you." Everyone snapped their heads in his direction.

I think I lost control of body the minute he shut his mouth. Forget trembling hands; my body began shaking out of control, my head shook, and my eyes nearly bulged right out of my head.

"No!" I squawked. After a shaky breath, I continued in a softer tone. "Eddie, he's not going to want to hear about me. I'll only be something that he never intended to happen," I muttered with my eyes locked on my plate.

Stefan leaned over and grasped my hand. "Stella, you don't know that. We're the perfect example of what could happen. Maybe he'd want to know about you." I gripped his hand tighter, my fear swelling to epic proportions.

"And if he doesn't? I'll be left to live with being unwanted. At least right now, I can take comfort in the fact that he doesn't know about me. I would rather not know about the phone call. I think I should lie down. I'm not feeling so great." Stefan rose when I did.

"Is it your blood pressure?" he queried.

"Probably, you should stay up. I can go to bed myself."

"Are you sure?" His brow furrowed in worry.

"Yeah, you haven't seen Michael in so long, and I need a few minutes alone," I uttered, afraid I would hurt their feelings.

"Okay. Goodnight, Stella." Stefan kissed me, his lips lingering for a few seconds before he sat back down.

● ● ●

Michele Richard

"Goodnight, Stella," Eddie and Michael said in unison.

I could hear their hushed voices, but couldn't make out what they were saying. It really didn't matter. My thoughts were a jumbled mess. Eddie had accepted me, just knowing we shared half of the same genes. I doubted Melvin would feel the same way. Not that I wanted to admit it out loud, but what if Eddie was just saying that stuff to be polite? He could very well hate me, just on principle. Moreover, how would they feel about my mother?

Without changing my clothes, I lay on the bed, closed my eyes, and allowed my thoughts to swirl around in my mind. I didn't want to tell Stefan, but I was petrified about what would happen. There were way too many variables to decipher what the outcome would be. Either Eddie was telling the truth and he'd be there for me, or he wasn't and he'd hide from me. Then again, the same could be said for Melvin. What about Michael? Stefan's brother would be stuck in the middle of a mess he hadn't created.

One thing I knew for certain; I did like Eddie. He's been there for us over the last month, giving us non-stop advice. The best I could hope for was that he'd meant what he said and that he didn't just say those things to be nice.

Before I knew it, I had slipped into an uneasy sleep.

I was jarred awake when Eddie and Stefan started bickering in our room. "You did what?" Stefan bellowed.

"Stefan, please, he had the right to know!" I could hear the desperation in Eddie's voice.

"Stella doesn't need this! I won't let you put her through this! This could cause her to go into early labor, or worse, kill all three of

* * *

them!" I had never heard such an edge to Stefan's voice.

"Stefan?" I groaned as my body protested against my sudden movements.

"Damn it, Eddie! Stella, sweetheart, go back to bed. We'll take this outside," he cooed.

"What's going on in here?" That was it; our room was officially a conference room.

"Would someone please tell me what all the screaming is about?" My sleepiness made me snippy.

Stefan cringed, muttering, "Your father's downstairs."

I snapped, "Excuse me?" I must have heard him wrong.

My head whipped to face Eddie. "I called him last night and told him everything. He was shocked, but happy. He drove all night to meet you."

He wasn't the only one who was shocked. I was dumbfounded, Michael looked embarrassed, and Stefan was just furious.

"Eddie, why?" My voice begged for an explanation.

Eddie sighed. "He needed to know. Please, don't hate me. He really is excited to meet you."

Michael shook his head. "Eddie, you knew they were coming here so Stella could rest. You of all people knew what could happen. Why would you do that?"

"I'm sorry. I wasn't trying to hurt anyone, especially not

● ● ●

Stella and the twins. But is it wrong to want her to be acknowledged as part my family? I don't want her to be a dirty little secret! She deserves to be welcomed in with open arms, not hidden away!" His voice pleaded.

"Eddie, what if . . .?" He quickly held up his hands, stopping me.

"He wants you to be part of the family. He'll tell you himself, but believe me; I wouldn't let him near you if he was going to say anything hurtful. You should have heard how thrilled he was when I told him. He remembered your mother immediately." I bit my lip, considering if I could handle this.

"Stefan, I need a shower. Can you help me?"

"Sure, baby, anything you need."

I giggled when he pulled me from the bed by both my hands. At seven months along, I was beyond huge. The elderly women in the supermarket were telling me "any day now" and patting my bulging belly. My retort was always the same: "I still have two months to go." They, of course, gulped and looked again.

Michael left towels next to the outfit Stefan had brought in. "Stella, I'll be downstairs when you're done. If you need me, just yell." Stefan shut the bathroom door behind him, looking rather defeated.

I spent the entire time in the shower trying to relax and not get too frantic over it. I couldn't change the fact that Melvin was already here. Eddie had sworn that my father had been ecstatic to hear about me, and I decided to trust him.

● ● ●

Dressed in a simple black dress that Stefan had forced me to buy along with the black ballet slippers he'd insisted I needed, I waddled out of the bathroom. Peeking over the half wall that viewed the lower level below, I could see that Stefan was already looking haggard.

Next to Stefan stood the man I knew to be my father. Melvin had aged well. His face the same as in the photos, with just a few more wrinkles. My mom was right; I did look like him. Even from this distance, I could see his light brown eyes. He nodded to Stefan, who was talking to him in a whispered voice, so I couldn't make out what they were saying. Eddie's student medical bag sat on the coffee table. No doubt, in case I had an issue.

Closing my eyes, I took a few deep breaths, squared my shoulders, and held my head high. Being careful not to trip, I headed to the stairs. At first, no one heard me approaching. Stefan looked up first. As everyone else followed, Stefan started up the stairs to guide me down. With his arms securely encircling me, I looked up at the bottom to see my father and Eddie smiling at me. You could see the understanding in their eyes. Neither of them could deny I had his eyes when they stared into them. After another deep breath, I let Stefan lead me forward.

"Good morning, Stella. I'm your dad — Mel or Melvin." He fidgeted, unsure what to do next.

"Hi." I was at a loss on what else to say.

"May I?" My dad extended his arms toward me.

"Um, okay." My eyes began filling with happy, hormonal tears.

● ● ●

Mel stepped forward and pulled me into his embrace. We both sighed as we let each other quell the fear of rejection. "I have a daughter," he sniffled against my cheek, stroking my hair.

"I have a father," I sighed.

"I always regretted not giving your mother an address where she could reach me."

"Well, that would have helped." I pulled back and moved to Stefan's side.

"When I was discharged, I went looking for her. I watched through the window of the salon where she worked. She was pregnant. I didn't want to have her reject me when she was clearly with someone else." He huffed, looking saddened by the memory.

"She wasn't. Brianna's father was long gone, too," I sighed.

"So, you've never had a father?" He grimaced.

"No, just my mom, Brianna, and my grandmother."

"I see I'm going to be a grandfather. Wow, you're so young. I've heard a lot of great things about you, Stefan, but if I had been in her life at the time, I would have tracked you down like a dog for getting my daughter pregnant." He glared.

"We were unprepared. Though if I had known, my parents wouldn't have been able to tear me away from her." Stefan brushed his fingers across my blushed cheek.

"So, you intend on being there for the kids? Supporting them?"

"Yeah, I do," Stefan vowed.

"Stella, you look tired," Eddie surmised.

Stefan looked anxious. "Stella, why don't you sit down, talk to Mel and Eddie. Michael and I will make some breakfast for everyone." I nodded, waddling to the couch. They chuckled, watching my best attempt to lower myself down gracefully. Yeah, it did not work.

Over breakfast, we filled each other in on the details of our lives. It turned out that Melvin owned a chain of twenty-one variety stores that stretched across the whole State of Virginia. He lived two hours from the beach in a tiny town I'd never heard of. His ex-wife had died of cancer when Eddie was only six years old, and he'd never remarried. Both his parents were also deceased, so it was just Eddie and himself left in his family, and now there was me, too.

Mel — or Dad as he told me I could call him — decided to spend the rest of the weekend with us. He claimed the couch for himself. He insisted on being the one to call my mom to tell her how we'd found each other. I paced the living room for an hour when he called Daisy. They even made plans to have a face-to-face on the subject of me. From the twinkle in his eye, I think the idea really excited him.

Before hanging up, he returned from the back patio and handed me his cell phone. "Stella, are you okay? Are they treating you all right?" God, it was so nice having her back in my life.

"Yeah, Mom. I'm good with it. They're very nice people."

"He's looking forward to spending time with you. Do you want that?"

"Yeah, I do. Thank you for not freaking out over this," I

● ● ●

sighed.

"This is a first for us. Nana's the only one who knew her father. I guess we'll fumble our way through it." She laughed.

She rushed off the phone to tell Nana what had transpired between Mel and me.

My dad offered to give me some money, but I flat-out refused it. Money wasn't what I wanted or needed from him. I wanted the dad I'd always dreamed of having.

Stefan stopped his sheltering of me and allowed us to walk around the complex alone on Sunday. We just wanted to get to know each other without being under the microscope. The complex looked so beautiful at dusk. We stopped at the little pond at the center of the complex to feed the ducks floating by.

"So, Stella, you and Stefan seem very happy. I'm sorry it wasn't easier in the beginning," he expressed with concern.

"Yeah, well, I can't deny it was hard, but I don't talk to Stefan about it. He already carries so much guilt over it. I never blamed him for any of this." I waved my hands around my stomach.

"However, his parents do blame you?" he questioned.

"Yeah. His father has come around, but his mom thinks I'm the devil in disguise," I joked.

"Why won't you let me help you two out?"

"Because I never wanted to meet my father for his money, I wanted to meet you because I wanted to know who you were as a person," I replied, looking at the fountain in the middle of the pond.

* * *

"And, now you have. I have to tell you, when Eddie called and told me about you, I was so afraid you'd hate me for not being there. I would have been if I'd known." I could see the sadness in his eyes.

"I know that now. We can't take back what's happened, but we can move forward." I smiled at him.

Once our walk was over, we headed inside. Stefan was upstairs in the guestroom, so I headed there to let him know I had returned. You can imagine my surprise when I overheard another one of his cell phone conversations.

"No, she has no clue. I'm not ready to tell her," he grumbled into the mouthpiece.

"Anastasia, I swear if she finds out about . . ."

"She can't take the stress right now . . . no . . . when the time is right, I'll tell her," he muttered, sounding irritated.

"Yeah, I can't wait to see you, too."

"Love you, too," he sighed.

As he hung up, I heard him strolling toward the door, so I ducked into the bathroom. There was no way I could face him after hearing him proclaim his love to someone else.

● ● ●

Chapter Fourteen

Trick or treat?

Stefan

THE THRILLING SIGHT OF SEEING STELLA SO HAPPY LEFT me riveted to me seat. She literally danced around the house, looking forward to our first Halloween together. Her skin glowed from her new healthier, fuller face, making it an exquisite sight I wanted to see every day. From my perch on the couch, I watched her decorating the cottage in orange and black skeletons.

Fear welled up in my chest when Stella froze suddenly and rubbed her baby bump. Furrowing my brow in concern, I moved to her side. "You okay, Stella?" I joined her in cradling her beautiful belly.

"Yeah, it's those Braxton Hicks contractions. They're a real

* * *

pain," she twittered.

"Maybe you should slow down and relax a little. I'll do the rest for you." I smiled and rubbed my children through her shirt.

"Just for a minute, then I'll be as good as new." She waddled to the couch, looking very uncomfortable.

Oh, who was she kidding? She would be couch-bound for the rest of the night, leaving me to hand out the candy. I couldn't blame her, really. At her current size, it made moving more difficult.

Her last appointment with Doctor Marcus had gone so well, she had been beaming when we'd left his office. Stella had managed to gain four pounds in two weeks.

Everything had been going so well between us, too. Every now and then, I would catch Stella staring off into space. She refused to share her thoughts when she did it and it was making me nervous. Eddie kept telling me not to worry, because she hadn't said anything to him. Maybe she was thinking about baby names?

We'd had a great time the weekend we had spent in South Carolina. Stella's dad Mel called or emailed her daily since then in his effort to get to know her better. She, of course, was very happy with her new relationship with Mel and Eddie. The fact that they lived so far away made her sad sometimes, so I set up video conferencing on the laptop for them.

Eddie was thrilled with having a sister as wonderful as Stella. However, you could see the guilt he carried over missing her earlier years. I can't tell you how many times I came in from school to see her and Eddie engaged in a video chat. Stella had even arranged with her doctor to share her information with Eddie so he could help me

● ● ●

monitor her. She'd been doing wonderfully on that front, too. Stress, we discovered, made her blood pressure spike, so I'd kept that to a minimum.

My dad had been a little pushy about telling Stella of our upcoming visit to D.C. for Thanksgiving. I know she'd worried about my mom, and honestly, so did I. Michael had promised to come with us and to bring Eddie along.

Michael had no intention of telling my dad about their relationship. Not out of embarrassment, but to protect Eddie from my dad. Eddie didn't care who Michael told; he'd never hid who he was, and he understood Michael did out of necessity. The military had a very touchy attitude when it came to being homosexual. He knew my dad already had an idea, but that didn't mean he wanted to flaunt it in front of my dad's subordinates.

Taping up the last orange skeleton, I glanced over my shoulder to see Stella sneaking candy out of the bowl. She was so cute when she grinned at her prized, pint-sized Snickers candy bar. The slight hum that vibrated out of her chest as she chewed was too much of a distraction, and I couldn't help want a taste.

She never saw me tiptoeing up, since her head was back in the bowl looking for another piece. "Come here, you," I purred, leaning in and pinning her to the back of the couch.

"It's mine! You can't have it." She giggled.

"I don't want the candy, my sweetness." I kissed her below her ear, eliciting an adorable moan.

I groaned when the doorbell chimed. Damn! "I've got it, Stella." I moved toward the door, but not before she managed to

* * *

heave herself off the couch.

I regretted opening the door instantly. There before my eyes stood the one and only Savanna. There was no hiding the shocked look on my face when she stood there in nothing but a very revealing and suggestive French maid's outfit. Before I could slam the door in her face, she launched herself into my arms and locked her lips onto mine.

Struggling, I tried to get her to release me, but she wasn't hearing any of it. When she forcibly shoved her tongue into my mouth, I gagged. I heard Stella whimpering behind me. The shattering of the glass candy bowl finally, allowed me to pry her mouth from mine. I spun to see Stella shaking her head, her eyes clamped shut, the shattered bowl and its candies on the floor.

"Get out! And don't come back!" Stella screeched, stomping off.

"Savanna, you're despicable! Get out!" I bellowed an inch from her face.

The way she smirked at me over her shoulder as she strutted away told me more than enough. She wanted to put a wedge between us. I ran for the bedroom in search of Stella. Her sobs could be heard through the locked door.

"Baby, let me in. She's gone. Please open up?" I begged through the door.

"I told you to get out! And don't come back!" she screeched again.

"No, Stella! Don't do this. I love you. Let me in! Please?" I

● ● ●

begged. The pain in chest threatened to overwhelm me. My chest refused to allow me to breathe, and I felt like I would suffocate.

"I'll never be able to look at you again without picturing her mouth on yours, her claws in your shoulders, her leg wrapped around you." she growled in agony.

"Stella! No!" I yelled, dropping to my knees on the floor in front of the door.

"Get out!" she croaked.

In a moment of desperation, I pounded on the barrier between us with my fists. "No, I can't live without you! Please? I love you. There is no me without you." Tears slipped from my eyes.

Over the next hour, I begged, pleaded, and groveled for her to let me in. I knew I could take her pain away, if she'd allow me to. The churning in my stomach reached a point where I had no choice but to run for the bathroom. The renewed separation took a physical toll on my body. In the end, all I could do was let the remains of my dinner come back up. Looking in the mirror, I looked as sick as I felt. My complexion pale and my eyes dark, I resembled myself from the days when I had been locked away from Stella.

This time, it was Stella locking me out. After scrubbing my mouth clean, leaving no residue of the lipstick and alcohol that Savanna had deposited there, I paused with my cheek against the door, ghosting my hand over the wood. Stella's crying never ceased, but now she was begging Eddie for help. I wanted to be the one that helped her.

With a sigh, I shut off the porch light. Until then, I had ignored the insistent ringing, but I needed peace. I couldn't look

* * *

those happy children in the face, feeling the way I did. Grabbing the vacuum, I removed the scattered candy and sucked up the glass pieces. When Stella finally came out, I didn't want her to think about what had happened.

The couch was my bed for the night — not that I slept. Without a blanket or pillow, I hunkered down and prayed she'd emerge to use the bathroom. Her tortured cries had me wanting to rip the door from the hinges. I would have done anything to make the mental images in her mind go away.

She never left the room for the rest of the night. By the time I needed to go to school, she still refused to talk to me, or see me, for that matter. No amount of begging on my part managed to change her mind.

Feeling defeated and emotionally spent, I made my way to school. By the time I pulled into the student parking lot, my pain had manifested itself into anger. Not at Stella, but Savanna. My first class of the day was the one I shared with her. Storming my way in, I stalked straight for her, shoving her desk as I went on the attack.

"You ever come near me again, I swear, it will be the last thing you ever do. There are some major benefits to having a father who's stationed at the Pentagon! If you even as much as breathe in the vicinity of Stella, I will end your future before it starts!" Seeing her cowering back against the seat brought with it more satisfaction than I ever imagined.

Her so-called friends even moved away from her when I unleashed my tirade. My sneers had them quaking in their seats as well. The fear in their three sets of eyes cemented the fact that they'd never approach Stella or me again.

* * *

"I . . ." I shook her desk beneath her, stopping her words in their tracks.

"Not another word, if you value your future." My voice reverberated through the room.

With a sharp nod, she lowered her eyes to the desk, no doubt afraid to see the raging storm in my eyes. With one last shove of her desk, I spun and retreated to my desk. In a surprising move, Savanna bolted out the door clutching her books to her chest, never looking back. Good riddance.

It was tortuous sitting in the class for another hour. The only thing I could think of was Stella and what I needed to do to fix the mess that had been created by Savanna. There was nothing I wouldn't do to keep her, and when I went home after my last class, she would know that, too.

My second class was just as bad as the first. I spent the entire time fidgeting with the pages of my book. Listening to the teacher drone on about her latest math problem held no interest for me. By the time we were released, I charged for my car. I needed to show Stella she was the only woman I loved. I did make one stop on the way home. I bought Stella a dozen long-stemmed, red roses. Money didn't matter when it came to being with Stella.

When I keyed open the door, I hoped Stella would be roaming around the house, but it was quiet — too quiet. Frozen in shock, I dropped the bouquet to the floor and gasped. On the coffee table was an envelope with my name on it. With shaking hands, I pulled the letter from its envelope.

● ● ●

Stefan,

I can't. The vision of her on you is more than my mind can stand. It's obvious; she wants you enough to stomp on anyone to get to you. Don't look for me. I don't want to be found.

Stella

Screaming out, I tossed everything from the table and flipped it over. This was not the end!

◊ ◊ ◊

Stella

When I called Eddie the night before, he freaked out. Before I hung up, I could hear him and Michael getting in the car. They arrived only minutes after Stefan pulled out of the driveway.

Shutting the door behind me started my tears falling again. Michael and Eddie tried to talk to me, but I was a babbling mess. Michael threw my bags in the truck while Eddie helped me into the car. Lying on the backseat, Eddie took a blood pressure reading. The results were far from where they needed to be. Michael and Eddie shared a worried glance before getting in themselves. Listening to their hushed words worked as a lullaby. My red, swollen eyes floated closed, and sleep finally over took me.

Stretching to wake up proved to be difficult in the cramped

● ● ●

confines of Eddie's white Dodge Charger. "Welcome back to the living," Michael's chortle startled me.

Groaning, I sat up to see Michael staring at me. "Thanks," I whispered my voice still hoarse from last night.

"Ready to talk about it?" Eddie asked in a soft tone.

"What's left to say? I told you last night, I can't be there right now." My grumble was almost too soft to be heard.

"Stella, you did leave him a note telling where you were going and that you'd be back once you felt better? Right?"

Without looking in their direction, I lied, "Um, yeah, of course I did."

"Stella, you can't do this to him," Michael blustered.

"Michael, you didn't see them. Every time I shut my eyes, the sight of them tears at me. She kissed him! God, she touched him!" I lashed out at him, letting my tears fall again.

"Stella, please? Let's talk to Stefan. I can't believe he would've enjoyed that," Eddie pleaded.

I shuddered as my mind replayed the event. "It doesn't matter if he did; she did. How am I supposed to look at her knowing she had her tongue shoved down his throat?" I growled.

Clutching my chest tightly, I curled up in the backseat. "He won't survive if you don't go back, Stella. It almost killed him when our parents pulled him away last time. What about the twins? They need their father. Do you really want them to grow up without a father like you did? Because of a misunderstanding?"

* * *

I turned away and refused to answer Michael. He knew I didn't want that, but I had to be away and let my brain clear.

Staring out the window, I watched the scenery slip by. When I checked the dashboard clock, it flashed two o'clock, and I knew Stefan would be arriving home any moment to find my note. The pain of writing it hurt more than when he had been torn from my life. I never thought I would be the one to walk away from him. If I walked away, he'd move on with his mystery woman. Maybe she wasn't a mystery at all. It was possible Savanna had grown tired of waiting for him to tell me.

Michael's phone chirped a few minutes after I lied about the note. He sighed, looking at the caller ID.

Looking at Eddie, he snapped it open. "Stefan?"

"Slow down! What do you mean?" he gasped, and I knew the truth was out.

"She what?" he snarled.

"Pull over, Eddie!" He snapped back to watch me.

"No, Stefan, calm down. She's not gone. She is taking a few days to get her thoughts together, then she will be home." I gulped at his glare.

"Yes, I know where she is. She's with me and Eddie." I cringed at the harshness of his tone.

"We were headed to South Carolina." He nodded, even though Stefan couldn't see it.

"See you soon." He snapped his phone shut.

* * *

"Stella! How could you?"

"What — what did she do?" Eddie almost gave himself whiplash, looking to Michael for details.

"The note she left said she wasn't coming back and for him not to look for her." Eddie hissed and jerked his head to face me.

"You didn't! You couldn't! Seriously? What did you want to do? Destroy him?"

"I didn't destroy him; I set him free," I murmured with my hands covering my shame-filled face.

"You didn't hear him. He's a mess. Don't you get it? Every couple in our family knew the moment they'd met their other half." Eddie gazed at Michael like Stefan always did at me.

"You, too?" Eddie whispered.

"Yeah, me too. That's why I know what he's been going through. It's the same thing I feel every time I go home for the summer." I had to look away their moment was just too intimate for me to watch.

"So, what's the plan?" Eddie asked Michael, ignoring me.

"We take her back. I won't hurt him because she can't see how much he loves her." His eyes locked onto mine. "Wake up. He will never move on from you. You will talk to him. If you need help seeing just how nuts he is over you, than allow me to tell you what he won't."

So, with us parked on the side of the highway, he told me every moment he had witnessed of Stefan's torture. Leaving out no

* * *

details, he told me of the nights Stefan would lie in his bed and cry over me. Even Eddie was tearing up as he continued down the dreaded memory lane and the way he described the haunted eyes Stefan wore for all those months. Sniffing, I wiped away the tears that were dripping from my cheeks. How could I have hurt him like that?

The only thing I never mentioned was the phone call I had overheard between Stefan and someone he said he loved. It was all so confusing. Eddie pulled back into traffic, only to take the next exit to drag me back. After learning of my deceitfulness, they kept quiet on the ride back.

A stray thought skirted around my mind while we drove back to the cottage. What if this was only about the babies? Maybe that's what he's afraid of losing and not me. Right at the moment we entered the Norfolk city limit, panic engulfed my chest. What was going to happen when I arrived home?

Michael grabbed my trembling hand when I gazed up to see his expression toward me had now softened. When Eddie retrieved the few bags I had out of the trunk, we headed for the door. Wheezing, I opened the door to see Stefan standing in the center of the room. With his arms crossed across his chest, he glared at me.

"Did you really think I would forgo looking for you and my children? It's one thing if you don't love me, but it's another when you try to make my choice for me. We all know how well that worked out when my parents tried," he heatedly spoke.

Before I said anything, I looked around at the living room. There on the table stood a vase with a dozen red roses prominently displayed. My eyes shot to his to see him watching me admiring

● ● ●

them.

"They represent the twelve things I love about you. Would you like to know what they stand for?" The most I could manage was a soft nod.

"One, your beauty that captured my heart the moment I first saw you." He pulled one rose out and placed it in my shaking hands. "Two, the way you loved me even after everything that happened." Again, he put another rose in my hands.

"Three, that adorable giggle you release when you're embarrassed." My bouquet grew by one more. "Four, the fact that you waited for me even after my mother lied and told you I'd moved on." I sniffed, gazing into his loving gray eyes.

"Five, I love the way you accept me just the way I am." I could feel my resolve faltering. "Six, your lips on mine; your taste is better than any chocolate I have ever had."

"Seven, feeling your body against mine, so warm and soft." This time when he placed the rose in my hands, he rubbed my shaking fingers with his own.

"Eight, the intelligence you hide from everyone except me and your teachers. And nine, that you gave me your heart when you denied it to everyone else." Seeing his eyes twinkle had my knees going weak.

"Ten, your determination to succeed against all the odds." He sighed.

"Eleven, the way you set my soul ablaze every time you walk into the room."

* * *

With one left to go, I had a feeling I knew what he was going to say. "I love the fact that you don't hate me for getting you pregnant." His smile faded.

That wasn't what I expected. I thought he would have said that I was giving him children. Wow, didn't see that one coming. With one step, his body loomed over me. "Let me give you a new memory that will wipe that last one away." He leaned in, and against by better judgment, I allowed him to brush his soft, moist lips against mine. It was over; I couldn't leave him, and I knew it.

"I love you, Stella. There's no one who can replace you." He encircled me in a tight embrace. Three more sweet kisses wiped out any possible resistance.

"Please, I don't want to think about her anymore." I whimpered when he nuzzled into my neck and hair.

"It would be my pleasure."

I yelped when he pulled me up into his arms and started walking toward our room. One of these days, he was going to do permanent damage to his back.

"Stefan, Stella, we'll see you at Thanksgiving." Michael waved, smiling at Eddie before they left.

Stefan was right; he kept my mind preoccupied for the rest of the night.

● ● ●

Chapter Fifteen

Stella learns her lesson

BRIGHT AND EARLY ON A CRISP SUNDAY MORNING IN November, Stefan drove us to the parking lot where he'd been giving it his all to teach me how to drive the Mustang. It was different from driving Nana's old car, which she finally found a replacement for after I'd totaled the grey relic months prior.

The lesson began after he settled in the passenger seat. The easy stuff I could handle: mirrors and whatnots. He tried to hide his frustration, but it never worked. I could hear his chest rumble when he flew into the dashboard, and then he would grunt when he'd be thrown back into the seat. I really couldn't blame him. It's tough teaching me how to drive. At least, he never yelled like Nana did.

● ● ●

Even though my mom and I were talking again, she still refused to resume her attempts to get me on the road. In fact, she promised to get off the road the day I managed to get my license. The nerve of her!

After an unsuccessful hour, we headed home. It was becoming clear that I wasn't meant to drive. We decided we would try again next weekend, but this time he wanted to try something different. I was all for anything that might work, so I agreed without a fight.

True to his word, we were back in the same parking lot the next week.

"Stella, you've procrastinated enough. Your mirrors are set, the seatbelt is fastened; now push that friendly long petal on the right, nice and easy," Stefan whispered ever so softly in my ear from his belted position in the backseat.

Our new plan was for me to be alone in the front seat, thus removing the stress of someone scrutinizing my every move. If this didn't work, I was going to give in and forget trying to learn. It's not that I didn't enjoy Stefan chauffeuring me around; I just wanted to be independent.

Pushing with just my big toe, I tapped the gas pedal with almost no pressure. For the first time, the car didn't jerk forward; instead it accelerated, slow and steady. I giggled. "Stefan, I'm doing it!"

"Yes, you are. I'm so proud of you; just keep it up. Now with one finger, test out turning the wheel," he urged. "See, it doesn't need much to turn it. Normally, you would use both your hands, but this is to show you how little it takes to make the car turn." I peeked

● ● ●

in the rearview mirror to see his pride in me beaming back.

"Wow, this is so much fun." I laughed.

"Here's the hard part; do the same thing to the brake pedal. Start with one toe, and add in another as you get closer to where you want to stop." His gentle voice relaxed my stressed shoulders, and I did what he instructed.

Amazingly, the car didn't send us flying forward into the dashboard. I was giddy when the car slowed and stopped on the yellow line I'd been aiming for. As I turned around, Stefan leaned in and kissed me, showing me how proud of me he felt. It was one of the best feelings in the world. For the next hour, I eased around the empty lot, trying all the things I'd seen other people doing in their cars. Parking was the hardest obstacle left, but we'd tackle that next week.

"See, sweetheart. I told you, you can do it. Now, it's time for a reward. Swap seats; I want to take you somewhere." I wasn't sure I was going to like the reward from the way he grinned at me.

"Where are we going?" I questioned with a laugh, waddling around the car.

"It's a surprise," he chuckled, wiggling his brows at me.

Yep, more nervous now. It wasn't that I didn't like surprises, because I did. However, the way he was so cryptic put me on the edge of my seat. Therefore, you can imagine my surprise when we drove straight to Nana's house.

"Stefan, why are we here?" I asked, bewildered.

"Sunday dinner; now come on." The way he chuckled sent

* * *

shivers down my spine.

"Since when did you start arranging Sunday dinners with my family?" This was never a regular routine for us.

Every day at Nana's was Pick Night, which was a night when everyone picks what they wanted and made it themselves. You know, a free for all. It was probably one of the reasons that I had terrible eating habits.

"Oh, stop complaining already, and let's go." There was that snicker again.

Stefan practically bounced up the stairs, when the door flew open. "Stella!" My mom rushed us for a hug.

"Hi, Mom. You're awfully happy to see us." I giggled, stepping inside.

"Surprise!" Startled, I tried to back up to escape, only to run directly into Stefan's chest.

I now understood the evil grin he was wearing all the way here; he knew.

"Nice try, my love. But there's no escape for you now," he cooed into the crook of my neck before kissing it.

Looking around, the house looked so pretty decorated in pastel pink and blue decorations. Everyone I knew was there, from my dad to my mom's friends from the shop. The ogling was a little unnerving, but in their defense, not many had even seen me pregnant outside my immediate family. The only one missing was Eddie and, of course, Stefan's side of the family. That was no real surprise. I knew how they felt about me.

● ● ●

"Have a seat here, Stella." My dad delivered a chair for me to sit on.

"Hi, everyone." I waved, feeling awkward.

The sudden chatter had me shrinking into the chair. I was shocked by the whole turn of events. In a fury that could only be rivaled by a hurricane, the guests were introduced to me; even my dad had brought a few friends. I don't ever remember having so many people in the house all at once. Brianna and her posse attended, which was another unexpected experience.

Nana's call to the lunch buffet saved me from having to talk to any more strangers. "Stay here; I'll get you something to eat." Stefan kissed me and headed to the kitchen.

"So, how are you feeling, Stella?"

"Good, Dad. Stefan taught me to drive today." I grinned, pleased with myself.

"That's great. You know, I would have taught you if you'd asked me." I couldn't help laughing.

"You say that now. But ask anyone; until today, it was downright scary to be in a car with me behind the wheel." Nodding, I accentuated my point.

"I think your mom might have mentioned something about it giving her more gray hair." He laughed at my expense.

"Thank God she can color her own hair," I snorted, mocking at the horror of my mom without hair dye.

"And here, I thought it was natural," he chuckled.

* * *

My dad drifted off when my mom walked by with two heaping plates of food. He reminded me of a dog following his master in the hopes she would drop a morsel for him. It was kind of cute in a gross way. Stefan arrived back right behind her with two plates for us. His plates were just as overflowing. I swear he thought he was feeding an Army platoon. The guy seriously had a problem with trying to force food on me. Yeah, I knew I needed to gain my marks, and I'd been trying to do better.

"Eat up. My kids must be starving." I sneered at his insinuation.

"I am not starving them," I gloated.

"Not anymore you aren't, but you were." He cocked his brow challenging me.

"I was not! Take it back!" I poked him in the chest.

"I surrender." Laughing, he held his arms up.

"That's right. Who's your baby momma?" I snickered at my win.

"You are, sweetheart." He smirked, then kissed me.

Following his lead, I started eating. Mealtimes were hard for me. Unlike before, I now had no appetite. After our visit to Michael's and the two overheard phone calls, I knew it was a matter of time before Stefan would leave me for his new love. Over the last few weeks, he's been more affectionate than usual. Under normal circumstances, you'd think he still loved me. He always said he loved me, but there were too many unexplained phone calls for me to ignore them anymore. I never let it show how much it hurt me. The

● ● ●

last thing I needed was Brianna saying 'I told you so.'

It took a while, but I plowed through the mound of food piled on the plate. The food was great, and I felt like a cow when I finally finished. Stefan sighed when he took my plate. "I'll be right back," he whispered before disappearing among the guests.

When Nana announced, "Time for presents," the cameras came out, and I regretted not being better dressed.

"One second; I need to use the rest room." I shuffled away, hoping to make myself more presentable.

The once-familiar trek to my room felt odd now. Strange how moving away did that. As I heaved my weight up the stairs, I could hear Stefan's voice coming from the bathroom.

"No . . . yeah. Today we got one day closer." He sighed.

"Don't screw this up," his voice demanded.

"I said I would, and I will. Look, I have to go before she notices I'm gone." I sighed knowing what would be said next.

"Yeah. Me, too." He agitatedly hung up.

I ducked into my room before he could exit the bathroom. Holding my breath, I shuddered when I caught my reflection in Brianna's mirror. It's no wonder he was talking to someone else. I'd been trying to keep us together with the hopes that he might still love me, but days like today made it increasingly difficult.

Grabbing Brianna's brush, I tried to primp a little. There's only so much you can do with board-straight hair. Even the makeup I borrowed from Brianna's bag didn't make me feel any prettier; at

●　●　●

235

least I gave it a shot.

Giving Stefan enough time to get back downstairs, I headed back to the shower.

"Stella, what are you doing up here?" Yelping in surprise, I spun to see Stefan was still upstairs.

"I . . . um . . . well, I needed to touch myself up before they started taking pictures," I stuttered like a child caught with their hand in the cookie jar.

"Well, let's go. You look fabulous. You know that, right?" It was all I could do not to flinch when he grabbed my hand.

"Yep, everyone adores a walking incubator." Stefan laughed at my utterance.

"Well, you are the prettiest walking incubator I've ever seen," he purred, leading me toward the staircase.

Everyone was waiting for us when we made our descent. As expected, the flashes started blinding me immediately. Picture after picture was snapped as my mom started shoving the pastel-colored presents at me.

I had to admit the gifts were unexpected. I assumed Stefan and I would be buying most our own stuff and it would be used. Since we didn't know what we were having, most of the clothes were white or yellow and a few were green. The soft fleece blankies were irresistible. Nana and Brianna had chipped in and bought us two black infant car seats that doubled as carriers. The most surprising gift came from Mel and my mom. They bought us two white matching convertible cribs. The cribs could be changed when the

● ● ●

twins grew into toddlers. That would save us from buying toddler beds for them.

I couldn't help but wonder if Stefan would still be with us when that happened. From his cryptic calls, I had serious doubts that he would. By the time everyone left, I was exhausted and ready to go home. Kissing my parents, I said my thank you's and goodbyes. Stefan was chatty on the ride home, but I kept quiet. His words from the phone call kept me preoccupied on the hour-long ride home.

While I made dinner, Stefan set off to assemble the room the twins would share after their birth. It was a good thing he wasn't under my feet while I cooked dinner. I needed the space at that moment.

The next few days crawled by with me being lost in my own little bubble, pondering where Stefan and I were headed. Deep down, I hoped I was jumping to the wrong assumptions.

"We need to talk, Stella." Looking up from my breakfast, my stomach churned.

"Okay," I blew out a deep breath, thinking the time had come.

"Don't freak out, but I told my dad we'd go there for Thanksgiving." I hissed at the thought of being in his parents' home for the first time.

Pursing my lips, I tried to figure a way out. "That's a bad idea. I don't think my blood pressure can handle that." I had to give it a shot.

"Michael and Eddie will be there to keep you calm. And, my dad says my mom is warming up to the whole situation." He smiled.

* * *

"I don't have a say here, do I?"

Smirking. "No, not really," he chuckled.

"For how long?"

"Four days." He started to catch on that I was ticked off.

"Fine," I grumbled, storming off to the bedroom and locking the door.

My second worst nightmare was about to come true. Four days trapped in a house with my arch nemesis. Great! What a nice way to spend a holiday.

● ● ●

Chapter Sixteen

Stella finds Stefan's other woman

TALK ABOUT A LONG RIDE FROM VIRGINIA BEACH TO Washington D.C.. Four hours in a car for an eight-month pregnant woman carrying twins was beyond agonizing. Stefan diligently stopped every hour for me to waddle round, eat the food he'd packed, and use the restroom. However, he couldn't stop the pressure on my hips after staying seated for so long. No amount of adjusting helped me get more comfortable. I know I tried!

I never asked about his parents' finances, so when we pulled down their road, I was very surprised by the houses. Slack-jawed, I stared at my surroundings, baffled. Being out of your element would do that to you. The homes looked very expensive. Every house

• • •

boasted grand porches, expensive cars in the driveways, and well-manicured front lawns that had to have been professionally designed. It was a neighborhood I would never have been able to live in.

Once school ended, I dreamed of starting my own landscaping design company. The nice part of that simple plan was that it wouldn't take a large amount of funding to get that type of business off the ground. It was also the kind of business that one could do on a flexible schedule. With the twins due any day, that was a major consideration of mine.

Stefan pointed out the ominous-looking white house. To most passersby, it looked like a nice, happy home; to me, it promised to be a living nightmare. Inside that house stood the one person I didn't want to spend my time with — his mother.

It wasn't that I disliked Shirley Sterling, but she hated me. It was no family secret that she felt her son deserved better. In the three months that Stefan and I have been living together, she's never once called and asked about the pregnancy or me.

When we got closer I saw several people standing around chatting. I recognized all of them save one, the small framed brunette. They all smiled and waved as Stefan passed through the black fencing. The second Stefan pulled up and threw the car in park; he leapt out and charged the tiny, striking brunette.

"Anastasia!" Stefan sprinted away from me and into her awaiting arms. In a sweeping motion, he scooped her up and spun her around, laughing.

Shocked by the entire situation, I stared on gawking like an idiot. It was the first time he hadn't helped me out of the car. Seeing my dilemma, Michael was nice enough to pull me out of the green

* * *

beast. I stood there, too dumbfounded to move, as they hugged and whispered to each other. I finally had to admit my suspicions about the phone calls were right. His attention was no longer on me. The short-haired brunette was more than a friend. She held a special place in his heart that I never could. My insides turned to pudding when the revelation hit me full blast in the face.

Sniffling, I tried to stop the stinging in my eyes. It didn't work; tears started to overflow my eyelids as the pain rippled from my chest outward. Biting my lip, I was able to hold back the whimper that desperately wanted out. Feeling heartbroken, my legs shook with the urge to run.

There was nothing left to do but quietly slip away and let them be. It was the last thing I wanted to do, but it was the right thing to do. He deserved to be happy, even if it wasn't with me. No one even noticed my predicament; even my brother was so distracted by the sudden scene that he didn't even greet me.

Without a word, I started backing away from everyone, including the happy couple. "Stella, what are you doing?" Michael tried to grab my arm, but I just swatted his hands away. Now he noticed the blimp standing next to him? At that moment, the only thing I wanted was to be ignored.

"Wait, Stella!" Looking away, I tried to hide my emotions.

I started moving back down the driveway, heading for the front gate. Upon closer inspection, I realized my entire body was shaking to the core. Through my teary vision, I could barely see where I was walking. Just as I reached the end of the driveway, I registered faint voices behind me, but they made no sense to me. Their voices were garbled and distorted, drowned out by my

● ● ●

heartbeat pounding in my ears. Could I just walk away from the only person I've ever loved? I would do it for him. I'd do anything for him.

The starry flickers in my vision alerted me to the fact that I wasn't going to get far. Stumbling over the uneven terrain, I tried to reach out to grab the wrought iron fence. I felt my knees buckle and give out when my vision went black.

"Stella!" Stefan's guttural scream was the last thing I heard as my body impacted with the unforgiving ground.

Through my ringing ears, I could hear them talking.

There was no mistaking the softness beneath me. Feeling warm and fuzzy meant one thing; I wasn't on the lawn anymore. When I finally convinced my eyes to open, I was startled to see Eddie rushing over to my bedside. Looking around, I discovered I wasn't alone; most unexpectedly, Stefan was here, too. He was sitting on the bed next to me. From his distraught expression, I gathered it wasn't a good thing that I had passed out. A second glance around the room had me wishing I hadn't woken up. Every member of Stefan's family stood by watching my every move. I had to do a double take when I saw two Shirley's in the room.

Stefan leaned in, and his voice shook as he asked, "Baby, how do you feel?" That one word "Baby" had me wanting to sob again. I knew everyone could see my lip quivering.

When my heart started racing again, Eddie took notice. "Stella, you need to calm down or I'll drive you to the hospital myself." Eddie's stern voice caused me to shiver.

Looking down at my arm, I figured out what the problem

* * *

was. Eddie had his blood pressure monitor on my arm. The doctor had warned us about my blood pressure being too high. When I looked around the room again, everyone's face was etched with worry. That was surprising. I'd expected them to be indifferent or even relieved. If the twins were gone, so would Stefan be.

"Where were you going?" Stefan's soft musical voice asked.

Clamping my eyes shut, I whispered, "Home."

"Your home is with me," he cooed as he caressed my arm.

My face distorted at the thought. "Not anymore. You don't have to stay with me. I know you don't want me anymore," I sniveled.

"Where did you get an insane idea like that?" Stefan ground his teeth, leering at his mother.

"Stefan, I think it had something to do with the way you greeted Anastasia," Michael surmised. Stefan's head snapped from me to her and back again.

"Stella, what exactly do you think is going on between us?" I shook my head and refused to answer him. "Stella, it's not what you think," he implored.

"I heard the phone calls," I chided, looking away to hide the pain that no doubt was written on my face.

I have never seen him move so fast as he crossed the room and grabbed her by the hand. His suddenness even surprised Anastasia. Strolling back over to me, he looked so ecstatic. Anastasia on the other hand looked baffled. Stefan's grin beamed enough that it would light a city block. I wished I could have made him that happy.

* * *

I huffed when he dropped to his knees at my bedside.

"Stella Richards, this is Anastasia, my cousin. We call her Annie though, and that's my mom's twin sister, Charlotte." He stroked the blush that crept across my cheeks. I must have looked like I'd been baked under the glaring sun for hours without an ounce of sunscreen.

"Oh, um . . . I didn't know," I managed to stutter. "Hi, Annie, Charlotte." There was something eerily familiar about Annie's perfect heart-shaped face and ocean-blue eyes. No amount of staring seemed to jog my memory.

Anastasia seemed to be doing the same thing. The only difference was that she kept opening her mouth as if she was going to say something, then decided against it.

"Wait, it can't be." She clasped her hand over her mouth before her voice whispered, "Stella Richards? From Virginia Beach?"

"Yeah." She surprised me when she started bouncing up and down.

"Oh my God! It is you. You were my best friend the summer we vacationed there." It was her. The first person I had ever befriended on the beach a decade ago.

I scrunched my eyes shut. "Yeah, and you were mine. Until you left and forgot about me." Her sharp inhale caught me by surprise again.

"I've never forgotten you. In fact . . . never mind." Her smile faded, and she waved me off with a subtle hand gesture.

* * *

"So, let me see if I'm following this. This is the same girl you raved about for years? The reason you never connected with anyone after that summer? The reason your mother searched every piece of paper in your house for months looking for an address after you moved?" She looked embarrassed by Stefan's questions. I, on the other hand, gulped, too tongue tied to speak.

"Yeah, she's the one." My cheeks flushed crimson at her admission.

I had to ask; the need to know was too overwhelming. "You really never forgot about me?"

"No, we moved the week after we arrived back in Boston. Your address was lost in the shuffle. I'm sorry you thought I'd forgotten you." Annie shifted between her feet, her nervousness evident.

"I'm sorry I doubted you. If it's any consolation, I never connected with anyone else after that summer, except for Stefan." From the glimmer in her eyes, it pleased her to hear it.

"It would seem I found something you lost," Stefan snickered and nudged Annie's hip with his shoulder.

Maurice's voice brought reality back to the forefront of my mind. "Eddie, how is she doing now?"

"It's coming back down. However, she's still high. I emailed her doctor, and he wants her watched very closely." My eyes fluttered shut when Stefan placed a chaste kiss on my clammy forehead.

"Bed rest?" My brother just nodded to answer Maurice.

● ● ●

245

"Okay, here's what's going to happen. Stefan, grab the bags from the car. Michael, get the cot from the attic, and set it up in here. Eddie, make a list of everything you need from the store. Annie, you're the shopper. Shirley, Charlotte, she's going to need her dinner and a pitcher of water brought in here." He clapped his hands sharply to signal it was time to move.

I half expected Shirley to complain, but she didn't. No one complained; instead, everyone rushed off to do his bidding. My head spun slightly when I tried to sit up. Eddie's strong grip on my shoulder told me that he didn't want me in the upright position I desired.

It wasn't a shocker when Michael re-emerged first. He strolled in carrying an army cot. "Where do you want it, Dad?" With one finger, he indicated the precise location where he wanted it placed.

Stefan rushed back through the door next, dropping the two bags we brought to the side. There was an air of desperation to his enchanting features. He appeared to be a man on a mission.

Regardless of the fact that I was in a twin bed and his family was watching on, Stefan crawled in and cradled me in his embrace. With his arms came the guarantee of safety. They always had.

Eddie tittered as I melted into Stefan's welcomed encirclement. "Keep that up, and she'll be back to normal in no time."

"That's my girl. Just relax, sweetheart. I'm not going anywhere," Stefan cooed into the crook of my neck and stroked my messy mane.

● ● ●

Sighing in contentment, my eyes floated shut. If Shirley hadn't entered at that moment, I might have fallen asleep right there. I only knew it was Shirley because Stefan tightened his grip on me.

Holding my breath, I waited for her to snarl her disapproving opinion. You can imagine my astonished gasp when she approached the bed with a faint smile gracing her face. It was the first time she had shown any form of acceptance toward me or the relationship between Stefan and me. I kept looking between her and Stefan to see if my mind was playing tricks on me.

"I took this off of the menu Stefan emailed me. It's still good, right?"

I had to admit the minestrone soup and turkey and cheese sandwiches looked delicious. I was definitely hungry. From the amount on the tray, I would say she intended for Stefan to join me for dinner.

"Yes, it's perfect, Mrs. Sterling. Her doctor hasn't made any new dietary changes," Eddie responded as he checked my pressure again. "Here's the list for Annie."

I almost laughed when every man in the room reached for his wallet. Maurice won; with a single glare, he froze everyone in their tracks. I had the distinct feeling that it was a common occurrence. It seemed as if no one liked to confront the well-trained alpha male.

"Here, Shirley, give this to Annie." He passed off the list and some cash. "I think we should give them a few minutes to eat." Maurice waved everyone out of the room.

Once everyone was gone, Stefan went into his nursing mode. "Come on, Stella, let me help you up." I grasped his well-toned

● ● ●

247

biceps for support.

Gazing into his eyes, I muttered, "I'm sorry," as he lifted me so I could sit against the headboard.

"Stella, don't be sorry. I'm the one who is sorry. I should have told you that my aunt and cousin were coming for the weekend. My uncle is still deployed, so they had nowhere else to spend Thanksgiving. If I had warned you, you wouldn't have been so upset." This time when he stroked my cheek, I sighed.

He tried to hide it, but I could see he was still frantic. "You're forgiven. I just wish I hadn't overreacted. Annie must think I'm such a freak," I twittered.

His grin warmed my heart. "Actually, no. She wants to start again with you. Do you think you can do that?"

I laughed at the silliness of his question. "Yeah, I can do that. Well, I guess we know whose side the twins run on," I snorted at his smirk.

"It's one of the reasons I never needed a paternity test. Twins don't run on your side. And what are the chances you would sleep with someone else who had twins that run in their family at the same time we were together?" he said as I playfully slapped his arm.

"I always wondered why you never asked for one." I feigned surprise.

In silence, we enjoyed our picnic dinner in bed. We never seemed to need words for expressing our feelings. They were felt or expressed through a simple smile or touch. Once the wooden dinner tray was emptied, Stefan put it on the floor and settled back on the

● ● ●

bed.

"Stella, you do understand what your brother was saying to my dad, right?"

I furrowed my brow, chewing my lower lip. "Yeah, bed rest from here out for me. What about school?"

He shook his head with his eyes cast down. "It's out until further notice."

"But?" I huffed.

"But nothing. Those two come before anything else," he demanded, his voice firm. I nodded without a fight, knowing he was right.

If I had to retake all the courses again, I would do that for the two unborn lives we were responsible for. They were the only thing that could keep me from school.

"So, we need to figure out who is going to sleep where," Maurice mused from the open doorway.

"Excuse me, Mr. Sterling. I need to make my bed," Eddie cackled as he passed Maurice.

His features confused. "You're sleeping in here?" Maurice pointed to the room.

"Of course. What if my sister needs me in the middle of the night?" Eddie dove right into making his makeshift bed.

"Your sister?" Maurice questioned. I laughed, thinking I had never seen him more confounded since he'd found out about my pregnancy.

● ● ●

"Yeah, Dad. Eddie is Stella's brother. It's a very, very long story," Michael snickered, carrying in the pillows for the cot.

He glanced back and forth between us. "I can see the family resemblance, though I am not sure why I'm just hearing about this."

"Goodnight, Stella. I'll see you in the morning." Stefan winked at me before he left the bed.

"Come on, Dad. We'll tell you all about it downstairs." Michael led the way out of the room, leaving Eddie and me alone.

He hopped into the cot with a thud. "Stella, I called Dad. He's very worried about you. He said to keep him updated as often as possible. He was contemplating driving here in case we needed him. I told him to stay home until we called him. He is also calling your mom and letting her know what's going on." My eyes widened as he lips curved up to an evil grin.

"What's up with those two anyway? They're talking all the time," I chortled.

"Well, it would appear they still like each other." He finger quoted when he said "like."

I was in hysterics. "Who knew?"

"Yeah, when they met back up to discuss everything, they had such a good time that they did it again and again." He wiggled his eyebrows and I almost chuckled myself off the bed.

When my phone started vibrating on the oak nightstand, a completely new bout of giggles broke out. "Speak of the devil incarnate," I shushed Eddie with my finger over my lips.

● ● ●

"Hi, Mom." I fiddled with the sheet covering my beyond-enlarged stomach.

"How are you?" There was no hiding the anxiety in her voice.

"Better now. Eddie is watching me closely." I grinned at him when he patted himself on the back.

With her voice less stressed, she praised him. "Your brother from another mother is a real good boy."

"Mom, he's a man. You know you can't go around calling a twenty-two year old guy a boy. And where did you learn that expression?" I giggled when she "Pfft'ed" me.

"Fine, fine, fine, whatever you say. I Googled it, baby. Mel and I have a bag packed in case anything happens. So make sure someone calls us if anything does."

"Will do, Mom. Look, I was just heading to sleep, so I'll call you in the morning." Eddie was biting his lip trying to hide his laughter.

"Rest up, sweetie. We'll talk in the morning." I sighed when she hung up.

"She okay?"

"Yeah, she's fine. I was thinking about when I first found out about being pregnant. She wouldn't even talk to me. That all changed the night Stefan came back." I peeked up to see he wasn't smiling anymore.

"I wish I had been there for you. You really could have used me back then." I shrugged.

* * *

"But you're here now." I smiled, causing him to do the same.

"As Michael likes to put it, enough with the heavy stuff. Get to bed; I'm shutting off the light." He did just that. Of course, I laughed when he stubbed his toe walking back to his cot in the dark.

In what could only be described as a scene from an old TV show or movie, everyone started calling out their goodnights.

"Goodnight, Stella," Stefan chortled.

"Goodnight, Michael," Eddie yelled.

"Goodnight, Annie," Michael hooted.

"Goodnight, Stefan," twittered Annie.

"Goodnight, everyone," growled Maurice.

This was going to be one fun-filled Thanksgiving!

● ● ●

Chapter Seventeen

Stefan's family reunion

IT WOULD BE A VAST UNDERSTATEMENT TO SAY I WAS happy to see Anastasia. We had grown up together after she moved to Italy. Her dad had been stationed there while we had been in Germany. Every summer we would stay with her family. Her mom Charlotte was my mother's twin sister. In an attempt to keep Stella from being too upset, I'd never mentioned to her that they would be attending Thanksgiving with us. She would worry about my aunt Charlotte hating her, and the doctor had said it would be unwise for her to worry about things that could spike her blood pressure.

* * *

I couldn't stop myself from darting out of the Mustang to greet her. "Anastasia!"

"Stefan, it's so good to see you." She giggled as I spun her in my arms.

"When did you get in?" I chuckled.

Once I put her back down, she gave me a once over look. "Yesterday. Wow, you look great. Where's your girlfriend?" She peeked around me, searching for Stella.

When I did the same, that was my undoing. I should have helped Stella out of the car and introduced her properly. But, being lost in the excitement, I forgot to. When I spun around Michael and Eddie were following her down the driveway. From the way she swayed and the shuddering of her shoulders, I could tell something was wrong.

"Stella!" She trudged forward, ignoring me.

"Michael, where is she going?" I shouted.

"I don't know. She won't answer us," he called over his shoulder.

"Stella, come back!" I yelled, starting to run down the tarred drive.

Panic took over my body when she started to stagger toward the fencing.

Pushing harder, I passed them as she teetered and fell. "Stella!" I skidded to my knees, stopping just inches from her limp body.

• • •

How could I have let that happen? For the life of me, I couldn't figure out why she had headed for the street. If she was having difficulty, she knew Eddie or I would know what to do.

"Stella! Sweetheart, wake up," I flustered, pulling her onto my lap.

Michael and Eddie had to pry her from my arms. "Get her to the house!" my dad ordered. Michael pulled her into his arms and took off running, while Eddie went for the special travel bag he had packed for this trip.

Dr. Marcus had told Eddie everything to watch out for, even going as far as giving him his email address in case anything happened. Everyone in the family sobbed when they saw how badly off Stella was. Seeing her unconscious tore me to pieces. My hands shook, and my breathing was labored. My dad grabbed me just in time before my knees buckled.

"Hold it together, Stefan. She needs you to be strong." He was right; she needed me. I nodded before plowing up the stairs. I needed to be with her. After everything we've been through, I couldn't lose her now.

Michael placed her limp body on my childhood bed. Eddie rushed in and started with the obvious. With his portable blood pressure monitor, he discovered her pressure was 195/150. That was way above normal.

I swept the hairs away that were clinging around her clammy, rounded face so I could see her glorious features. Since she'd started finally gaining some weight she had filled out, no longer looking like a gaunt teenager, but a healthy young woman. It made her more beautiful.

* * *

"Eddie?" my quivering voice asked.

"Calm down, Stefan. It's going to take a few minutes for it to come back down. And if it doesn't, then we need to take her to the hospital."

This time when the machine beeped I breathed easier. 180/135 was an improvement, but not good enough in my eyes. Still, Stella hadn't woken up three minutes after she'd passed out.

A quick glance around the room showed everyone had followed us in. Even my aunt and my mother were there. Sitting on the bed, I had a better view of what was going on. Eddie was running the machine every minute. As it crept lower, Stella started to shift around. It was the longest five minutes of my life.

"Eddie, what are you doing?" I snarled when he took out his phone.

"I'm emailing her doctor. He's going to want to know about this."

"Stefan, how bad has her pregnancy been?" the timid voice of my aunt asked.

"It's been a mess from the beginning," I answered my aunt honestly, but I looked at my parents.

The words had just left my mouth when Stella opened her shimmering honey-brown eyes. However, I didn't expect her to react to me like she did. Her face screamed of being in pain. It was the same way I'd looked when I had entered military school.

When she started pushing me away, I thought I would die from the way my heart was breaking. Each of her words caused my

* * *

chest to heave. I thought I would fall apart when she said she was going home and leaving me. It took every ounce of control I could muster not to cry to her. What could have ever made her think I wanted out of our relationship?

When she explained about overhearing the phone calls, I knew what she had heard. She just misunderstood them. An introduction was definitely in order to help her see where she jumped to the wrong conclusion.

Once I introduced her to the rest of my family, she sighed and flushed red. The poor thing needed to know I wasn't in love with anyone but her. You could see how relieved she was when it sunk in.

Confused, I stared on as Annie connected the dots that explained why my two favorite women were so lonely. They had connected as children, and small twists of fate had pulled them apart, leaving neither one of them whole. Poor Annie had been a mess when her first best friend had been unreachable. From the way they both looked, they were at peace when the pieces of the puzzle had finally settled into place. There was no doubt in my mind; these two lost souls were going to be great friends again. Once all the misunderstandings were explained, Stella calmed and snuggled against me.

Soldier mode kicked in when my father started shooting off orders. We were used to that, so we scrambled off. My biggest issue was that I didn't want to be separated from Stella, even for a minute. Annie stopped me on my way out the door to the car to get our bags.

"Stefan, will she want me back as a friend?"

"Would you like that?" I smirked already knowing the answer.

* * *

"Very much."

"Okay, I'll talk to her. But, I'm sure she would want you back. You know, I never connected the dots when she told me about being so hurt after that summer that she refused to get to know anyone else." I eyed her with compassion. Like Stella, Annie had done the same thing.

When my task of collecting the bags was completed, I went to the one place I wanted to be, the one person I wanted to be with: in bed holding Stella.

The moment my mom entered the room carrying Stella's dinner, I stiffened, squeezing Stella closer to my chest. She wasn't going to stress her out again. She knew I was watching her closely. Stella stiffened also when she opened her eyes to see my mom. Looking to me for confirmation, I nodded that it was my mom and not my aunt.

Yeah, we were both shocked when my mother smiled at us. She hasn't given me a genuine smile since the trip to Virginia Beach. Eddie did one last reading before he left at my dad's request. Thankfully, Stella's blood pressure had crept down to 165/120, still high but headed in the right direction.

Stella and I chatted easily again, now that she knew the truth. Once dinner was done, everyone started coming in and out again. When my dad asked who would be sleeping where, I almost told him I wasn't leaving Stella's side, but Eddie came in and claimed the spot, stating his sister might need him. Michael and I just looked at my dad, who looked dumfounded, and we realized neither us had informed him of their connection.

After saying goodnight to Stella, it was time to explain

● ● ●

everything to everyone. One by one, we all followed Michael down into the living room. When everyone had claimed a seat I began the long-overdue conversation.

"Dad, Stella never knew her father. All she had was a picture her mother had from when he visited the beach. When we visited Michael last month, there was a picture of Eddie's father on the table. They're one in the same. He drove all night to meet her. Talk about a family resemblance; yeah, there was no denying it. When he saw his own eyes, he knew she was his. After the summer she met Annie, she'd never let anyone get close to her. Until I came along, that is. So when I was dragged away, she felt abandoned all over again."

"That's unbelievable. That poor thing grew up so lonely," my aunt surmised, looking at Annie.

"How did I misjudge her so badly?" my mom sobbed into her hands.

"We are both to blame when it comes to that mistake. We thought she was like the rest. Nevertheless, I'm the one who made such a mess of the whole thing. Maybe if . . . we could have . . . I am so sorry, Stefan." My dad held my mom close.

"Dad, I forgave you already. I know you didn't understand the depths of how Stella and I feel for each other." I smiled.

"We should have asked," my mom wept.

"Did we do this to her?"

Michael and I were already shaking our heads. "No, Dad, but the stress doesn't help. No more putting her through the wringer, not if you want them to bring your grandchildren for visits."

* * *

"Michael's right, the only reason I agreed to this is because Annie desperately wanted to throw her a baby shower on Sunday. If you can't keep the house stress free, I'm taking her home tomorrow," I informed everyone, my resolution firm.

"That won't be necessary. Stella and those babies are family. We take care of family. Right?" Everyone nodded with my dad.

"Speaking of the shower, who's going out shopping with me Friday at five a.m.?" Annie twittered.

"I'm in," laughed my aunt.

"Me, too. My grandchildren need . . . well, everything." My mom sighed.

"Do you know what they are?" Annie chirped.

"No, we don't know. They didn't want to cooperate at the ultrasound." I laughed, remembering how they kept turning away whenever we were close to seeing their sexes.

"So, we'll buy a little bit of everything," Annie hooted with a twinkle in her eyes.

"Me and Eddie already took care of our gifts, so if anyone even considers waking me up, you will pay dearly," Michael threatened. Coming from him, it was almost comical.

Slowly, everyone drifted off to their beds. I had to sleep with Michael. After we all called out our goodnights, I had a hard time sleeping. I missed Stella.

Stella's shrieks caused me to fall out of bed. Scrambling, I hurried down the hallway only to discover the screams were coming

* * *

from the bathroom. With my fist, I banged on the door.

"Stella! Open the door!"

"I can't! My water broke," she howled, panicked.

"Stefan, what's going on?" my dad growled.

"Stella's locked in the bathroom and her water broke. She sounds like she's in pain," I snarled and tried to jiggle the knob again.

"Look out!" my dad demanded, readying himself.

With a slam and a grunt, he broke open the door with his shoulder. I charged in and froze; Stella was lying on the floor of the tub. Quickly, I tossed her robe over her naked body before anyone else could see her.

"Stella, what happened?" I panted.

"My back was sore from the fall, so I thought a shower would make it feel better," she whimpered then whined, clutching her distended stomach.

"Stella, it wasn't from the fall. If you woke me, I would have checked you for back labor." Eddie dropped to his knees next to me.

I stroked her hair and looked up to see my dad on the phone with the paramedics. Stella released a gut wrenching scream just as he hung up.

"Breathe through it, Stella," Eddie ordered to her.

"The paramedics are on their way. How close is she?"

* * *

261

"Very close. Stefan, you need to look, see if you can see a head." Eddie nudged me.

"You're the med student." I gasped.

"And her brother." Oh right, too creepy!

One quick peep said it all. "I see black hair!"

"Stefan, you need to pull the baby out while I help Stella push." Eddie pulled her up, so she was seated almost upright. I slipped into the tub and knelt at her ankles.

"Stefan! Help! It hurts!" she screamed.

Everyone was in the hall pacing as Stella pushed when Eddie instructed her to. "Now, Stella, push!" he grunted with her.

"Ow. No — no — no. Get it out!" she growled.

"Stella, the head's out; you can do this." I couldn't believe what I was seeing. There, coated in film, was an angelic face with its eyes scrunched up tight.

"Now, Stella." Eddie demanded when a new contraction hit. She snarled as she gave it her all.

"That's my girl," I laughed with tears running down my cheeks.

"Twist and pull on the next push." Eddie nodded to me.

"You can do this, baby. One more time," I called over Stella's screams.

"Next time, you have the babies!" Stella roared.

● ● ●

"Deal. Now, push." I could hear my aunt leading the paramedics up the stairs.

"Oh my God!" Stella shrieked, pushing the tiny body out of hers and into my shaking hands. She slumped back and cried as the contractions slowed for the moment.

"Let us through, folks. Nice job. Let us finish up." Reluctantly, I handed over the child and got out of the tub.

"She's having twins?" the female paramedic asked.

"Yeah, they're five weeks early," Eddie answered when I couldn't.

The need to be close to Stella was overwhelming. "Eddie, let me help her with this one," I implored.

"You got it." He didn't hesitate to move for me.

"Stella, are you doing okay?" I asked as I watched the other paramedic clamp and sever the umbilical cord, separating my child from its mother before swaddling it in a thermo blanket.

"Yes. But, they're starting again." Her voice was now hoarse.

"Stella, my name's Arlene; when I say to push just do what you did before. Okay?"

"Yes," she moaned when a new contraction struck.

This time as she pushed, panted, and groaned I was there for her. I kissed her tear-soaked cheek when the second child slipped out. Sleepily, she glanced up at me.

"You did it, sweetie," I crooned.

* * *

"What are they?" she panted out.

"Twins girls, love. Twin girls." I hugged her against my chest sighing with her.

"Do they look like you?" she mumbled exhausted.

"Um, if you mean hair color, then yeah they look like me, but they have your beautiful features," I purred in her ear.

The paramedics had handed off my first daughter to me to show her to Stella while they finished up with the second one.

"See, she has your adorable button nose." She was going to be heartbreaker when she grew up; I could see that already.

Once they were both bundled up, I held the three of them while Arlene readied everything to go to the hospital. The other paramedic called in the firefighters that were waiting downstairs to bring up the gurney for transport. Eddie was on his phone calling Stella's parents so they could come up to meet their grandchildren.

Arlene pulled out two tiny oxygen masks for the twins. It was hard to miss that their lips had a bluish tint to them. With one twist, the portable oxygen tank started hissing. I smiled at Stella to keep her calm, but inside I was a mess. They were too early, and their lungs weren't fully developed. Without removing them from Stella's chest, the paramedic slipped on the masks and nodded to her partner.

The twins rested on Stella's chest until the time came to move her. My family tried to catch a peek at the new arrivals. When the time for them to remove Stella from the tub came, Army or not, I saw my dad wipe away a tear. My mother just bawled like everyone else. With the exception of the rescue personnel, it was a tear-fest.

● ● ●

It took four of the burly men to carry the gurney downstairs while we held the twins securely on the gurney tucked into Stella's side. I held her hand through the whole process. She would never leave me if I had anything to say about it. I knew at that moment that one day soon, she would be my wife.

* * *

Mocked By Destiny

• • •

Chapter Eighteen
Stella's a mommy

"STELLA?" I ROLLED OVER, WINCING TO SEE MY MOM coming through the doorway.

"Hey, Mom," I slurred from the pain medication.

"How are you feeling, sweetheart?" She gently joined me on the bed.

"Sore, but good. Where's Stefan?" I peeked around, to see that we were alone.

"Down at the nursery with your dad. The twins are so stunning. They look like a perfect mixture of you both." She beamed with pride in her eyes.

"They're a little small and need some help breathing, but

• • •

267

otherwise they're perfect." I grinned.

"I've wanted to talk to you about how I reacted to your pregnancy. I'm so sorry I turned my back on you when we found out. I guess I thought eventually you would see it my way and you wouldn't choose to go through what I did. It was stupid to think that way." I focused on the tears slipping down her cheeks. "I love you and them, even Stefan. You made the decision that was right for you, and I see that now. You and Stefan will be great parents. You were right about him; he's not like the rest."

"I know, Mom. He is different from everyone I have ever met. I knew that the moment I gazed into his eyes. I knew that day my life would change. I just didn't know how." I giggled.

"Mel is so proud you. He brags about you to everyone. The first time I met with him to talk about you, we spent hours in a coffee shop looking through Nana's albums. I just wish he had come into the shop the day he came back from Hawaii. He would have been there for you, and probably Brianna, if we had worked out."

"Eddie says you're seeing him again?" I said with a quirk of my eyebrow.

She laughed. "We are giving it another try. No guarantees, but you never know where life will lead you. This time, I'm going to let life take the reins."

"There's the mommy. Hi, sweetie." I giggled when Mel's chin stubble tickled my cheek.

"Hi, Dad. Is Stefan coming?"

"Yes, as soon as he grabs a wheelchair for you. He wants to

●　◉　●

268

take you down to see the babies. They're still on the machines to help their breathing."

"Ah, my lady. Your chariot awaits you." Stefan laughed as he pushed in the wheelchair.

Biting my lip, I glanced up to see my parents watching our every move as Stefan helped me from the bed to the chair with caution. My eyes ghosted shut as he stroked my cheek and kissed my lips. When he laughed, I knew it was because of the way my body reacted to him.

"Next stop: the nursery." He spun me around and pushed me out of the room.

"Mom, are Nana and Brianna coming?"

"As soon as they can. We didn't call them until a few hours ago. I was staying at Mel's when Eddie called." Did she just say she was having a sleepover with my dad? I was so not going there, not even with a ten foot pole. I wonder if the nurses will give my brain a sponge bath to wash away those pictures!

The nurses waved when we strolled by with my parents behind us. The nursery was only a short walk down the hall, so the reason for the wheelchair escaped me; that was, until we reached the glass window that looked into the nursery. A sharp gasp escaped my lips as my smile faded.

"Stefan?"

"Stella, calm down. They need extra attention, and they're very tiny." A tear slid down my cheek. I looked in to see my girls were not with the rest of the babies.

* * *

They were in a private room, a NICU room, their tiny bodies draped in nothing but a diaper so their IV's would be uninhibited. Hoses were taped over their quivering lips. The glow of the warming lamps shaded the twin's wrinkled skin a brighter shade of pink. They looked nothing like their plump, pale, clothed counterparts.

"This is entirely my fault," I sobbed as Stefan held me.

"No, Stella, you were not the only one in this equation. If I had run away earlier like I wanted to . . ." He whimpered into the crook of my neck.

"If I had told everyone the moment you called, we could have told the doctor about our family history. You would have never been under the stress you endured because we forced you two apart. This is my fault." Shirley grimaced from behind us.

"No, we kept them apart together, the blame falls on both our shoulders." Maurice cradled his wife.

"I didn't help either. I should have been there for you." Mel pulled my mom into his embrace.

"No, we should have been there for them." Eddie joined Mel in holding my mom.

"Give me a minute, and I'll think of something I did wrong." Michael pursed his lips in thought. "Nope, I'm coming up empty, so it must be all your faults." Thank God for Michael's sense of humor.

"Stella, they are doing okay, considering. I mean sure, right now, it looks like they are sickly. They're preemies, but you did manage to keep them in until they were 36 weeks and you did get them up to 4.7 pounds and 4.9 pounds. It could have been worse — a

● ● ●

lot worse." I sniffled and nodded into his shirt.

"Thanks to Stefan." I smiled at him.

"Come on, love, they need to be held. It's another form of warming; we hold them skin to skin." I had to admit I really wanted to snuggle with them.

The neonatal nurses, Lisa and Beth, greeted us with warm smiles when Stefan wheeled me in. Our first stop was Baby Girl Sterling #1's incubator. She was the largest and the first one born, making her three minutes older than her sister. After I opened my pink, fuzzy robe, Lisa placed the tiny being against my chest, careful not to tug on any of her tubing.

I stroked her black wisps on her head. "Hello, little one. I'm your mommy. So were you the puncher or the kicker?" I giggled, when she stretched her tiny frail legs into my cleavage, I knew she had been the kicker.

I watched Stefan opening his white button-down shirt a few buttons in preparation for his miniature snuggler. Baby Girl Sterling #2 was placed against Stefan's chest while he sat in the rocking chair next to me. Everyone outside had their faces pressed against the glass to watch us.

"So, do they have names yet?" Beth inquired, waving the name cards in the air.

"Stefan, are we still going with the ones we picked out?"

"Absolutely, love." Just then, baby number two stretched her hand up into his ear. "I guess that makes you the puncher." He chuckled.

* * *

271

"So, don't keep us waiting. What are their names?" Beth lifted her eyebrows in question.

"Adrianna and Alina Sterling," I answered, grinning.

Lisa hummed as she changed their nameplates. "In a few days you will be able to feed them, but for now the tubes are taking care of everything they need."

A knock on the glass caused us to look and see Annie and Charlotte were there, too. Annie waved for Beth to meet her at the door. When Beth came back, she was carrying two pink fleece blankets.

"Look what I have: their first presents." I mouthed my thank you to them.

I felt a little bad that they couldn't all come in and hold them, but there was too much of a chance of infection. While Lisa changed Adrianna's diaper, Stefan went out and hugged his cousin and aunt, giving them a proper thank-you. Once Adrianna was cleaned and loosely draped, Lisa held her in front of the window so everyone could take photos with their cell phones. I felt naked when Beth took Alina to do the same. Stefan was still outside when I noticed they were waving goodbye to me. He strolled back in, looking like the cat that ate the canary.

"Are they leaving?" I was saddened that I could not say a goodbye.

"They're going home to cook the turkey, but fear not, lass. They will be back with dinner for us both." He smirked when I gawked at his Irish brogue.

● ● ●

Smiling, I smacked my forehead with my palm. "Oh, I forgot, it's Thanksgiving," I prattled.

"Yeah, well, you were a little busy this morning." I looked up to see it was only nine in the morning.

For the next few hours, we went back and forth from the NICU, alternating which twin we held. We needed them both to feel our love for them. Stefan insisted I nap while he went out to buy us lunch.

I opened my eyes when I felt a familiar hand swiping a hair from my face.

"Nana," I sighed.

She grinned at me. "Yep, it's me. You really couldn't wait for me?"

"It wasn't me who couldn't wait," I snickered.

"Always so impatient, you are," she guffawed.

"That's me. Hey, Brianna." She nodded her head, our relationship still as stressed as ever.

"Where are they?" she enquired.

"They're in the NICU. They need to be on a ventilator for a few days." I chewed my lip waiting for a snide remark.

"But we can see them, right? They're going to be fine, right?" It was the first time Brianna seemed worried about her nieces.

"Yeah, they said the twins will be fine with a little extra care." My eyes snapped to the door as Stefan opened it and froze.

* * *

273

Stefan was not so willing to forgive her for her betrayal. He just needed more time. After all, if he could forgive his parents, then he could forgive her.

"Hi." She ducked her head down avoiding his glare.

"Nana, it's nice to see you. How was the drive?" Stefan refused to look at Brianna.

"Easie peasie." She waltzed up and hugged him. "Thanks for the directions."

"No problem; it was my pleasure. Brianna?"

"Congratulations." She shrugged and shifted uncomfortably between her feet.

"Thanks," he replied with his voice flat.

"Stella, after we eat we can take them down to see the twins." I could tell there was no room for a compromise.

The promise of seeing my babies again had me scarfing down my turkey and mashed potatoes. I wished I could have had the babies in my room for visits like every other mother in my ward. I just kept chanting in my head that it was only for a few days.

Stefan just shook his head and grinned when I finished before he did. That was a first for us. "Like I said: impatient," Nana cackled.

The sudden sounding of an alarm in the hall had Stefan dropping his food and his feet moving toward the door. When he flung the door open, the nurses were scrambling around the floor in a flurry. Several security guards sprinted by headed to the nursery. Stefan ran out of the room and followed them. As fast as I could, I

● ● ●

crawled out of the bed and limped toward the door. Nana and Brianna were right behind me. Before I could make it out of the room, Stefan rushed back in with a look of horror etched across his face.

"Stella, get back in bed and stay there. There is problem in the nursery."

"What kind of problem?" I whined, desperately seeking an answer.

"Stella, please, just do as I say. For once, don't push this," he growled.

"Stefan!" I faltered, causing Nana and Brianna to grab me and guide me to the floor.

Stefan rushed to my side to cradle me against him. "Stella, baby, please relax. It will be fine," he pleaded.

"No. Tell me," I cried.

"The maternity floor is under a lockdown. A distraught mother is in the nursery, refusing to relinquish the child she gave up for adoption. She signed him away to an adoption agency, and now that she had him, she wants to keep him." He held me as I sobbed.

"I want my babies!" I shrieked.

"Get back in bed, and I'll go see if they have gotten her out yet. Right now, there is nothing to worry about. When I followed the security guards, the NICU was sealed off so she couldn't get in." He kissed my cheek and helped me to my feet.

I prayed as he left that the mother was taken care of. I wanted

* * *

to see my babies with my own eyes, the pain of giving birth long forgotten as I worried about my children. After everything we had been through, I could not lose them now. Life or destiny couldn't be that cruel. Could it?

From the fear on Stefan's face when he reentered the room, it wasn't over yet. I had seen Stefan scared before, but this was beyond anything I had ever seen.

"The police are here now, but the nurses in the NICU called out to the nurse's station to tell us they were safely barricaded in there." He was trying to appease me, I could tell.

"What aren't you telling me?" I questioned.

"No one comes in, and no one goes out, until further notice." His grim expression was mirrored by everyone in the room.

The fear welled up in my chest as reality came crashing down on my shoulders. Stefan clutched onto me as I hyperventilated. One of the floor nurses came running in with a needle in her hand. Apparently, they knew I wouldn't react well to being told I couldn't see my children until the drama ended. I wouldn't have put it past Stefan to have been the one who warned them. I thrashed, trying to stop the nurse. With one prick of her needle, my resistance crumbled.

Numb from the shot, I laid my head against Stefan's chest, whimpering, while Nana called my mom. Brianna sat on the window ledge gnawing on her nails.

Stefan practically jumped out of his own skin when the door flew opened to expose us to the view of an officer in full garb.

"Sterling family?"

● ● ●

"Yes. Is the nursery cleared yet?" Stefan asked, with hope lacing his voice.

"No, not yet. Families with a baby in the nursery are being guarded."

"We see. I'm Stefan. This is Stella, the mother; her sister Brianna; and Marie, her grandmother." He pointed each of us out.

"Officer Kyle McAide." He nodded. "I'll be right in front of your door if you need me. I felt a little safer as he slipped out.

Stefan looked out the window and sighed when his phone vibrated. We all listened in as he told his family why they could not get in.

"Michael, relax. There is nothing we can do about it. Until they can get the baby safely away from the mother we're stuck," Stefan griped. "No Alina and Adrianna are safe in the NICU. They locked her out. The nurses had to give Stella a sedative. It could be hours before we can get to them," he grumbled. "Why don't you all go home, and I'll call when it's over."

"I know. Tell Stella's mom that Brianna and Nana are just fine. They are locked in our room with us. I don't want her to worry." He sighed, looking at the floor. "Sure, I'll give her the phone." He handed over the phone to Nana.

"Yeah . . . got it . . . no worries . . . at all costs." Nana nodded, pacing the room looking haggard.

"Yes, here's Brianna." She passed the phone.

"Of course, Mother. I'm not that stupid," Brianna snarled into the phone.

● ● ●

"Yeah, here's Stella." She pranced across the room, dropping the phone in my hands. Brianna rolled her eyes immaturely.

"Hi, Mom," I breathed.

"You okay?"

"No, I'm scared out of my mind. They gave me something to calm down," I muttered.

"From the amount of police cars down here, your ward must be flooded by the cops."

"Yeah, we saw quite a few run by." I sighed, thinking about how my infants needed me and I wasn't able to get to them.

"Your dad wants to talk to you." I heard her pass off the phone.

"Sweetheart, we'll be here when it's time to come back in." I grimaced.

"I know you will be. How's everyone down there handling it?"

"We're a mess. Eddie is about to tear my arm off, so tell him to relax."

"Stella, you good, little sister?" he babbled nervously.

"Yeah, we're all good, so relax. You will see us soon enough." My attention was drawn to Stefan and Nana, who were whispering in the corner animatedly.

"Eddie, we need to save the battery. We'll call you when we know something." I snapped the phone shut.

● ● ●

278

Stefan had a fire in his eyes I haven't seen since my nutritional issues came up. He was upset by whatever my grandmother had said to him. When he walked back over and crawled into my side, Nana pulled a chair over near the door and took a seat.

"Stella, your eyes are drooping. Please take a nap? I'll wake you if anything happens." He placed a soft kiss on each of my eyelids.

"He's right, Stella. You nap, and we'll wake you the second anything happens," Brianna droned from her perch on the windowsill.

I tried to fight the medication the nurse had given, but it was a fruitless venture as I listened to the beating of Stefan's heart. It had long since become my favorite sound in the world, each beat reminding me that he loved me. Each breath that filled his lungs provided the rocking motion that reminded me of the ocean's tide we had often watched. I slipped off to sleep seeing the innocent faces of my twins.

I don't know how long I slept, but the emptiness of my arms pulled me back to consciousness. Brianna, Nana, and Stefan were all watching out the window.

"Stefan?" I slurred from the medication.

"Hey, you. Well, it would appear that every news van in the state is taking up residence outside. Kyle says there is no change in the nursery. They're hoping she'll get too tired to continue, and then they can slip in when she's sleeping." He seemed more relaxed.

I rolled out of bed and started my trek to the window when he

● ● ●

moaned. Looking out the window, I could understand why, just not the reason behind it. "Why are they here?"

"I don't know. My dad doesn't have that much clout. I'm guessing a hostage situation this close to the Capital is making a few very important people nervous." That had never occurred to me.

"There's my dad." He pointed at him as if I couldn't recognize him.

"Who's he talking to?" My voice wavered.

"Kevin McKnight, one the guys he went through basic training with and longtime friend." Stefan wrapped his arm around my waist for support and comfort.

"Do you think he'll tell us what's going on?" I peeked up, hopeful.

"Yeah, we were watching the news for reports. This has turned into a big story, but he should be able to tell my dad more," Stefan explained, never taking his eyes off the scene below us.

When Maurice trotted over to the rest of the family, Stefan's phone went off. Instead of answering it, he put on speakerphone. "Good news, son. Kevin says they have orders to move as many as they can out of the ward. I explained our situation and he said he'll have the twins pulled out first since they need more medical care than anyone else. So far, two new babies have been born, and they need to be moved, too. Have everyone ready to move when they get there," Maurice instructed.

"Will do, Dad. Is there anything else I need to do?"

"No, just protect them until you're all out. We love you all;

● ● ●

be safe."

"We love you all, too. We'll see you soon." Stefan sounded calmer now that he knew the plan. Even after the clicking off the disconnecting phone, we continued stared at it.

"You heard the man. Let's get everything ready to run." He crossed the room in three strides and began throwing my toiletries into a teal plastic bag he had found underneath the sink.

● ● ●

Mocked By Destiny

Chapter Nineteen

Stefan's at all cost

FRANTICALLY, I PREPPED EVERYTHING FOR US TO LEAVE as quickly as possible. I could see the fear in Stella's eyes. I raced around the room, throwing her things into the plastic bag I had found. Calming her nerves would have to wait until I finished or we were out, whichever came first. We only had until the troops arrived before we would need to leave.

Nana had already told me of her backup plan, which needed to be avoided. She'd meant it when she said, "At all costs." It wasn't until after the call, that she filled me in on what the question was. Daisy had asked her to protect her four baby girls. Nana flat-out told me she would be the last to leave. Only when Brianna, Stella and our babies were safe, would she be willing to be rescued. What did she think she was going to do?

• • •

"Stefan? Please, I'm scared," Stella sniveled, trying to crawl from her bed.

"Stella, get back in bed until it's time. You need to save your strength for when we leave." I ushered her back to bed.

Nana took a shaking Brianna into her arms and held her, stroking her hair. With everything settled near the door, I curled up in the bed and cradled a trembling Stella to my side.

"Shush, I've got you, love. I will never leave you or the twins. We're a family, always and forever," I whispered for her benefit alone.

"I love you, Stefan. Nothing will change that, ever." She reached up and ghosted her palm across my cheek, causing me to lean into it.

"I love you, too, Stella. You're my angel, my resurrection, my savior, and one day you will be my wife," I vowed before I passionately kissed her in a heated exchange of unsaid promises.

Clutching her head, we breathlessly held our cheeks together and waited for the world to right itself.

It wasn't long before a sound I knew very well echoed down the hallways outside. There's no mistaking the sound of Army boots sounding off against the flooring. I had grown up hearing that sound every day.

Stella yelped and cowered into my embrace when the door flew open, exposing us to a soldier in full camouflage fatigues. The determined look etched on his face reflected the seriousness of the situation at hand.

* * *

"Stefan Sterling?"

"Yeah, that's me." I unlatched Stella's death grip on me so I could slide out to meet him properly.

"My name is Sergeant Christopher. My team is moving on the nursery now. It will be a few minutes before we can move you. Reports have it that the distraught mother may be dealt with quicker than anticipated." His deep voice echoed his authority even though he never raised it.

I was about to ask him how long it would be but his radio went off and he excused himself to talk to his troops outside. Spinning around, the sight of Stella sitting up drew me back to her bedside.

"Not yet, sweetheart; soon, but not yet. They are analyzing the situation before we can move." I caressed her cheek with the backside of my fingers.

"Promise me they'll be fine," she begged in a whisper.

"I will do everything I can to see them safely back in our arms," I vowed, holding her as close as I could.

There was no close enough when it came to holding Stella. If I could, I would crawl under her skin and stay there forever. From the way she gripped me, I would say she felt the same. The minutes clicked by on the clock on the wall overhead. There was an eerie silence hanging over our room while we awaited the news of our twins' fate. Our eyes snapped to the door when we heard the approaching footsteps.

This time, when the door opened, Stella stayed quiet. When

* * *

she glanced at the door, a smile like none other crept across her face. Lisa and Beth were ushered in, pushing the two incubators that housed the twins. A group sigh reverberated throughout the room as the tiny twosome joined us in Stella's hospital room.

"Relax, everyone. We kept them safe. We need to plug in their incubators. Right now they're on battery backup, but it won't last forever." Lisa went straight for the wall with all the electrical outlets on it.

"Give us a minute, and then you can hold them. Okay?" Beth smiled on her way by.

Stella couldn't wait, and by the time the nurses were done, she was already underway to retrieve the precious cargo she desperately wanted to hold. I was right next to her, helping her in that endeavor. I will admit it; I wanted nothing more than to hold them, too.

Peeking into the plastic enclosures, it was evident the twins were unaffected by the whole ordeal. Of course, it wasn't over yet. We were still trapped here, but at least we were together.

There was no stopping Stella when she reached in and grasped Alina. Seeing her in Stella's arms, I took stock of just how tiny and fragile she truly was. Even stretching, she measured shorter than Stella's forearm. For the first time, Alina opened her pretty gray eyes and gazed at her mother. You could see she knew and loved her already.

A light laugh escaped me when I retrieved Adrianna from her bed as well. She, too, was tinier than I remembered. Careful not to tug on her hoses, I pulled her close to my chest, humming to her. This was Nana's first chance to meet our bundle of joy and newest

* * *

family member. Looking over my shoulder, I watched her caressing the black fuzz on Adrianna's soft spot.

"She's beautiful," she gushed, smiling. Carefully, I passed Adrianna to her. "Such a petite thing, isn't she?"

I nodded and watched Brianna kneeling at Stella's feet, admiring her niece as Alina rested on her mother's chest. When Brianna started singing to them, I felt a tear slip down my cheek. I had never known she could sing so beautifully.

You could feel every emotion in every tone as she serenaded Alina. Her love could be felt by everyone in the room. Stella's eyes fluttered shut as she listened to her sister declare her love for her family. The words were not from any song I had ever heard. Either she sang from her heart, or she had written the song.

The exchange between the women was undeniable. Brianna was forgiven, and Stella was pleased that the dispute was in the past. When Brianna finished her soulful apology, Stella relinquished Alina to Brianna. With a smile gracing her lips, Stella made her way over to Nana and me. Nana sighed when Stella placed a loving kiss upon her cheek.

My attention shifted focus when the door opened again. This time it was the Sergeant again. Moving closer gave him the chance to fill me in alone. "We need you to stay here a while longer. The floor is still under siege."

"When will we be able to leave?" I whispered, hoping Stella wouldn't hear me.

"As soon as the mother is restrained. Everyone else has been removed, but our delay in moving the twins caused us to miss the

* * *

opportunity to leave when the window was still open."

"What do you mean?" My gut feeling being this wasn't going the way they'd hoped.

"The mother is no longer in the nursery. She is hiding somewhere on the floor." His attention seemed distracted.

When I looked at the door, I understood why. There in the doorway stood a manic looking, ash-brunette haired, young woman holding an infant to her chest. The disturbing part was that in her other hand she held a gun. Everyone in the room froze. A pin dropping would have sounded like a piano plummeting forty feet to the ground.

"No one move. I don't want to do this," the young mother threatened.

When the sergeant twitched toward his sidearm, she started shaking the gun in our direction. Protectively, I made one step to my right to block Stella from her view.

"I said, don't move!" she shrieked at me more than anyone else.

"I won't, but you need to understand I will protect my family if you attempt to harm them in any way." She nodded, no doubt thinking about the extremes she had gone to in order to protect her cherished child.

"He's hungry," she muttered, bouncing the whining blue bundle.

"We have formula, if I may?" Nana called to get her attention away from the rest of us.

* * *

"Put the baby down, and get it." She wagged the gun around again.

Nana just nodded and passed Adrianna off to Beth. If I didn't know better, I would have thought it was just an old woman offering help, but I did know better. She had already told me that if cornered, she would sacrifice herself before any member of her family would be hurt.

Holding my breath, I waited to see where she was headed with this. Behind the gun-toting kidnapper, the troops were lining themselves up. This was not where I wanted my family trapped. One stray shot, and I could lose any member of my family.

Nana saw what I saw, but she kept mum, moving toward the supplies under the incubators. With a nipple and a bottle of formula in hand, she inched over to the distraught mom.

After fastening the top on, she stretched out the hand holding the offering just short of reaching the now wailing infant. The mother was left with a dilemma. She couldn't hold all three: the gun, the baby, and the bottle. This must have been Nana's plan all along.

She gnawed her lip while she decided what her best options were. You could see the gears in her mind working as she decided on a solution. The grin adorning her chapped lips suggested she had a plan. Taking one step forward, she raised the gun until it was aimed at Nana's chest. Everyone in the room wore different versions of the same shocked expression; that is, except for Nana. She seemed to have expected it.

From the corner of my eye, I saw the twitch of the Sergeant's fingers around his own gun. There was no way this was going to end with a happily ever after. Something had to be done. The question

* * *

was what?

"Feed him, but I swear if you make one wrong move, I will not hesitate," the girl ordered.

"Sure thing, sweetie," Nana purred.

The mother paused and then passed the child off. Her mistake was she never looked around before she gave up the only thing that was keeping her safe. Now there was nothing to keep them from ending her.

In a flash, the Sergeant's gun was out of its holster and aimed at the girl who had wreaked havoc on the floor. She saw his sudden movement, too, and before anyone could breathe, almost simultaneously a flash rushed out of the barrels of both handguns.

Everything moved in slow motion as the ending played out. The soldier's military training gave him the quicker response time. Even if it was just by a hair, it was more than enough. The young girl jerked and staggered backward toward the bed Stella had been in. When her back impacted with the metal frame, her aim jerked away from Nana. A twitch of her finger was enough to set her gun off. Stella's screams drew my attention to her bewildered face. Actually, everyone was staring at me with the same expression.

With my eyes locked on Stella's, my knees buckled. A sudden searing pain radiated from my stomach. Looking down, I found my hands were clutching my shirt. When I released my grip, my hands were already soaked in blood. My head snapped up to see Stella screaming and charging over to me just before I slumped over into her arms.

"Stella!" I roared as the pain washed over me.

● ● ●

"Stefan! No! You promised!" She clutched me closer to her chest, shaking me.

"I — love — you," I choked out.

"I love you, too," she cried into my neck while she held me.

"Don't let me go," I begged as everything went black.

* * *

• • •

Chapter Twenty

Stella's not letting go

"DON'T YOU LEAVE ME!" I SHRIEKED AND SHOOK Stefan's unconscious body lying on my lap.

"Please, baby? I need you." I sobbed, clutching his head to my chest.

"Miss, you need to let him go. We need to try to help him." I looked up to see the man I held responsible for this mess.

"You did this! You just had to shoot. Why couldn't you wait?" I howled with no embarrassment.

"You need to let him go," Beth pleaded, very concerned.

* * *

"I'll never let go, Stefan!" I kicked and screamed when they dragged him away from me.

The weeping of Nana and Brianna barely registered as I watched the nurses work on Stefan. The soldier holding me back was too strong for me to fight off — I knew; I'd tried. No amount of struggling would allow me to break free.

My own pain was irrelevant and forgotten. Stefan was all that mattered. The room suddenly filled with more nurses, doctors, and soldiers, everyone concentrating on him. I was released when they rushed him out of my reach. Slumping to the floor and pulling my knees into my chest, I rocked back and forth.

It wasn't until I looked the room over that I saw the rest of the horror of what had happened. The girl laying just feet from where I sat couldn't have been much older than me, but now she would never age. She had a son who now had no mother. I couldn't help but wonder what had pushed her to such extremes.

The once-white floor was now covered in puddles of crimson that made moving around for the rescuers difficult at best. Even as the zippering sound echoed throughout the room, all I could think of was that it could have been me.

If someone had tried to take my children away, I would have fought back. Though I would like to think I would've done it differently, there was no way to know. The young mind of a hormonal teenager is a scary place, even more so when there are pregnancy hormones and another life involved.

You could not deny that the way she had gone about retrieving her son was wrong, even if it had been for a good reason. In her moment of desperation, she had torn my family apart. Why

● ● ●

was it that no one ever saw the bigger picture? When you lashed out, it's not just you that got hurt. With one wrong decision, an innocent person had to pay for your choices.

My body quaked as Lisa rushed up and tried to comfort me. There was no comfort anyone could provide, except for Stefan. He was always the one who kept me sane when I went off the rails. I needed him, plain and simple.

Shifting through the multiple conversations, I found what I was searching for, the reason she'd snapped.

"Yes, sir. She used a syringe to get the gun away from the security guard," announced a Private.

"Apparently, the father broke things off as soon as her signature hit the paper," a nurse whispered.

"He laughed at her naivety when he stalked away. He even told her the only reason he had stayed with her was to get her to sign the baby away. That was cruel," another nurse replied.

"Postpartum depression is the official diagnosis," a doctor answered an interviewing detective.

As my brain connected the dots, I shivered. The catalyst was the cruel behavior of a teenager who didn't want to be a father. The mother had had her emotions toyed with until she didn't know up from down. The father should have been charged with cruel and indecent behavior, in my opinion.

Together, Lisa and I staggered out of the room so they could handle the girl who had shot Stefan. Looking over my shoulder, I saw that Brianna and Nana were still crying as they deposited the

* * *

twins back into their incubators so they could be moved with me.

The staff moved me to another room five doors down. With the incubators plugged in again, they ushered me numbly into a running shower to wash off Stefan's blood. I hadn't even been aware of the fact that I had been covered in it. The shaking of my body was so bad, I couldn't even wash or dry myself. I just stood there quivering from head to toe as I cried Stefan's name. A new nurse fumbled with my cleansing, but all the sensations of my body were gone. Nothing touching me registered in my mind while I was washed, dried, dressed, and brushed. She could have thrown me to the floor, and it wouldn't have broken through my haze.

When we left the bathroom, Brianna rushed up and embraced me. She was still crying. "Mom's on her way up with Mel and Eddie. Stefan's family is waiting by the OR for any news from the surgeons. They said it could take a while before they know anything," she rattled, still pumped full of adrenalin.

"I need to be there. I can't do this without him," I wept into her shoulder.

"We'll get you there." I looked up to see Eddie, with my parents right behind him.

"Eddie!" I collapsed in his arms as visions of Stefan forced me to focus once again.

"Stefan will fight for you; you know that." I knew, but it wasn't a consolation to me.

All of my family converged together as we held each other, even Brianna. Knowing the twins were safe now, all I wanted to do was go to the OR and wait for news about Stefan.

● ● ●

"Eddie, will you take me to him?" He scanned the room to see if anyone would object.

"Yeah, I can do that for you. Everyone will sit with the girls." I nodded and accepted his arm to steady myself.

No one batted an eyelash when we made our way through the halls to where the doctors were operating on Stefan. The last hall that led to the waiting room seemed to get longer as we walked it slowly. When we entered the waiting room, everyone jumped to their feet. Michael was the first to approach me, with everyone watching for my reaction.

The tears were falling from my eyes before he reached for me. Pulling me close, we both fell apart. "Why? He never hurt anyone," I gurgled.

"He'll make it. We just have to have faith in him to pull through. Destiny may mock us sometimes, but it's never cruel enough to destroy a love so pure." I sighed at Michael's wisdom.

I knew from the gentle stoking of my hair that Annie had joined us in the middle of the room. One by one, the whole family gathered around. For the second time in an hour, I was at the center of a tight-knit group hug.

The buckling of my knees brought it to a quick end. Maurice led me to an armchair near the door. He surprised me by sitting next to me and holding my hand. Old softy. Sure he looked tough, but all fathers can't keep up the appearance of being tough when it comes to their children.

The seconds stretched into minutes and then into hours as we waited for some sign of what the outcome would be. Finally, two doctors came through the operating room doors. Maurice grasped my elbow, helping me stand. Holding my breath, I waited as they strolled our way.

"Sterling family?" the lead doctor asked.

"Yes." Maurice's voice sounded soft and insecure for the first time since I'd met him.

"Stefan's going to be just fine." Both doctors grinned.

"That's great news. Thank you so much." Maurice vigorously shook both their hands smiling.

Everyone started laughing and hugging, except for me. There was only one thing I wanted to know. "When can I see him?" I pleaded.

"He's in recovery. We had a hard time stopping the bleeding. The bullet bounced around a bit, but missed all his vital organs. You should be able to see him in a few hours." I heaved a sigh of relief, collapsing back into my seat.

My presence felt like an intrusion on their celebration; they were his family after all. Without a sound, I slipped out of my chair and scurried back down the hall. Before I could escape, I heard my named called.

"Stella, where do you think you're going?" I found myself face to face with Shirley.

"I was just giving you guys a little space." I gestured toward the elevators.

"Why would you do that? You're family and you belong with

● ● ●

us. Stefan is going to be asking for you when he wakes up. You wouldn't want him disappointed. Would you?" Before I could say no, she grabbed my hand and dragged me back to the fold.

"Stella, if you're worried about the twins, Michael and I can go sit with you for a while." Eddie's strong grip on my shoulder caught me by surprise.

"Yeah, I'd like to see them and tell them their daddy is going to be fine."

"Why don't we all go? The doctor said it would be hours before we could see Stefan. We'll be back before he's awake." I smiled at Michael in response.

Our motley crew headed upstairs to spend our restless hours with the twins. My family was pacing when we arrived. Mel was the first to rush across the room.

"He's out of surgery and in recovery. He's going to be fine," I giggled when my dad smothered me.

"That's wonderful!" Like with Stefan's family, everyone laughed and hugged, but now they included both our families.

Once they released me, my first stop was the incubator of Adrianna. With caution, I removed her and cradled her close to my chest. "Daddy's going to be fine, baby girl. He'll come see you as soon as he can," I fussed over her. This process was repeated for Alina also.

For the next hour, everyone sterilized and prepped to hold the two little critters Stefan and I had created. Everyone took turns adoring the two tiny beings that wouldn't wait to join the world. We

● ● ●

filled in Stefan's family on everything that had happened. It was agreed my family would stay with the babies so I could go with Stefan's family to wait for him to wake up.

He was still out when we arrived at his room. I was the first one to enter his room, and it broke my heart to see him lying there with the same tubing that the twins had. Sitting in the chair next to the bed, I intertwined our fingers, gazing at his angelic features. He looked like he was sleeping instead of just coming out of surgery.

I held his hand to my cheek, sighing. I needed to be close to him, to feel him. Leaning in, I placed my head on top of our hands, laid them on his sheets, and closed my eyes. Somewhere in the middle of my visit, I drifted off.

A shifting in the bed caused my eyes to snap open just in time to see Stefan opening his, too. Even though his eyes were glazed over from the morphine drip, you could see the love there when he gazed down at me. At that moment, I couldn't deny his devotion to me and mine to him. One sweep of his thumb across my cheek was enough to bring a smile to my face.

"You didn't let me go," he said in barely a whisper.

"Never," I breathed across his hand before I kissed and nuzzled it.

The staff must have been monitoring him from the station outside because a nurse came rushing in to check on him. With a smile gracing her face, she slipped back out without a word.

"Stefan, I need to let your family in now. They've been waiting to see you. I'll be right outside if you need me," I whispered into his ear.

* * *

"I always need you," he grunted softly.

"Me too." I kissed his forehead before backing away.

An ache erupted in my chest as I pulled the door open. He nodded when I peeked over my shoulder for confirmation that he was all right with me leaving.

Maurice and Shirley looked up from the nurse with relieved smiles playing on their lips. Rushing up, they stopped long enough to hug me quickly before they disappeared into Stefan's room.

"Stella, are you okay?"

"Yeah, Michael. I am now. It's going to take a while for everyone to visit him, so I think I should go be with the girls." He nodded his understanding.

When I arrived back, everyone was already celebrating the news about Stefan. It should have been no surprise that Eddie would call them the minute I entered the elevator. The girls were now back in the NICU room, so that was my destination. An hour later, I went back to Stefan's room. My visit lasted until his eyes drifted shut again, then I headed for my room.

The next day, I was officially checked out, but I never left. When Stefan was sleeping, I would be in the NICU, and at night, the nurses overlooked my sleeping in his chair. That's how I spent the next few days. Thanks to Eddie bringing me my clothes and my showering in Stefan's room, the days flew by, and next thing I knew, it was Sunday.

"Stella, you have to go home for Sunday dinner," Stefan demanded.

* * *

"No, I'll eat here with you, then I'll go feed the girls," I pushed back.

"No, Eddie will be here to get you any minute, and you will go. There is no room for negotiation on this." He eyed me sternly.

"Why are you trying to get rid of me? Do you have something going on with the nursing staff?" I snipped, feeling hurt that he wanted me gone.

"Oh, yeah, Nurse Liz and I have a whole steamy affair going on," he mocked, taken aback.

"Fine, whatever you say," I snapped, storming out.

When Eddie pulled up, I was waiting by the curb. He knew better than ask me what was wrong. By the time we reached the house, I was still fuming over the spat Stefan and I'd had. Stomping my way in, I burst through the door, looking more like a bull than a human being. The only thing missing was steaming coming out of my nostrils.

I couldn't hide the shocked expression on my face when I looked up to see the living room decked out in everything pink. Even though I smiled, I groaned too low for anyone to hear.

Annie was nice enough to introduce me to the friends and neighbors that Shirley had invited. After she explained that this was the reason Stefan agreed to come home for Thanksgiving in the first place, my anger had dissipated. How could I be mad at him after he had gone through so much to show us off to his side of their family? Yeah, I couldn't.

For him, I would endure anything, even his family without

● ● ●

him. It was actually quite a nice way to spend a few hours. The hospital had started to wear me thin, not that I would have admitted it to him.

While there, I took a few moments to email our teachers and tell them of the recent events. We would have to make up the work we'd missed, but as long as we made it back before finals, we wouldn't have to retake the classes from the term.

No words were spoken when I slipped into his bed upon arriving back at the hospital. He, as always, held me while I snuggled into his chest until he drifted off to sleep.

Mocked By Destiny

Chapter Twenty-One

Celebrations and confusions

Stella

I COULDN'T STOP THE GIDDINESS I FELT WHEN, FIVE days after their birth, the twins were released from the NICU room. Finally, I could hold, feed, and change them for myself. It was slightly disheartening doing it without Stefan being there, but there would be other times when he could be with us.

The NICU had been abuzz all morning, with the nurses and doctors checking and rechecking every one of the twin's test results. With the last few seconds ticking away, the countdown to their freedom began. Annie was supposed to be there with me since Stefan couldn't be, but she had yet to show. Pacing the room, I fidgeted with

● ● ●

everything in reach. My nervous hands need something to do, and at this rate my shirt would have holes in it from where I kept tugging at it. The nurses smiled at my jumpiness from the anticipation.

"Miss me, love?" I spun on my heels to see Stefan being wheeled in by none other than Annie.

"Stefan!" I twittered and did my best to leap into his lap.

"Easy does it," he chuckled.

"I'm sorry. I just miss seeing you out of bed," I laughed, snuggling for a moment.

"And I miss seeing you in bed." His wiggling eyebrows earned him a hand swat and caused a whole new set of chortles.

"It's time," Doctor Lewis called when he entered the NICU.

With shaking hands, I slid off Stefan's wheelchair. With care, Stefan struggled to stand with me. I melted against his side when he wrapped his arms around me. At that moment, I couldn't think of a better place to be than with the girls and their daddy. Together we leaned on each other to help the twins to freedom. Wrapping my arms around my chest, I tried to keep myself together. The last thing the room needed was me falling apart from over-excited hormones. My lip quivered when they started readying Alina.

I winced when they started to remove the tape from Alina's mouth. Her delicate pink flesh flaked off with the adhesive that held the tubing in her tiny mouth. For the first time since she'd arrived, her musical wail reverberated through the room. Against my will, my tears of happiness started falling. Stefan wiped away my tears of relief, and I did the same for him.

* * *

The sound of each of her breaths was music to my ears. Mesmerized, I watched her tiny breast rise and fall on its own. It was one thing to know that it happened because of the machines, and another to know she was doing it of her own accord. She did do it, even if it was labored; those pants were the most amazing thing to see.

Struggling, she tried to pull her hand away when the nurse removed her IV. It tore at my heartstrings when she screeched again. She really didn't like them fussing with her tubing.

Once the IV's were removed, the time had come. My tears were still falling when Doctor Lewis handed Alina to me to hold. I couldn't stop my hands from trembling when she finally made it into my longing embrace. Holding her close, I snuggled and sniffed her. She had that wonderful baby smell, a perfect mix between baby powder and the fresh air after a cleansing rain.

Kissing her forehead, I breathed her name, "Alina."

Glancing up, I noticed Stefan struggling to stifle his own happy tears. Grinning, Stefan cradled us together. He lifted her tiny hand to his lips, kissing the Band-Aid covering her IV mark.

We watched anxiously while Doctor Lewis did the same for Adrianna. This time when the doctor tried to pass us Adrianna, I insisted Stefan sit and hold Alina. He wouldn't admit it, but I could feel his legs shaking beneath him. With Stefan seated again, I received my next joyous bundle. Taking the time to memorize every nuance of her, like before I held her close, smelled her, and introduced myself again.

Her steely eyes snapped open at the sound of me whispering her name. You could see she knew who her mommy was. I carried

* * *

Adrianna to Stefan to hold. If he were a peacock, his feathers would have been fully erect with pride.

The slight sadness I felt about my parents not being there couldn't put a damper on the day. I understood that they need to get home for work. Now that everyone was out of danger, there really wasn't any need for them to stay.

A flash overhead caused both of us to snap our heads up to see a beaming Annie with a camera clutched in her hands. "Hey, you need a first family photo for their albums." She shrugged, looking quite pleased with herself.

"You could have warned me you know. I could have primped myself up. Now, I'm going to scare everyone," I griped.

"You don't need primping; you're perfect," Stefan purred to me.

"Right, like there's ever been a line of suitors looking at me," I scoffed.

"That's because they all know you belong to me." He laughed, cocking his eyebrow.

Our family was now whole again. We could love them the way they needed to be loved. They would never want for anything. We took advantage of every moment with them. The Sterling clan arrived in a flurry of activity. The girls were well doted upon by his family. Everyone took their turn holding the little ones. With all the pictures that were snapped, we'd have no problem filling two photo albums.

A nurse from Stefan's ward came looking for him an hour

● ● ●

into our celebration. He tried to fight her, but we all knew he would lose that fight. By dinnertime, I had returned to Stefan's room, expecting to see him eating his dinner. What I didn't expect was to walk in on a family discussion with his parents. Still hidden behind the drawn curtain, I found myself listening to their conversation.

"Stefan, are you going back to Virginia Beach once you're released?"

"Mom, yes, for the last time. I'm going back to Norfolk at least until Christmas, and then we'll see what happens." There was something in the way he sighed at the end that irked me.

"Relax, son, we're onboard with your plan. We're just checking that you haven't changed your mind," Maurice whispered.

"No, I haven't changed my mind. I just don't know how she is going to react, that's all," Stefan whined softly.

It didn't sound like he really wanted to go back. Keeping my distance, I slipped back out into the hall before they noticed me. I know he said all the wonderful things I wanted to hear, but I just kept wondering about what Savanna had once said to me. Had I really forced him to want this? Would he be happier somewhere else? With someone else? What was he planning on doing?

All my old fears and doubts came rushing back. Still lost in thought, I made my way back to the nursery. I was surprised to see that Doctor Lewis had come back into the nursery. After his new examination of the girls, he decided that the twins would be ready to be released on Thursday. So many things rushed through my mind all at once. I didn't even know where to begin trying to figure out what had happened.

* * *

For the next two days, I kept my feelings and worries to myself. Stefan had asked more than once what was wrong. I couldn't explain my sudden mood swings to myself, never mind to him. For some unknown reason, I kept the fact that the doctor had set a release date secret.

Therefore, on Thursday morning as scheduled, I wrapped the girls up in their new pink buntings and settled them into their carriers all on my own. Without a word to anyone, I slipped out the front doors of the hospital with the filled carriers and the overloaded diaper bags that the nurses had given me.

Without thinking, I jumped into the first cab that stopped. I slipped away with no destination in mind. Slumping into the seat of the cab, I felt the warm, salty tears falling from my eyes. I cried for everything: my lost childhood, my children, and the aching that I felt whenever I thought about Stefan. I knew the cab driver was watching me, but at that moment, I really didn't care what he thought.

"Where to, hun?"

"Anywhere but here," I sighed.

Using my last $20.00, I made it to the bus station. Once the cab pulled away, I sat on the nearest cold, metal bench. Running away was the last thing I wanted to do. So why was I there?

It didn't take long before the girls started crying. Sighing heavily, I gathered up my stuff and headed for the restroom. Teary eyed, I changed each of their wet diapers and fed them each a bottle of formula. Still they weren't happy. Burping and bouncing had no effect on them, either. I couldn't understand it. I had done everything the nurses had told me to, but still the three of us cried as if we were hurting. I knew what caused my pain, yet the girls cried, too. Could

● ● ●

310

they be feeling the same thing I was? Did they miss their daddy, too? I buried my face in my hands. The harsh reality hit me, I couldn't do this alone. Scrambling to my feet, I lugged everything back outside.

Using the last of the loose change in my pocket, I called the hospital. I was shocked to hear that Stefan had been released. They hadn't been planning on releasing him for another two days. Slamming the receiver down on to its cradle, I shrieked. Slumping against the glass door of the phone booth, I slid down onto the rain-soaked floor. I gave up fighting it anymore. Misery could have me.

◊ ◊ ◊

Stefan

"No! What do you mean they're gone?" My screaming started my stomach aching. Not from the gunshot wound, but from hearing my family had disappeared.

"We'll find them, Stefan. You need to relax." My father's stern tone did nothing to calm me.

"Get me released, now! If I wasn't in this stupid bed, this wouldn't be happening," I seethed.

"We'll talk to the doctor." Eddie and Michael raced off to do my bidding.

"Mom, get me my clothes." I probably shouldn't have growled at her.

By the time Eddie and Michael returned, I was dressed and

ready to run from my room. Okay, so running was out of the question, but the sentiment was there. The nurses all wore a bewildered expression when I reached the nursery. None of them knew why Stella hadn't told me they were being discharged today. They had assumed she had told me, since she had known for two days about it.

"Doctor Lewis?" I could see in his eyes that he felt terrible about what had happened.

His sympathetic eyes said it all. "Don't blame her, Stefan. I think she is confused by a mild form of Post-Partum Depression. I noticed a change in her after the twins came off their ventilators. I didn't mention it, because she seemed to be dealing with it with your help. Now, it's apparent I should have brought this up sooner."

"Will she hurt them?" my mom queried, grabbing my father's hand.

"No, Mrs. Sterling. She's not violent. She just seems unsure of where she belongs." Beth's words flipped a switch in my mind. I had done it again; I had missed the obvious.

Slamming my fists against the countertop, I lashed out. "Because her whole life, she never knew where she belonged. Her life was always about being left behind. Now she thinks I'm going to do the same?"

"Probably; that would be my guess." I nodded in agreement with the doctor.

Clenching my eyes shut, I tugged at my hair in frustration, sighing. "I'll show her where she belongs, and who she belongs with." That had been my plan along anyway.

● ● ●

"She was spotted leaving in a cab by the surveillance cameras. She could be anywhere by now." My mother huffed.

"No, she only had the twenty bucks I gave her for food. That won't get her very far," I concluded.

The way my father headed for the door I knew he had an idea of where to start looking. We split up; I went with my parents, and Eddie and Michael were in Eddie's Charger. Separately, we started combing around the hospital, then we fanned out in a spiral. Staring out the window of my dad's black Cadillac Deville, my eyes swept the streets and alleys. Even in the pouring rain, I would know her the moment she came into view. How could you miss a young woman lugging two infant carriers?

By dinnertime, my fears had doubled when we had failed to find her. Reluctantly, we made our way back to my parent's house. Annie and my aunt wanted to join us in searching for them, but I begged them to stay at the house in case Stella showed up or called.

Storming in, I demanded to know if they had heard from her. "Any word?"

Wearing a desolate expression Annie shook her head. Looking around at all the baby gifts sitting on the dining room table started a new fury in my chest. Picking up and rubbing one of the pastel pink fleece blankets against my face, I thought of how soft the twins were, how fragile their skin was.

Forgoing the food that was offered to me, I decided I couldn't sit there and wait. I needed to be doing something to bring them home to me. A few pain meds later and I was itching to head out again. Pacing the living room wouldn't bring them home to us. I needed to be in the city looking for them. They required my

● ● ●

313

protection in the harsh, cold world.

"I'm going back out to look for them. I can't sit here waiting anymore." Eddie and Michael agreed with me.

The three of us headed for the door, not even bothering to grab our coats. I opened the door and froze in my tracks. A cab had pulled into the driveway. There was only one reason someone would take a cab here. It had to be her. My feet pulled me of their own accord, unable to wait.

Even with the rain running down my face, I could see Stella. Moving at a painful pace, I made my way toward the cab door. To my relief, she leapt out and ran straight for me before I had made it three feet. With every ounce of strength I had left, I grabbed hold of her, latching her to my chest in a desperate grasp.

"Don't ever leave me again," I barked into her hair.

"I won't." She grimaced, grasping me tighter.

I refused to release her when my dad walked past us to pay the cab driver. Even when he ran back lugging the carriers; we stayed locked together in the rain. When she finally looked up, I couldn't resist the urge to kiss her with every feeling I had for her. It was something I hadn't done enough of lately.

I poured every ounce of love I had for her — not the girls, just her — into every movement of my lips, swirl of my tongue, and heartfelt moan I let escape. She needed to know I loved her, not just the children. The last few months had been about the twins and not about us. We needed to get back to a place where we mattered just as much as the girls did.

● ● ●

Looking back at the last few months, even though I'd told her how I felt, I had failed to show her. With the exception of the Halloween fight, I had perceived our relationship as being solid since I had told her all the little things that I had noticed were missing. But they were just words to Stella. She needed proof of love; the little things that would show her I loved her, the tender caresses, the make-out sessions, and the worshiping of her body, not her stomach. How could she truly know how much I loved her, if I didn't show her?

"Let's get you inside. You must be starving, my love." I pulled away from her lips. Snuggling my face into her rain-soaked hair; I peppered her neck and ear in sweet kisses.

"But . . ." Before she could fight me again, I cupped her face and kissed her lips again. I had missed kissing them like this. I reveled in the feel of her lips moving against mine in a fiery tango that set my heart racing out of control.

Pulling back one last time, I spoke from my heart. "No more buts. You're home, and that's all I care about. When will you see how much I love and need you?" I breathed.

"If you keep kissing me like that, I just might believe you," she moaned.

"Deal. Now it's time to get you inside." This time she didn't fight when I led her away by the hand.

Everyone sighed in relief when she nervously walked in behind me. Using my body for coverage, she refused to let the family see the shame she felt. No one said a word to her about her missing hours; instead, everyone tended to her needs for a change. For the last week, everyone had been focused on the early delivery of the girls and the shooting. That would change from this point on. It

* * *

would be my new mission in life. She would never have to wonder again if I loved her.

I couldn't take my eyes off her for the rest of the night, partially out of fear that she would run again and partially because she was still the most stunning woman I had ever met. My parents didn't fight me when I insisted on spending the night in my room with Stella. They knew they would lose that fight.

Two days later, we headed home to finish up the semester at school.

● ● ●

Chapter Twenty-Two

Stefan's holidays

THE THREE WEEKS AFTER RETURNING HOME FROM D.C. seemed to fly by. It wasn't easy, but together Stella and I conquered the hectic schedule of caring for the girls and finishing up the semester. Stella had started to look a little worn by the time the Christmas break finally arrived.

The constant sleep deprivation didn't make it any easier on her. We did alternate the nightly feedings by whoever had the later schedule. That usually meant Stella did them. In my defense, I did the weekends and every night once school let out.

Stella was a little hesitant about going back to D.C. for Christmas, so it we agreed that everyone would come to the beach for Christmas. Daisy and Nana were more than happy to take on the job of hostesses for the holidays.

• • •

"Stella, come on; we're only going out to dinner and to buy a tree. I'm sure your mother can find everything while we're gone," I called from the Mustang for the third time.

Part of my plan to ensure Stella knew how much I loved and cared for her was a date night for us each week. Her mother more than happily agreed to help with Adrianna and Alina. I had a sit-down with her parents when we got back and informed them of her needs. They were working with me on making sure she knew they loved her, too.

On most days, Stella did much better, but there were still days when she needed reinforcing. Whenever I would see the doubt growing behind her honey-colored eyes, I instantly dropped whatever I was doing to push the thoughts from her mind. Stella did visit her doctor after we arrived home, and he agreed that if we kept up with it, she wouldn't need any medication for her issues.

"Okay, already. Geez, you act like I'm being over-cautious," Stella grumbled, climbing into the Mustang.

Grabbing her tiny fingers and intertwining them with my larger ones caused a blush-filled sigh. "Hey, this is our special alone time. I don't want to miss a minute of being alone with you," I purred, stroking her cheek.

As I pulled away, Stella started her signature fidgeting. "So, Stefan, I wanted to talk to you about something. I met with my caseworker yesterday, and she had some good news for me. I got my childcare voucher. I called the school and they said the campus daycare will accept them and the girls can start next semester." She peeked up with her honey irises, looking unsure.

"Stella, we can talk all about this after Christmas. There is no

• • •

rush before then. Right?" I needed her to wait until after the holidays before she cemented her mind on the future.

"Oh . . . um . . . okay." Boy, it really sounded like a question the way she muttered it out.

She remained quiet as we drove to her favorite restaurant. It took a lot to pry that information out of her. Who knew a favorite place to eat was such a secret? There was nothing I wouldn't give her; if she liked buffets, then buffets were fine with me.

"Stella, why are you so quiet tonight?" She had taken to avoiding eye contact with me.

"It's nothing." She suddenly found her hands mesmerizing.

I blew out a deep breath. "Don't go that route, Stella. I know what you're doing. We're not leaving here until you tell me what's going on in that brain of yours." I even made a point of tapping her on the forehead with my finger.

Her head snapped up, and she hissed at me. "You wouldn't." The hell I wouldn't!

"Oh, really? I think you're starting to know better than that. I won't let you spiral again. So, I'm asking you again, what's wrong?" I grabbed her hand and held it hostage.

"I thought you would be happy about the girls going into daycare. It will make things so much easier, and I could get a job." I scrunched my other hand into tight fist; I had had enough with this crap.

"You're not going to add working to your plate right now. For all that is Holy! Why are you insistent on running yourself into

* * *

the ground?" I scowled.

I knew I was in trouble when her lip started trembling. Quickly, I shifted out of my seat and into the booth next to her. I grasped both her hands; it was time to calm her down before she started crying in the restaurant.

"Stella, look at me." I tapped her chin so she would look up at me. "I won't let you run yourself into the ground. Taking care of the girls and passing school are the only things I want you to worry about." I placed a chaste kiss on her soft lips.

"But you pay for so much. I feel like I should do something," she pleaded.

"I tell you what; why don't you start your landscaping company. You can work from home, and I can work with you to get it off the ground." The smile that graced her lips warmed my heart.

"Yeah? You think it would be okay?" She nibbled her adorable lip, making my insides quiver.

"No, I think it will be great." I kissed her again with a little more enthusiasm this time. "Let's go get the girls their first tree." Grinning, she nodded and slid out of the booth.

After tossing down a few bucks for a tip, we departed the buffet, both of us already feeling lighter as we did.

One thing about Christmas tree vendors: they are on every corner. Strolling hand-in-hand, we combed the lot looking for just the right tree. Since the cottage was small, it couldn't be too big, but Stella wouldn't settle for anything less than perfect when it came to our first tree. After making the attendant search through every one,

● ● ●

she started racing toward the back, focusing on one in particular. The gleam in her eye told me the search was over. She had an adorable smile when she patted the pine needles.

Seeing her so happy was well worth the cost. I would pay anything for that smile to never leave her beautiful features. Stella was jumping up and down giggling while I strapped the tree to the roof of the Mustang. She glowed the whole way home.

Daisy blinded us by taking a photo of us when we entered the cottage. "For your album," she chuckled as we blinked away the white spots left in our vision.

The rest of the night we spent decorating the Douglas Fir Pine. Daisy had brought over a box of ornaments from Stella's childhood, and my mom had sent me a box from mine as well.

◊ ◊ ◊

"Stella, wake up, sleepyhead. You have a shopping date with my mom." I traced her jaw line with my nose.

"The girls aren't up yet, so I don't have to get up," she grumbled.

"They've been up for an hour. Oma and Opa have been spoiling them rotten." I chuckled.

My parents, Michael, Eddie, Charlotte, and Annie had all arrived on the morning of Christmas Eve. My parents, my aunt, and Annie had rented hotel rooms. Michael and Eddie were staying at our house in Norfolk.

"What? When? Why?" From the way she growled, I half expected her to be foaming at the mouth.

"Stella, it's Christmas Eve, and you need to finish shopping for the little princesses. I, on the other hand, have plans with my dad." She popped up her elbows, and for a moment there, I thought my life might be in danger.

"I'm going alone?" Shaking my head, I pulled the covers off her and dragged her from the bed.

"No, Annie will be there to protect you from the big bad wolf." She giggled and wiggled when I tickled her sides.

"Fine, but I'm not going to have fun." She huffed and snuggled into my chest.

"Stella, stop being a baby and get dressed. My mom wants to buy the girls all those frilly things you have been avoiding. Let her." I hated to let her go, but she couldn't get dressed if I was still attached to her.

When I arrived back in the living room, my mom was just finishing up with changing Adrianna as Annie worked on Alina. "Stefan, are you sure they're gaining weight?"

"Yes, Mom, the doctor said they've gained eight ounces since they were born. He said for preemies they're doing great." Crossing my arms across my chest, I waited for a fight.

"Okay; the doctor knows better than I do." Okay, someone had swapped my mom for an alien. I wondered if we could keep her.

● ● ●

Since Thanksgiving and the births, there had been a great improvement in my mom. It still took some getting used to. Stella had more adjusting to do than I did. She was always on guard, waiting for the other shoe to drop.

With a quick kiss goodbye to everyone, I left with my dad. He wanted help in picking out the gift my parents were buying us. Honestly, I had no idea what he was thinking until we pulled into a used car dealership.

"Dad? Why are we here?" I asked, gawking out the window.

My attention snapped to him when he sighed. "Stefan, don't give me that look. You boys weren't the only ones who got letters when your grandfather died. Since he had given Michael the Mustang, he wanted me to buy you a car from him when you went to college. I just thought with everything that was going on with Stella that it would be nice to make it a Christmas gift for both of you." I smirked, knowing the perfect vehicle we needed.

"Okay, since it's from Grampy, we need a pickup truck." From his questioning glare, he needed more information on that one. "Stella is going to start her landscaping design company from home until she graduates." From his laugh, he found that idea to be a good one.

"A pickup it is then, but you'll need an extended cab for the girls," he chortled and jumped out of the car.

Walking around, we found three possibilities. The dark blue Ford's high mileage turned us right off. The green Chevy's transmission slipped when we test drove it. The last thing we needed was a vehicle that needed work, so that left the red Dodge. It had another advantage; it came complete with a plow set up. It rarely

●　●　●

323

snowed in Virginia — an inch of snow would shut down most cities and towns — but when it did, the plow would come in handy for servicing Stella's future customers.

I stood back and watched when my dad — being a master at negotiations — worked his magic on the salesman. He even had the dealer throw in a big red bow for the top. The salesman grinned when they shook hands and walked inside to do the paperwork. I spent my time learning how to work the plow with the on-site mechanic. Deep down, I knew I'd be the one doing all the plowing.

By noon, we were the proud owners of a nearly new red Dodge Ram truck. It was different from driving the Mustang, but in a good way. I had no problem envisioning Stella driving it. I would miss that old buddy of mine. It still shocked me that Michael had given it me. Of course, he had purchased a new car with some of his money from Grampy.

The only thing left to do was to run home and retrieve the Mustang for the trade in. Being sneaky had my nerves working overtime. I blew out a sigh of relief when the ladies were still out shopping. For one last time, I drove the Mustang back to the lot. Running my hand along the fender, I said my goodbyes to an old friend.

I drove it straight to Daisy's and parked it across the street from the house. I hoped Stella would think it was someone visiting the neighbors. It wouldn't explain away the missing Mustang, though. This gift would make Stella's Christmas the best one of her life.

After stopping briefly at Daisy's, we explained everything, including that Stella and I had decided for her to start her dream

● ● ●

business. Mel and Daisy looked all dreamy eyed at each other, and I didn't want to go there.

With my parents' gift out of the way, we were off to the mall for my gift to Stella. Technically, I wasn't buying her gift since I already had it; I just needed a way to wrap it. Michael was giving Eddie the same thing I was giving to Stella, so we snickered about it a lot. We were caught on more than once occasion whispering about our plans. We Sterling's do love to plot.

Michael and Eddie joined us for lunch at the food court. Turned out, Michael knew about the car deal. I couldn't help but wonder what else he knew that he refused to share.

"Dude, I thought you had my back? What's with holding out on me?"

"Kid, there was no way I was going to ruin the surprise. You know me better than that." When my dad smirked, I knew what he was thinking before he even opened his mouth.

"Stefan knows something you don't, boy." Cocking his eyebrow, he let me take over.

"Dad knocked up Mom before they were married." I bit my cheek to keep from chuckling.

"Get out! You dog! And you were the one going nuts over Stella and Stefan? I wondered why you gave in when you found out she'd gotten pregnant. That's just wrong on so many levels." He shook his head, smiling.

"Yeah, well, it wasn't just me. Grampy did it, too." My dad gloated.

* * *

"Oh, God. That is not something I want to envision." Michael shivered at the thought.

With everything ready for tomorrow, we headed back home. I rode with Michael and Eddie to the cottage. Together we came up with the plan of telling Stella it had a flat so I'd left it at a tire shop to be fixed.

Amazingly, Stella came home in high spirits just before we needed to head to our Christmas Eve dinner. My parents had rented a private room at their hotel for the dinner.

My eyes widened and my jaw dropped when Stella strutted out of the bedroom wearing her new dress. My mom had insisted on buying my three ladies matching Christmas dresses for the dinner. One twirl was all it took to make me fall in love with her all over again.

"Wow, Stella, you look beautiful," I babbled like a school boy in love with his teacher.

"Thank you." She curtsied.

"There's just one thing wrong with your lipstick. Let me fix it for you." Before she could object, I charged in and kissed her, leaving us both stunned into silence.

"Come on, let's load the car." Eddie laughed, nudging Michael's shoulder.

As usual, we were the last to arrive. It wasn't easy going out places when we needed to bring everything for the twins. Everything needed to be doubled when it came to taking them out. Of course, the minute we arrived, they were instantly scooped up and passed

* * *

around.

That gave me the perfect opportunity to pull Stella to the small dance floor. We only had a radio playing from the overhead speakers, but it was enough for us. She hummed against my chest when I pulled her flush to my chest.

"Dance with me," I breathed into her ear.

"Our first dance," she sighed, gazing at me.

Feeling her molded against me pushed away everyone else in the room. Floating across the dance floor, we danced as if no one else was there. For one brief moment in time, we didn't have a care in the world. Staring into her eyes, the love reflected back had my chest constricting. Stella would always leave me breathless.

Twirling her around once, I declared, "I love you, Stella," in nothing more than a whisper.

Stroking my cheek, she replied, "I love you, too." Her radiant smile turned my insides into Jell-O, just like the day we'd met.

When the song ended, cupping her cheeks, I kissed her until my body gasped for air. It wasn't until that moment that I noticed that everyone had been staring at us. Ducking our heads, we tried our best to hide our embarrassment at being caught up in our own little bubble.

I grabbed her hand, and we dashed from the dance floor. "You guys had better keep your mouths busy with the food." Michael pointed to the buffet.

"Good idea." My dad seconded that motion.

* * *

Watching Stella's face flushing red, I had to agree. Before she could move on to being mortified, I nudged her along the buffet table filling our plates. No one said a word when we sat down with Stella's family to eat. After dinner, we mingled around and chatted with everyone.

More than once, I was caught staring at Stella as she sashayed around the room. How could you blame me really? She looked stunning in her flowing red velvet dress that matched the girls'. With all her baby weight gone, she was back to the Stella I'd met all those months ago.

No one was more surprised than I when my Aunt Charlotte dropped her wine goblet to the floor, shattering it into a million tiny pieces. Looking up, we all saw what had startled her. There at the doorway stood none other than my uncle Alfonso Bissett in his full dress Marine's uniform.

"Al," she shrieked and launched herself at him.

"Dad!" Annie was the next to rush him.

"Dad's home." He smirked, holding his family.

Pulling Stella in close, I held her. With a round of applause, my uncle was greeted with a hero's welcome. It was definitely well-deserved. His newest deployment had kept him away for the last eighteen months with no visits home. It was going to be a very merry Christmas for all of them.

One by one, everyone shook his hand and introduced him to anyone he didn't know. The twins and Stella were introduced last, because Stella was shaking a little from the nervousness she always felt around new members of my family.

● ● ●

"Uncle Al, this is Stella, and these two little ones are my kids Alina and Adrianna. Stella, this is Alfonso Bissett." When Stella went to shake his hand he shook his head and hugged her instead.

"Handshakes aren't for family. My wife has told me so many wonderful things about you. I still can't believe you never forgot Annie."

"Well, that goes two ways. I can't believe she didn't forget me." With a smile, Stella stepped back into my embrace.

He was quite smitten with Alina and Adrianna. There was no surprise, since my aunt had filled him in during their video links.

When we finally broke up the party, Stella and I headed to Nana's for the night. Now it was my turn to be nervous. It would be the first time we'd spent the night in the house where Stella had grown up.

Daisy had the playpen set up in the room Stella had once shared with Brianna. Everyone was in the kitchen when Stella decided it was time for us to turn in.

Holding my hand, she started for the stairs when Daisy called out, "Stefan, I'm in no rush to be a grandmother again." I froze, looking back. "Just remember that." She waved goodnight.

"Understood," I croaked.

* * *

Chapter Twenty-Three
Stella's surprise

SNUGGLING AGAINST STEFAN'S CHEST WITH THE morning light beaming through the window, I fought the urge to open my eyes. Last night had been the first time since the conception of the twins that we'd slept in the bed at my Nana's house. I couldn't help but groan last night when my mom had all but threatened Stefan. The shock factor alone had been priceless.

I heard the two tiny fidgeters before they officially announced their desire to be fed. Smiling against Stefan's T-shirt, I prayed someone would come running in and grab them before I had to move from my source of comfort.

Until I'd run away in D.C., I'd had no idea how true that statement was. I was lost without him. Those few short hours had taught me a lifelong lesson. Even if I wouldn't admit it to him, I

● ● ●

depended on him for everything from physical contact to emotional support. Deep down, I think he knew it, too.

It was a little disappointing that he wasn't excited about the girls going to daycare, though his idea of me starting my business from home filled me with the excitement I had been searching for from him. If he thought I could do this, then I knew I could.

"Stella, I know you're awake." I peeked up to see Stefan staring at the ceiling.

"No, I'm not." I tried not to giggle, but failed.

Before I could blink, he flipped us over so I was the one staring at the ceiling. "Merry Christmas, baby," he purred, running his nose up my neck to my ear.

"Merry Christmas," I gushed, looking into the steely gray eyes I had always adored.

My eyes fluttered shut when he kissed me with all the emotions he felt. I made sure to return the favor as I moved my lips against his. The sudden wailing of the girls pulled us apart.

"Yes, your Highnesses, your servants are here to tend to your every need," Stefan chortled, leaping out of bed.

Together we changed their wet diapers and prepared their bottles of formula. Thank God we were decent when my mom busted in, waiving around two new Christmas dresses for the little ladies. They were adorable green velvet dresses trimmed in white lace.

"Look what Grammy bought." She strutted over to the bed.

Due to the fact they were still tiny, most of their clothes had

● ● ●

to be bought in a specialty store for preemies. It was one of the reasons I resisted buying them a lot. The store was flat-out expensive. Of course, Stefan's mother didn't bat an eyelash at the price tags when we had gone there the day before.

Annie had been the one to fill me in on how they had become well-to-do. It turned out that Shirley and Charlotte collaborated on a series of very popular children's books. Shirley wrote the stories, and Charlotte drew the artwork. It explained why two military families would have so much money.

Meeting Al was a treat; his personality mirrored Charlotte's. She may have been Shirley's twin, but they were as different as the day was long. Charlotte never acted like I was a hindrance in Stefan's life.

"You two should get dressed. Mel's out getting coffee and bagels for breakfast." She grabbed Alina and started pulling off her onesie.

"Right, I'll go first." Stefan grabbed his clothes from the overnight bag we'd brought and headed for the bathroom.

"Stella, how are you and Stefan getting along?" Glancing her way, I noticed she wasn't looking up from Adrianna while she dressed her.

"Um . . . great. Why?" Whenever she asked stuff like that, I couldn't help but worry.

"No reason. I just wanted to make sure you're happy, that's all." At least she wore a genuine smile.

"Mom, please don't scare me. If there is something going on,

* * *

just tell me," I pleaded; my nerves were getting the best of me.

"There is nothing going on, Stella. Right, Daisy?" I snapped my head up to see Stefan leaning against the doorway, looking apprehensive and gorgeous at the same time.

"Stefan is right. There is nothing going on except a very merry Christmas for everyone," she fussed at Alina, picking her up to take her downstairs.

"Oh, they're ready." Nana rushed in and scooped Adrianna up into her arms.

"Oh, for Pete's sake, it's not even nine. You know I need my beauty sleep," Brianna grumbled from her side of the room.

"Nope, you're pretty enough, now move that scrawny butt of yours." Nana rushed off before Brianna could make her retort.

Stefan made his way over and sat on the bed. "Stella, you have nothing to worry about. I'll never hurt you." I leaned against his hand when he caressed my cheek with his thumb. Biting my lip, I nodded. "Get dressed, baby. It's the first holiday for our girls and I don't to miss a single spit-up or messy diaper." I could not help but laugh at his enthusiasm.

Brianna had already slipped into the bathroom, so when Stefan left, I had the room to myself. Kicking off the covers, I slipped out and knelt next to the bed to retrieve his present from under my old bed. Caressing the red foil wrapping, I couldn't help but pray it would be good enough. For me it had been expensive, but would he be happy with it? Sighing, I placed it on the bed and got ready for the day.

● ● ●

A sigh escaped my lips when I found Stefan had picked out my outfit already. For a guy, he had the best taste in clothes that I'd ever seen. I'd admit the white chenille sweater and black skinny jeans were the most comfortable clothes I owned, and they looked dressy enough for the holidays. With a little makeup, I was ready to face everyone. Stefan swore I didn't need to wear makeup, but I felt better about myself when I did.

The first floor was a hub of activity when I drifted downstairs in search of a cup of coffee. After slipping Stefan's gift under the tree, I followed a heavenly scent to the kitchen. Stefan smiled and held out my coffee for me. God, he knew me too well. I was useless without my first cup of the day.

My dad grinned, kissing me on the cheek. "Good morning, sweetie."

"It is now." I snorted, taking another sip of the nectar of the Gods.

It was sort of fun having everyone sit around the table, laughing and sharing their favorite Christmas stories. Eddie and Michael's arrival made it even better. In the few months since we'd found out that Eddie and I were brother and sister, we had become closer than Brianna and I had ever been. Sadly, it was the truth. Brianna and I loved each other, but we had different lives. Her sole focus was her friends and partying. It had her out of the house all the time. Where I had locked myself off from the visitors to the beach, she had embraced them. Even in our appearances, we were opposite sides of the same coin.

With breakfast out of the way, it was time to start cooking for the masses that would be arriving for dinner. The amount of food we

* * *

needed to cook was staggering. Everyone took a job and set off to work. When Brianna finally graced us with her presence, Nana stuck her with taking care of the twins. She called it preventative medicine; I called it birth control.

Once the hysterics had finally calmed down and everyone had finished preparing their dishes, I set off to find my girls.

"Hey, Brianna, how's everything going?" I smirked, trying not to laugh.

"How do you do it? You have to do everything twice. Do they always do everything together?"

"Yep, they do. If one's hungry, so is the other." I relieved her of Adrianna.

"Forget kids. I'm all set on that. I'll stick to trying to sing; it's easier." Dropping down next to her on the couch, I hugged her with one arm.

"As much as I want to be an aunt one day, there's no rush." It was the first time in years that we'd showed each other any physical affection.

Looking into Brianna's sapphire-blue gaze, I realized I had changed. Gone were my days of shutting people out, subtly replaced over time with a new desire to accept those I had once pushed away. Patting her sandy blond, curled locks, I made room in my heart for her, should she want it one day. With a new understanding, we took a few moments to reacquaint ourselves.

When Stefan raced by, we both went into hysterics. We had been so lost in our conversation we hadn't heard the knocking on the

* * *

door. With a grin plastered on his face, he led his parents into the living room, his head shaking at us starting us off on another volley.

"Come on you two; we have guests." He grabbed Alina, and I stood with Adrianna.

Before I could say hello, the girls were gone. Grandparents could be so possessive. The rest of Stefan's family arrived at noon, and boy, were they in a festive mood. I had never seen Shirley so happy, but I liked it. She even asked if she could help us cook, which we told her wasn't needed. Stefan had taken up the job of host as he entertained everyone in the living room.

Dinner was served at one o'clock on the dot. Nana was always punctual in everything she did. Nothing irked her more than my mom always being late. I took after my Nana in that regard. Once everyone was sated and the dishes cleared, we all settled in the living room for presents.

I was so overly anxious about my gift to Stefan that I didn't pay too much attention to what everyone was receiving. From everyone's laughter, the families were having fun and enjoying their gifts.

The first gift Stefan opened was from Michael and Eddie. He was ecstatic over the new smart cell phone loaded with every app available. When I opened mine from them, I hooted. It was the same phone, only in pink.

My mom had floored me by giving us two hundred dollars in gift cards to shop for the house. My dad was a little timid about his gift, but handed it to me anyway. It was just a tiny box, so I didn't understand the problem until I opened it. Nestled in the silver shiny box was a key.

* * *

"Dad?"

"It's the key to your very own townhouse. It's a fixer-upper, but I think Stefan can handle it. And if not, he can call me, and I can come help out with fixing it." Stefan was as speechless as I was.

Looking between the box and my dad, I finally barked out, "Dad, I can't take this . . . it's too much." He was already shaking his head.

"You can, and you will. It's eighteen years' worth of birthdays and Christmas gifts all rolled in one."

"But?"

"No buts about it, it's already done." I pursed my lips at his smug expression.

"Then we'll pay you rent." I was grasping at straws, and I knew it.

"To who? It's your name on the deed." He defiantly crossed his arms across his chest.

Stefan spun me so I was looking him in the eyes, cupping my face. "Stella, say thank you. You're not going to win; I can see it in his eyes," he whispered in my ear.

"Thanks, Dad," I choked when he pulled me into a bone-crunching hug.

His gleaming grin pissed me off. "You're very welcome." Argh! Fathers could be so, so, so infuriating.

Stefan reached out to shake his hand. "Thanks, Mel. I'll take care of the repairs."

● ● ●

When a tear slipped down my cheek Stefan caught it with his thumb. "Calm down, baby. He loves you, and this is his way of taking care of you," he whispered, pulling me down to sit on his lap in the chair behind him.

Anxiously, we watched as Annie, Brianna, Michael, and Eddie opened their gifts from Stefan and me. The four just looked at the bibles, then each other. They were, without a doubt, confused.

"We thought you might need those when the four of you become godparents to the twins." I grinned.

"Oh, this is so cool. Give me my goddaughter, Mom. You've had her long enough," Brianna playfully demanded, reaching out to Alina.

"Yeah, Mom, what she said." Michael snorted, retrieving Adrianna.

It really didn't matter to us who was whose; they were all just so happy with our gifts. My smug expression proved to Stefan that I was right, Christmas gifts were not about the money; they were about the sentiment.

When I finally handed Stefan my gift, I held my breath and prayed he would like it. Smiling at me, he tore off the paper to expose the black photo album. As he flipped the pages, a tear slipped down his cheek. The album documented everything he had missed while he was away, and the last few pages were professionally done photos of the girls and me.

"Ah, baby, this is perfect. I love it, thank you," he mumbled against my lips, kissing me.

* * *

"Stefan, why don't you and Stella open our gift next." Maurice passed us another little box wrapped in gold shimmery paper.

My nerves were getting the best of me when Stefan handed it to me to open. Looking through my lashes, I could see he already knew what was in it. Without shredding the delicate paper, I opened the package, only to be confused yet again. Inside the box was a key ring, containing another set of keys.

"Stefan?" My hands were shaking so hard the keys jingled.

"It's outside, sweetheart." He lifted me up as he moved from the chair.

When he threw the door open, there stood a red pickup with a huge red bow on top.

"It's not new, but it will be perfect for our new business," he hummed in my ear with his arms wrapped around me.

Too many emotions for one day coursed through my veins, and I couldn't stop the tears from falling. Clinging onto me, Stefan just allowed me to cry my happy tears until I was ready to stop. It took a few minutes before I was able to sniff back any new tears.

"See, they don't hate you. They just needed time to adjust." He wiped away the remaining tears.

"Did you look at the key ring?" I shook my head, because honestly, I was too preoccupied by the truck to see anything else. "You might want to, since my gift is on it," he whispered.

Opening the box again there was no mistaking the glimmering reflection. On the key ring was the most beautiful ring I

• • •

had ever seen. You could see it was very old. Looking around, I discovered Stefan had knelt next to me.

"Stella, will you do me the honor of becoming my wife? I promise to love you every day for the rest of our lives. I will protect you, support you, and always make you happy." It was my turn to wipe away the tears that were running down his cheeks.

"Stefan, there will never be another man for me. You're the father of my children, the man who showed me how to truly live, and the man I want to be by my side for the rest of my life. So, yes, I'll marry you," I sobbed.

Fumbling with the key ring, Stefan slipped off the engagement ring. His eyes floated shut when he gulped in a large breath and released it slowly. "This ring will never come off your finger." He sighed, slipping it onto my finger.

In a flash, he shot up and spun me around. The smile on his face melted my heart.

Everyone applauded for our new status. Ducking my head, I hid behind Stefan as much as possible. Before I could object, in a whirlwind of excitement we were passed around and hugged by everyone.

"Welcome to the family, Stella. That ring belonged to Stefan's grandmother." Shirley was the last to hug me.

Closing my eyes, I allowed myself to let go of the resentment I had been harboring. Those days were behind us; they were the past, and Stefan was my future.

Turning, I found myself face to face with Stefan again. I

● ● ●

exhaled into his chest when he encircled me with his arms. Snuggling against his chest, we watched as another round of presents were passed out. Following Stefan's stare, I watched when Eddie opened his gift from Michael. From the gasp that rumbled from his chest, he was flabbergasted by the diamond-encrusted, antique, man's wedding ring.

"Michael, this was your grandfather's." His breath hitched in his throat, and you could see he was ready to cry.

"And if you'll have me, it will be yours," Michael vowed and stroked his cheek.

They were never into public displays of affection, but this was different; it was deeper than that. Looking around, the only one who seemed at all surprised was Shirley, but even though she gaped at them, she didn't say a word.

Eddie was too emotional to answer, so the best he could manage was a sharp nod. Michael grinned and hugged him tightly. Looking up, Michael watched as a tear slipped down Eddie's cheek. Unable to stop himself, Michael cupped his cheeks and brushed his lips across Eddie's.

"No tears; this is our forever," Michael mumbled before pulling back, smiling.

Like they had with us, everyone clapped and cheered.

Mel rushed back from the kitchen, waving a bottle of champagne, with my mom right behind him with the glasses.

"A toast is in order. Wow, I'm going to go broke after paying for two weddings." Maurice shot him a look.

● ● ●

"Why are you paying for both?" he sneered.

"Your sons asked my children to marry them. That makes me the father of the brides, or whatever you want to call it." He shrugged, smiling.

Maurice thought for a moment before answering. "Rock, paper, scissors, or flipping a coin?"

Mel eyed him carefully; the tension in the air could be cut with a knife. "Rock, paper, scissors," Mel challenged.

With the whole room watching, Al counted off to the count of three. The jockeying men threw their hands down. Maurice had thrown paper and Mel had thrown rock. In a show of force, Maurice wrapped his fist around Mel hand. "Paper wraps rock, I win! I pay for Michael and Eddie's," he gloated.

Shaking his head, Mel gave in. The twins wailed when he popped the top off the champagne. Once everyone had a glass of champagne, my dad made his toast.

"If you had told me a year ago this would be how I would be spending this Christmas, I probably would have thought you were on drugs. In one short year, my life went from just Eddie and me to seven in total. My family is bigger than I could have imagined. And it's the best feeling in the world. Eddie and Michael, Stella and Stefan, may life give you everything you need to be happy, and if it doesn't, come see me. Salute!"

"Salute!" the whole room repeated.

The celebration stretched on for hours. Toast after toast were made, most of them making me cry. For the first time in my life, I didn't hate Christmas. It was a time of hope, and I had a lot of that.

By the time we were ready to leave, I was exhausted, but a lot of things made more sense to me. It explained Stefan's conversation in the hospital, and it also explained him not wanting me to take on any more than I was already bogged down with. I would have to slip in planning a christening and a wedding between caring for the girls and attending school — not that I was complaining, because I wasn't. My days of self-doubt were behind me. I now knew where I belonged.

• • •

Chapter Twenty-Four

Stefan's wedding bells

ON AUGUST TWENTY-THRID, JUST OVER A YEAR AFTER I had met Stella, I stood on the main beach at the base, watching the sunset colors shifting between red and purple. It was a picturesque view as I waited for Stella to join me. After a few calming breaths, I turned to see her making her way across the sand.

I forced down a lump in my throat as I took in her beauty. With a light breeze licking at my face, I openly gawked at the woman in white making her way to my side. She truly looked like goddess in the simple, strapless, satin wedding gown. One thing about Stella was that she didn't need the sparkling adornments to enhance her beauty; she had an ethereal beauty that most women would pay for.

● ● ●

345

Annie and Brianna were the first to head down the sandy aisle. They both looked beautiful in their pink satin strapless, tea-length gowns and sandals. Eddie looked so proud as he escorted the ladies to the front. There was no mistaking the happy smiles that graced their faces.

All our guests were openly speechless when Stella and Mel made their way through the crowd. Stella had never looked so confident, gliding toward me on her father's arm.

So much had changed in the last six months. Our townhouse in Norfolk was finally finished. I'd never forget the look on her face the day after Christmas when Mel showed it to us. The cream-colored townhouse was located in a family-friendly neighborhood, complete with a renovated park. The hardwood floors needed resurfacing, but that was to be expected. It boasted three bedrooms on the second floor. Maybe Mel was hoping for more grandchildren?

The first floor again had three rooms, which would give Stella a room for an office. Seeing Stella walking around the spacious house filled my heart with joy. It was what I had wanted her to have. Even if it wasn't perfect, it would be when I was done with it.

Mel had been right; there hadn't been anything I couldn't handle on the repairs. Stella had long-since given up fighting against using my trust fund to pay for the repairs, my logic being that she had supplied her half by getting the house and my half would come from the repairs. Stella never enjoyed me spending my money from my grandfather. Though she couldn't fight it, she had insisted on paying for half of everything in the early stages of our relationship.

Mel and Daisy had moved into the cottage we had left vacant.

● ● ●

Mel could afford any house he wanted, but Daisy loved the place. They were even talking about getting married next year. Stella and Eddie couldn't have been happier for them.

Eddie and Michael had been married in D.C. last month. We had all driven there for the simple service. My mother, having learned from her mistakes with Stella and me, openly embraced Eddie into the family. My dad . . . well, he just never commented either way or gave his opinion on the matter. It was never an issue to Stella and me; we loved them, so it never mattered to us. Their happiness was always our main concern.

The twins were still smaller than their nine-month-old counterparts, but they were doing great. The doctors had determined they were fraternal twins, even though they looked identical. Apparently, it wasn't uncommon, considering it had been the same with my mom and Aunt Charlotte.

I was pulled from my recollections of the last few months when Stella finally reached me. Mel happily handed her over once they arrived. With one last kiss on her cheek, he stepped back and joined Daisy on Stella's right side. Grasping her tiny hand in mine, I couldn't help but marvel at my grandmother's ring gracing her finger. Placing a lone kiss on it, I locked my eyes on Stella's.

With the exception of the cooing twins, everyone silently waited for the ceremony to begin.

Lost in Stella's honey irises, I barely heard the priest rambling on about why we were there. I knew why we were there. I was making Stella mine forever. And in return, I was becoming hers forever.

"The bride and groom have written their own vows. Stefan,

* * *

please begin."

I swallowed roughly. "Stella, like you, I walked through life alone, with the exception of my family. I wasn't looking to fall in love, but I did the moment I laid eyes on you. Many people laugh at the idea of love at first sight, and until I met you, I was one of them. It happens to so few couples that it is easily dismissed. You changed me the moment I met you, and for that I am thankful. I wouldn't want it any other way. You have given me two beautiful daughters and a reason to live life to its fullest. From this day forward, I will love, honor, and cherish you all the days of my life." I sighed in relief, my part was complete.

"Stefan, you are the only person to ever penetrate my well-constructed walls that protected my heart from the outsiders. Before you, I only had one other friend, and it turns out, she was your cousin," she tittered nervously. "I tried to outrun my destiny, but at every turn, destiny seemed to mock me. When destiny has plans for you, there is no outrunning it. I thank God every day for sending you to me. Without you, I wouldn't have our daughters; I would never have found my father and brother, or a love that knows no bounds. I love my family, and I love you. From this day forward I will love, honor, and cherish you all the days of my life." Stella beamed like a lighthouse on a foggy night. She would always be my beacon of hope.

"Stefan, do you take Stella to be your lawfully wedded wife for all the days of your life?"

"I do," I solemnly vowed.

"Stella, do you take Stefan to be your lawfully wedded husband for all the days of your life?"

* * *

"I do," she declared.

I couldn't take my eyes off her pink-painted lips as I waited for those fateful words: "You may kiss the bride." Leaning in, I captured her lips, kissing her from the deepest part of my heart. I poured every ounce of love I had into the first kiss of our new life, leaving us both breathless with smiles playing on our lips.

"By the power invested in me by God and the State of Virginia, I now pronounce you husband and wife. It is my honor to introduce the happy couple for the first time: Mr. and Mrs. Stefan Sterling." With that, everyone clapped and cheered.

"I have been waiting for over a year to hear those words," I whispered, only loud enough for Stella to hear.

"Do you think your grandmother would approve?" she asked, staring at my grandmother's ring on her finger.

"I know she would," I assured, admiring the one carat solitaire, princess cut stone that was surrounded by twelve miniature diamonds.

There was no receiving line since the reception was being held right there on the beach. Instead, our families crowded around us, hugging and kissing us before we were handed off to the next person in the mob.

Hand in hand, we walked the few feet to the waiting reception area. My mom and Stella had arranged for a good old-fashioned barbeque style meal. It seemed fitting. The beach had never looked more beautiful decked out in pink flowing tulle.

"I love you, Stella," I murmured against her exposed neck,

* * *

causing her to shiver in my arms.

"I love you, too," she hummed.

The musicians had just started playing, so I pulled her to me and started swaying to the slow rhythm. "Dance with me, Mrs. Sterling," I requested.

"Anytime, Mr. Sterling." She curtsied.

Holding her in my arms, I spun her around the sand. Enya's *May It Be* had been Stella's choice for our first dance. I had to admit that it was beautiful. Stella snuggled her head against my chest, humming the song straight to my heart that beat below her cheek. Whispering in her ear, I sang it back to her.

"May I cut in?" Looking up, I could see Mel was wet around the eyes.

"Absolutely." I bowed out and watched as he danced with his daughter.

Grabbing my mother's hand, I asked for the honor of a dance. "Mom, will you dance with me?"

Seeing her blush like a teenager was heartwarming. Oblivious to our surroundings, we moved in harmony with Stella and Mel.

"Stefan, I know I was awful in the beginning, but I do love Stella and the girls. I can see now how unhappy you were before you found her. I know I have said this before, but I am truly sorry for trying to keep you two apart."

I groaned and held her tighter. "And, as I have told you before, you're forgiven. Mom, just be happy. We cannot change the

● ● ●

past, but we can make the future better if we learn from it." I kissed her cheek, showing her I forgave her again.

I was ousted from my dancing partner when my dad waltzed up and seized control of her. I watched on as more people joined in on the dancing.

"Hey, you," Annie snickered, slapping me on the back.

"Hey back. Oh, this must be Donnie." I reached out to shake the hand of the first man to gain my cousin's affection.

"It's a pleasure to meet you." Annie glowed as we shook hands.

"So, Annie tells me you're in the Navy?" Not that his dress blues didn't give that away.

"Yes, I just rotated back last month. Hopefully, I'm back to stay." Annie snuggled into his arms.

I knew the look in her eyes; it was the same look I'd had when I met Stella. Reaching out, I pulled Stella to me when she walked by, looking a little lost. That was all it took for her to relax into my embrace.

"Miss me, baby?" A sigh slipped out of her parted lips.

"Always," she prattled.

"Stella, this is Annie's boyfriend Donnie Trumbull. Donnie, this is my wife Stella." The words rolled off my lips so naturally.

"Hi, Donnie." Stella flushed when I kissed her forehead.

"It's a pleasure, ma'am." His accent told me he was from

* * *

351

deeper south than Virginia. It was closer to those from Louisiana.

"Stella, Stefan, it's time to eat." Daisy ushered us away to our seats.

Only the bridal party was being served; everyone else had to fend for themselves. Taking a sparerib from my plate, I hand-fed Stella, careful not to get any sauce on her dress. From across the tables, I watched as Nana and my mom fed the girls. Their eyes were as wide as saucers as they watched everyone mingling, dancing, and eating. That was their new obsession: watching people eat. Their tiny lips would move in sync like they were eating with us. They had graduated to small amounts of table food, so they loved that.

"Stella, your mom is waving us over to cut the cake," I whispered to her.

"Oh, okay. Let's do this." She jumped to her goddess sandal-covered feet.

As much as I wanted to smear it across her face, I had promised I would be nice and not do that to her. With our hands locked together, we sliced when we were told to, with everyone watching. From the glimmer in Stella's eyes, I knew something was off, but I couldn't put my finger on it, until it was too late.

In one fluid motion, she had cake on my lips, up my nose and across my cheek. Glaring at her, I could see the fear in her eyes when I lifted her piece for her to see. She was going down, and she knew it. Shaking her head, she tried to back away. Not a chance of that happening; it was war!

Grabbing the back of her head, I removed any chance of her escaping. Only instead of one fluid motion, I tortured and taunted her

● ● ●

when I slowly started at her pink pout and ended in her curled bangs. She released an ear-piercing screech, wiggling to try to break free. I couldn't help but laugh at her adorable lip when she pouted.

My laughing was probably not the best idea because suddenly, she grabbed a hunk of cake in her hand and whipped it at me. Her aim could have been better, since she missed me and hit Eddie in the face instead. He wasn't as forgiving as I was when he grabbed a fistful and chucked it at her. Stella was more agile than he'd anticipated, and a last-minute duck led to his mush hitting Annie on the shoulder. Grabbing Stella, I ducked down so we were out of view as the cake hit the fan. Before anyone could respond, the cake pieces started flying around the tables when the guests started to join in.

"This is all your fault." I licked the frosting from her lips.

"You only get married once." She snorted and started to remove the mess from my face.

"That's right, love." I kissed her, holding her pressed against me while the bellows from above continued.

After a few moments of quiet, we emerged to see everyone was covered in white and pink goo. Even the twins were happily playing with the mush that had landed on the table in front of them. There was no stopping the sudden hysterics when everyone looked at each other.

Who knew a wedding could be so fun? Not me. I had thought that Stella would have cried that the day hadn't gone as planned, but she didn't. My wife took it in her stride and laughed along with the rest of us.

* * *

When the music started again, I swept Stella away for a dance. "Even with cake in your hair, you're the prettiest woman I've ever met," I laughed to her.

"I think you might need to see an eye doctor when we get back from Boston. You definitely need your eyes checked," she cackled, throwing her head back.

"There is nothing wrong with my eyes, except maybe I'm a little blinded by love." Fisting my hands in her hair, I kissed her again from the heart.

After the cake fight, the night breezed by. Before we knew it, it was time for us to leave. We had decided to skip the outfit changing for a quick trip home to shower before we drove to Boston. We had decided to honeymoon in Boston since Stella had never been there, and Annie was thrilled to play tour guide. Stella and Annie had indeed regained their childhood friendship.

Stella was a little nervous about leaving the girls with my parents, but that was to be expected. She had never left the girls anywhere for longer than a few hours. We even took them to the landscaping jobs Stella had. She had been doing so well with her company that she had been able to stop using her government assistance months ago.

"Hey, Michael, you all set with dropping the gifts off?"

"Yep, little brother, we got this. Get your bride out of here." He waved his hand toward the parking lot.

Grunting like a caveman, I threw Stella over my shoulder and trudged through the sand. She waved goodbye from the top of the wooden stairs, but not before she tossed her bouquet at the crowd

● ● ●

below. Looking back, I had the pleasure of seeing Brianna catch the pink roses. She'd never seen that one coming.

After a quick stop at home to shower, we were back on the road and headed to Boston. Stella ended up falling asleep, leaving me to listen the rock music she hated. Her music of choice was hip-hop, and I wouldn't think of depriving her of that. However, with her sleeping, it was my turn.

My parents had called when they reached D.C., letting us know all had gone well with the twins. Honestly, I didn't know why Stella had been so afraid to leave the girls; maybe it was her own abandonment issues.

Stella took over driving the last four hours of the trip so I could crash. It was a grueling twelve-hour jaunt. However, seeing Stella grinning as we passed over the Zakim Bridge made it worthwhile.

True to her word, Annie spent the week showing us all the local hot spots and tourist traps. Stella's favorite was Cape Cod. What can I say; she was always a beach baby. Watching her on the dunes, I snapped my all-time favorite photo of her. It was a simple shot of her staring off at the sunset. The fact that she wasn't looking at the camera only enhanced the photo.

As much as we loved the time with Annie and her boyfriend Donnie, we were looking forward to getting home to Alina and Adrianna. As with Annie, we also had school starting in a few days.

● ● ●

• • •

Chapter Twenty-Five

Stella fulfills Stefan's dream

THE VIEW WAS BREATHTAKING WHEN I GLANCED OFF into the distance. I was so lost in my thoughts that I didn't hear Stefan creeping up behind me. However, there was no mistaking the feeling of him wrapping his arms around my waist.

"I told you that you would look beautiful on the beaches of Italy," he gushed.

"That you did, and it only took four and a half years to get me here," I laughed, remembering the first time we'd talked about Italy.

"Yeah, well, we were busy." He nuzzled my neck.

"Not to mention, nowhere in there did you mention that I would be pregnant at the time," I playfully chided.

* * *

"Like I said, we were busy. The girls don't seem to mind. They're having a ball." Following his glance, I couldn't argue.

It was only our second day in Italy, and I had to admit, it was a perfect way to spend our third wedding anniversary. We had discovered the day before our graduation that I was expecting again. No one was more thrilled than Stefan.

"Stefan, I saw the doctor the day before we left for an ultrasound." Peeking around, I could see the surprised expression on his face,

"Why didn't you tell me? Is everything okay? She's fine, right?" I couldn't torture him any longer.

"Yeah, everything is great, but I think your son might have an issue with you calling him a girl all the time." I snorted, leaning my head against his shoulder.

"My son? We're having a boy?" Ah, he was so cute when he gasped like a fish out of water.

"Yes, it's a boy. A very healthy little boy." I spun in his arms so my baby bump tucked into his stomach.

"Stella, you're the best. I'd hoped for a boy, but honestly, I was afraid you'd be upset. I'll love the baby regardless of what it is, and you know that, though a boy to carry on the family name is the best present you could give me." The way his lips latched onto mine, there was no way he was lying.

"I had a feeling this time was different, but I wanted proof before I said anything." Watching the girls from my spot, I smiled.

Almost on instinct, his hands suddenly caressed the baby

● ● ●

through my skin. The baby moved to his hands for some attention. "Did he?"

"Yes, he likes when his daddy rubs him. But he nudges me when you call him a she or a her." Stefan dropped to his knees and kissed my bulging belly.

"Okay, little guy, I get it. You're a strapping young man. Now be nice to Mommy so she doesn't get mad at me," he whispered, causing the baby to flutter against his hands again.

The girls looked up, shook their heads, and returned to playing in the sand. They were used to Stefan cuddling with my tummy, so it doesn't bother them anymore.

My mom and dad had been the picture of proud grandparents when we told them. They had gotten married the summer after Stefan and I were. Their wedding was different from ours. They opted for an outside ceremony in the mountains of West Virginia. To say it was beautiful was an understatement.

As for how Stefan's parents took the news, they were thrilled. They were still living in D.C., and Maurice had just celebrated his twenty-fifth year in the service of the Army. Shirley and Charlotte had released countless new books, many of them with characters named after the twins.

Stefan stood and grabbed my hand. "Hey, the honeymooners have decided to leave the Inn for the first time. Annie, Donnie, out for a breath of fresh air?"

"Yes, we are, and we're starving. Thought you guys might want to join us for dinner?"

* * *

"I could eat." I rubbed my belly.

"You better say that." Stefan snuggled against my neck.

"Let's go, ladies. Daddy's hungry, so we're heading back," I guffawed when he mocked having his feelings hurt.

"Ah, Daddy's always hungry," Alina grumbled grabbing her sand bucket.

"Mommy's probably just blaming Daddy because she's hungry again," Adrianna sniggered and followed her sister up the beach.

"Annie! We found seashells," Alina shrieked and charged Annie with her bucket in hand.

"Me, too, Donnie." Adrianna launched herself into his waiting arms.

"That's great, peanut," he said as he spun her around.

It was fascinating how much alike those two really were. Most people couldn't see the difference in their appearances, though everyone in the family could.

Hand in hand, we walked the stretch of beach that led back to the villa. It was a beautiful evening, so we ate at the outside café adjacent to the villa. Staring up the stars, the girls pointed out their favorites. Stefan stared at the girls in awe when they fell asleep at the table. That man thought his girls could do no wrong. If he only knew half the things they did, he would have been mortified.

Dinner was spectacular, and everyone excitedly chatted about tomorrow's plans. We had all decided to take the train from Italy to

● ● ●

Germany for a few days. I wanted the girls to see where their father had grown up at least once in their lives. Hopefully, we would be back to show his son, too.

Once the girls were nestled in their bed, it was time. "Stefan, I thought you might want to see what he looks like."

"Seriously? You brought the pictures?"

"Um . . . yeah. What good would it have been if I'd told you and didn't have pictures?"

"Bring them on," he demanded playfully.

I pointed out the features the technician had showed me. "I think he has your nose." I stroked the sonogram.

Grabbing my outgoing postcards, he cut a picture off the strip and taped one to each. Simply he added, "It's a boy" at the bottom of each.

"Well, that's one way to tell them," I laughed as he led us to the other bed.

"They'll never see it coming." He settled in beside me.

"That they won't," I hummed, snuggling in for the night.

We departed Milan by train before dawn. The girls stared out the windows, watching the picturesque scenery fly by as we headed to Munich, Germany. Annie and Stefan pointed out the highlights when we passed by. That trip was something both their families knew well, having made it dozens of times over the years of their childhoods.

We drove from the station ninety miles north to the city of

* * *

Ansbach, his dad's old posting and his former home. After the nine-hour trip, it was decided we would go straight to the inn that Annie's family used to stay in when they would visit. I was in awe as I walked around the historic inn, soaking up the old world features unique to this region. Germany's architecture ranges from antiquity to modern and everything in between.

"Stella, don't get lost on me, sweetheart." I stopped drifting and moved back in Stefan's direction.

"Stefan, this place is so beautiful. I can't believe you lived just minutes from here." He just smiled and shrugged.

Once we were checked in for the night, we made sure the girls were sleeping before we slipped out onto the tiny balcony. Sure, the view was fantastic, but Stefan was a captivating view, too.

Pulling me into his arms, he whispered, "Ich liebe dich." It was very rare for Stefan to speak German to me, but this one I had heard before.

"I love you, too." I grinned and melted against his chest.

On that trip, I finally had a chance to hear how beautifully he could speak both Italian and German. Then again, everything Stefan said was beautiful in any language.

For the next three days, it was nonstop running.

At the Margrave Museum, we were treated to the sights of exhibitions from the era of the Margraves and the Kaspar Hauser collection.

The Castle of the Margraves of Brandenburg-Ansbach left me breathless and the girls bored. Seeing so many places of an era they

● ● ●

knew nothing about would do that to any child. They wouldn't be able to truly appreciate it until they were older.

At the Kasper Hauser Monument, Stefan told us the mysterious story of a "feral child" who was found barely able to walk or talk. His story was a sad one. Five years after his appearance, he had been found stabbed to death in the court gardens. On his tombstone, the words read, "Here lies Kaspar Hauser, the riddle of his time. His birth was unknown, his death mysterious." The mystery of one of the most famous young men in Europe was never solved. A few of his possessions, including the two letters he had been found carrying, were on display at the museum.

The St. Gumbertus Church, was built in the 15th century over another church, and they still held services. It was a stunning sight to behold. It was a Baroque hall style and had the largest organ I had ever seen.

From the outside, the St. Johnannis Church retained its former splendor. The gothic brick church was built in the 15th century. The inside was a shadow of its former self, but it was still worth visiting.

There was no way I could pick one as my favorite; they were all breathtaking.

On our last day in Germany, we took a tour of the base where Stefan had once lived. All his friends from his other life were gone, but he didn't seem to mind.

"Stefan, will you miss it here when we leave?" I had to know if being with us was still where he wanted to be.

"No, not really. If I had never left, I wouldn't have found you.

* * *

I'm home wherever you are. Our lives are on the beach now. I'm glad I could share it with you and the girls, and maybe one day we'll bring our son here." My eyes fluttered shut when he stroked my cheek.

"That would be nice," was all I could manage to breathe.

"Let's go home, baby," he laughed, pulling me toward the train.

* * *

Epilogue

ON NOVEMBER TWENTY-FIRST, WE CELEBRATED Adrianna and Alina's twenty-fifth birthday with a cake, but it wasn't a birthday cake. It was Adrianna's wedding cake. As Stella and I had, she'd found her love just before she started college. Being Sterling through and through, it was love at first sight. Kevin never let her want for anything, and when she wanted to wait to sleep together until they had graduated, he complied. I can't tell you how happy that made me. Adrianna had learned to avoid the Richards' family curse after watching her sister succumb to it.

As every other female in Stella's family, Alina had become pregnant with my first grandchild while still in high school. The father was long gone by the time we found out. My dad had searched him down through his military connections, but the boy wanted nothing to do with my granddaughter.

Marie, named after Nana, was born surrounded by her family, and we would make up for anything her father wouldn't provide.

● ● ●

Unfortunately, Nana passed away a few years after Marie was born from a heart attack. In their short time together, Nana had made sure Marie knew she loved her.

Marie was the spitting image of her father, and he never denied she was his; he just refused to partake in her life. Her bouncing strawberry curls and bright green eyes were the picture of her father's.

Alina never went to college; instead, she followed Stella into the booming family business. Everyone knew of "Stella's Secret Gardens." Stella, Alina, and Marie were together working on every project.

Alina did find Mr. Right when Marie was three. Kyle came into their life in a whirlwind and never left. In a small ceremony, they were married a year later, and he filed to adopt Marie a month after that. They were due to add another member to our family in two months. It was a boy this time.

Our son Joshua was born on January ninth when the girls were five. For now, he was happy with starting college. He wanted to be like his dad, a financial analyst. He was the spitting image of his mother. All the girls loved his wispy, brown locks and amazing, honey-colored eyes. Of course, he had been smart enough not to be wooed by anyone, so maybe he was waiting for his princess to floor him like Stella had done to me.

Stella's parents had retired to Fort Lauderdale, Florida, a few years ago. They would visit as much as they could, but they didn't get around as easily as before.

The day was filled with tearful memories as I watched my daughter become a woman. Adrianna and Kevin had that special

* * *

something that told me they would beat the odds and make it to forever.

"Where's Eddie?" Shaking my head, I turned to Michael.

"Dancing with your wife." He pointed to Stella and Eddie whirling around the floor.

"What about Mom and Dad?" He tilted his head to a table in the front of the hall.

"Spoiling their great-granddaughter." I laughed when Marie pranced away waving a fistful of cash.

"They'll never change. Even retirement hasn't slowed them down." I snorted.

"Not one bit."

"How's South Carolina?"

"Beautiful as always. When are you two coming to see us again?"

"October, I think." I knew I had to check with Stella, since she made the plans for our vacations around her work schedule.

"It's good to see Annie and Donnie could put their issues aside so they could both come." I nodded, remembering the bad years they had gone through recently.

"They filed for the divorce last week. I guess she just couldn't stand all the years apart." Annie had told Stella as much over the years. Annie refused to leave Boston, and Donnie refused to leave the Navy.

● ● ●

"I see Brianna brought the flavor of the month," he snickered, pointing her out.

"Yeah, she's says she's in love, but she's said that before." I grinned, remembering the last three times she'd said it.

Sighing heavily, he asked, "So that's it? Next up, Joshua's wedding? If he finds someone, that is."

"Yep, that's all she wrote. My boy's life will be a whole other story," I chuckled.

● ● ●

www.ingramcontent.com/pod-product-compliance
Lightning Source LLC
Chambersburg PA
CBHW051129030726
47504CB00004B/785